"THE KILL caught my attention at once. Its first sentence is a grabber. . . . The ending reveals the most original horror device I've ever seen."

—*David Morrell*

"The book's unrelenting progression of short lulling scenes of the mundane punctuated by powerful gasps of the macabre built a tension in the narrative that didn't allow me to put the book aside until I had finished it. Mr. Ryan's prose is spare and convincing, and I can't think of any greater praise."

—*Michael McDowell*

"A winner, Alan Ryan's THE KILL . . . contemporary in the best sense, and has an ending James Whale would be proud of. This is thunder and lightning all the way . . . very well done."

—*American Fantasy*

THE KILL

ALAN RYAN

A TOM DOHERTY ASSOCIATES BOOK

Copyright © 1982 by Alan Ryan

A Tor Book

Published by Tom Doherty Associates, 8-10 W. 36th St., New York, N.Y. 10018

First printing, December 1982
ISBN: 0-523-48055-5

Printed in the United States of America

Distributed by Pinnacle Books, 1430 Broadway, New York, N.Y. 10018

To Charles L. Grant

*for finding a way
through the shadows*

I saw the hideous phantasm of a man....
—Mary Shelley

THE KILL

Prologue

Carla Helbig, nine years of age, spent the last hour of her life crying. Tears mixed with the pouring rain that lashed her face and plastered sticky strands of hair across her forehead. She blinked repeatedly, sniffled, coughed, caught her breath, stumbled forward again through the woods.

An hour ago, she had stepped into a deep puddle and the mud had sucked the red-and-white Little Pro sneaker from her right foot. The touch of icy water took her breath away but she pushed herself to her feet and stumbled on.

She was heading downhill, and at the bottom of the slope she came to a blacktop road, rain dancing in little silvery geysers on its surface. Unthinking, unseeing, she crossed the roadway and started up the slope of Deacons Rise.

Fright wrapped its smothering arms around her. She cried because she was lost and because she knew that the unavoidable penalty for running away from home was getting lost, getting lost and dying. She knew, with the chilling certainty of terror, that the Big Bad Wolf and the Wicked Witch darted here among the dripping trees, paced her step for step and laughed, cackled, each time she fell. She *knew* it! Their frosty breath prickled at the back of her neck, their bony fingers plucked at her legs. Then their storybook faces melted, blurred hideously into monstrous nightmare shapes, and turned into the red and snarling face of her father. His big meaty hands would snatch at her shoulder, his swollen knuckles lash at her face, and he'd catch at her hair like the whipping branches and he'd beat her and beat her and never ever stop! *She knew it!*

Panting, she squeezed her small body between two trees. Rough bark caught at the sleeve of her muddy sweatshirt. Goosebumps swirled across her skin as she shrieked, frantically yanked herself free, then quickly picked her stumbling way farther up the slope.

She wished she had Raggedy Ann.

The doll suddenly filled her mind. Aggy, she called her. Aggy could hug her and soak up her tears and save her. In her mind, she saw the doll's soft and saving face.

Aggy! she shouted.

Aggy could hug her and save her. If only Aggy was here!

Oh, Aggy! Oh, Aggy!

Icy water streamed down her face and neck. Her green sweatshirt was black with chilly rain, her mud-soaked corduroy jeans clung cold and wet against her legs. She was shivering and her eyes were closed when she stumbled against the rough surface of a boulder. She fell panting against it.

And that was when the thing touched the back of her neck.

Her body jerked in alarm and revulsion, one of her

knees cracking painfully against the rock. The treacherous mud slid away beneath her and she splashed to the ground. Instantly, instinctively, she tried to slither away, crablike, on heels, buttocks, elbows. The slippery mud betrayed her again and she fell back flat on the wet ground.

And then she heard the breathing.

It was a hissing sound, harsh and dry, like sand on a wood surface. It came from in front of her, from a spot in the air above her. All around, the rain slashed at new green leaves and burbled into the earth with a sound that was wet and natural. A stream gurgled over the stones and gravel that littered the hillside, carrying on its bubbling surface dead leaves and broken twigs not yet rotted and returned to the soil. Two boulders, each the size of a wheelbarrow, stood beside the stream. In some age long past, they had tumbled down from higher up the mountain; they might, at some time in the future, tumble farther down the slope. Now they stood silent, patient, rough sides nuzzling each other like lonely animals, and the rain-swollen stream swirled around them in its headlong plunge downhill. That sound too was wet and normal. But the sound from above Carla's head, the breathing sound, was dry and harsh, like calloused hands rubbed roughly together, back and forth, back and forth, but she saw nothing that could be breathing, only waving tree limbs and fluttering sheets of gray and silver rain.

Aggeeeeeee!

She screamed and tried to fling herself away. She tried to scream again but choked on rain and tears and mucus. She gagged, and hot, sour pain convulsed her chest and throat. Something blunt and solid struck her on the side of the face, and an icicle of pain pierced deep inside her ear. She stared, wild-eyed, seeking her attacker, but still there was nothing to be seen.

Then something grasped her rain-slick hair, twisted, pulled, so that her head was jerked sharply to the side and her life ended with one clear *snap!*

For a few moments, there was only the sound of the rain and the stream and the breathing.

Something lifted the child's body, lifted it easily by the throat—the way Carla might once before have picked up the Raggedy Ann doll—and dragged it a few feet through the mud. The body hung limp, mouth open, eyes goggling, blood trickling from the nose. Then, with a single, easy swing, the body was tossed to the ground. It fell in a soft and crumpled heap, muddy and shapeless, discarded, against the uphill side of the rocks. The water of the stream foamed eagerly against it.

Then the breathing moved slowly away, accompanied by another sound that receded with it, a gritty sound like that of salt crunching underfoot. Then the sounds were gone and only the rain made noise on the mountain.

PART ONE

1

Megan Todd tossed the set of color transparencies onto the piles of papers that already cluttered her desk. She stared at them for a minute in silence, then allowed herself to sigh out loud. The pictures showed two innocent-faced young women, barely more than girls, both of them naked except for white lace-edged garter belts, engaged in explicit love-making on a wooden floor that was polished highly enough to reflect their bodies in its sheen. Luxuriant potted plants surrounded them, framing each picture in silhouetted leaves. The camera lens had been covered with nylon for the photo session and the pictures had a soft, dreamy look that was enhanced by the golden reflections in the floor. After a moment, Megan leaned forward and reached for the chromes to study them again. There were fourteen of them, all variations of the same basic poses, the women's arms and legs intertwined in endless combinations. She held them up one by one to her overhead light and peered closely at them, then set each one down on the desk as she finished with it.

"Dave!" she called without looking up, her eyes wearily scanning the litter on her desk. So much work still to be done and it was already three-thirty on Thursday. I am not coming in on Saturday, she promised herself for the hundredth time that day, I swear to God I am not coming in again on Saturday. One way or another, all the deadlines will be met, all the magazines will go to the next stage of production on schedule, and absolutely everything will be absolutely hunky-dory but, as God is my witness, I am not coming in again on Saturday. "Dave!" she called again.

"I'm coming, I'm coming," Dave said as he arrived at her desk. He always looked at her so admiringly that Megan fancied he had a crush on her. She was short, blond, pretty, with a slender boyish figure that was still unmistakeably female, clean and classic features in a fine-boned face, hair that looked elegant worn straight or easily casual when pulled back in a ponytail. Now she was wearing faded jeans, a blousy white shirt and red suspenders; she might have been somebody's kid sister.

Megan glanced at the container of coffee Dave was holding.

"Want some?" he asked.

"Do I have to share yours or can I have my own?"

"Cup of coffee coming up. One arsenic or two?"

"Three," Megan said. "Thanks, Dave."

"Be right back."

He finished his own coffee in a gulp and headed for the hall.

Megan closed her eyes and hoped that the telephone wouldn't ring for at least ten minutes.

The telephone seemed to be ringing all the time these days, ringing endlessly and urgently, and always heralding the arrival of yet another crisis. Dave, Megan's assistant, was able to take some of the weight of daily details from her shoulders, but no one else could take final responsibility for decisions. That was why the Dunwoodie Publishing Group paid her to be art director for its line of magazines. Each of the titles in the group had its own nominal art director to do preliminary selections and layout, but it was up to Megan herself to oversee all eight magazines through all stages of production, and see to it that Dunwoodie maintained its reputation as a class act in the magazine business while at the same time pinching every penny that would stand still long enough to be pinched.

The job wasn't easy to begin with, and the company's recent purchase of *Ladylove*—which Dunwoodie's owner and president, Harvey Mendel, described as a "struggling but promising" men's magazine—hadn't made it any easier. Megan's requests for another assistant were all met with woeful stories about the company's finances, the high cost of paper, the high cost of this and the high cost of that.

She had kept her growing anger and frustration to herself for a while but had finally, at his urging, spelled it all out to Jack Casey, with whom she had been living for four years. Jack, trying to lighten her mood, had dubbed her the "Quim Queen" of the magazine business. She hadn't spoken to him again until he came home from work the next day with a single daisy and a bag of M&M's, saying, "I brung ya dese here posies and candy, but only if you'll be my friend."

Now, sitting at her messy desk, Megan smiled slightly as she thought of Jack. At times like these, she thanked her lucky stars that she had him. Let the feminists say what they wanted, there was nothing like burying your

face against a man's shoulder at night to make you
forget what happened during the day. And, damn it,
he's right, she thought. Here I am, the Quim Queen herself, sitting on her throne, waiting for her faithful
lackey to fetch her coffee. Some kingdom. Queendom.
Whatever.

She forced her eyes to focus on the pile of 4x5
chromes on the desk. If my mother only knew, she
thought, that her little girl now makes her living by picking the sexiest pictures of young girls she can find . . .
damn. Look at the magazine through a man's eyes,
Harvey had suggested. Sure, she thought. Maybe I
should hold the pictures in one hand while I look at
them, and keep the other in my pants. And damn again.

All in all, the net effect of the last several months was
that a job that Megan had found challenging and even
fun was now threatening to go out of control. Where before she had been constantly busy, working at peak
efficiency, able to concentrate for hours on a single
project but equally capable of switching her attention to
a new problem the instant it arose, now she was
eternally harried, distracted, worried, feeling that more
and more things were being left undone, and that the
things getting done at all were being done poorly.

It hadn't always been like this. It hadn't always been
like this at all. . . .

"We're fresh out of arsenic, so you'll have to make
do with sugar, okay?" Dave said at her elbow.

Megan took the container of steaming coffee.
"Thanks, Dave," she said. "But listen, let's can the
jokes for a while, okay? I'm really not in the mood."

"Sure," Dave said pleasantly.

She stirred the coffee in silence, then dropped the

wooden stick into the overflowing wastepaper basket
beside her desk. The coffee was still too hot to drink,
but she sipped cautiously at it anyway. With the second
sip, she remembered that she was drinking too much
coffee lately. And that reminded her that she was using
too much sugar in it lately. Damn again.

"Do you still want me?" Dave asked.

Megan closed her eyes for a second, told herself that
she really wasn't as tired as she felt. She reached for the
chromes, then stood up, still holding the container of
coffee because there was no place on her desk to put it
down.

"Come with me," she said.

He followed her across the office to one of the large
glass-covered lightboxes used for viewing transparencies. Megan swore under her breath when she saw the
untidy pile of tracing paper and clear acetates that
covered its surface. Dave quickly cleared them away,
and Megan spread out the transparencies across the
white glass surface. The pictures of the two naked girls
glowed in rich shades of pink and gold and gem-like
green.

"Dave," she said, "a photo set like this is not what
we're looking for. It's just not right for the magazine.
The pictures have that nice soft, romantic look, warm
glowing flesh tones, soft focus, reflections in that
wooden floor, everything framed by green plants. But
those are pictures you could use to sell perfume or
douches or feminine deodorant. It's known as women's
porn, the kind of thing you see in TV commercials and
in the women's magazines. It's not for us. We don't
want pictures of two romantic women lost in dream-
land. They should look like they're actively enjoying it,
not as if they're about to doze off any second. At least,

that is the bible according to Harvey Mendel who, as we all know, is our own personal god. Dave, I'm sorry. We're not in the pretty picture business. We're in the tits-and-ass business."

Behind her, the telephone rang on her desk.

"Dave, go through the pictures again and see if we have anything stronger on hand, okay? And God bless us, one and all."

"Okay," Dave said as he gathered up the chromes and switched off the lightbox. "But I don't think there's anything better."

Megan sat down at her desk and picked up the telephone. "Yes, Lynn."

"Suzi Steiger," Lynn's voice said through the phone. "I told her I thought you were at a meeting."

Lynn had been told to screen her calls for the afternoon and make excuses where she could. "I'm still at the meeting," Megan told her, and hung up the phone.

The disarray of her desk assaulted her again. She closed her eyes to shut it away. It wasn't always like this, she thought. . . .

Three months before graduating from Bennington, Megan had found a job as an assistant in the art department of a book publisher, so she had gone directly from college into exactly the work she wanted to do. Always realistic, she had no delusions about making a career as a freelance artist at the age of twenty-one. She meant to learn the business and at the same time continue studying drawing and painting.

She'd done well from the start. People liked her work and they liked her. After a year, she moved to another company. She had to drop her classes at the Art Students League, but she loved the vitality of the new position and new responsibilities.

But those responsibilities left less and less time for her own drawing and painting. On the rare occasions when she had the time and energy to start something on her own in the evenings, it didn't bother her that she had to paint by artificial light in a corner of her small apartment. What bothered her was that she could do it so seldom.

Then Harvey Mendel had called one day and asked her to lunch. He'd been watching her work, he said, and before the lunch was over he'd offered her the position of art director. The position seemed a natural next step for her. She had confidence in her own taste and didn't mind exercising it in public, and she liked the thought that so many valuable enterprises depended for their continued success on her judgment and decisions.

And three weeks before she left her old company to start at Dunwoodie, Jack Casey joined the company as an editor. He asked her to lunch on the Friday of his first week. He had an easy wit that could be suddenly biting and a casual acceptance of her as a professional equal. There was an almost instant meeting of the minds between them.

Three weeks later, on the Friday ending her first week at Dunwoodie, after a long evening that started with pizza and the new John Carpenter film, and ended in bed at Jack's apartment, Megan stretched luxuriously, sighed happily, and said, "Sir, I declare myself well and truly fucked."

Jack propped himself up on an elbow and peered solemnly into her face. "Good," he said. "Likewise, I'm sure." He kissed her. "There's more where that came from, you know."

"Already?"

"Well, I'll need twenty minutes or so. But what I had in mind, actually, was the future, in a general sort of way. Which is why I think we should live together."

"Oh?" Megan said. Then, more slowly, "Oh." And realized that she had been thinking the same thing.

They spent the rest of the evening sitting on the bed, doing arithmetic and deciding how much they could spend on an apartment in Manhattan if they combined their resources. Six weeks later, they moved into a place on East 80th Street, near York Avenue, that cost sixty-three dollars a month more than they had planned on. But it had a tiny balcony where Jack could grow the "green things" he said he wanted to grow, and there was room for Megan to set up a permanent place for painting.

Jack encouraged her to get back to it, but the job at Dunwoodie offered too many reasons to stay away from the easel: she was tired, she came home late, she brought work home with her, always something. Jack pointed out advertisements for art supplies. He suggested that they eat out so she could relax and have more time to herself. He tried to talk her into taking a day off now and then. And, slowly, she renewed the habit of sketching. And, more and more often, the sketches looked interesting enough to get her to stretch a new canvas and actually start painting the picture. A few of the paintings got finished, but only a few. Gradually the hall closet, and then the space behind the living room couch, was filled with half-finished pictures, testimony to the press of business, the distractions, the movies that had to be seen, the parties that had to be attended, the meetings and the dinners, both hers and Jack's, where they were expected to show up.

And here she sat, as she so often thought these days, shuffling pictures of naked women around on her desk, trying to decide which of the models and which of the poses would bring the greatest pleasure to that proverbially lonely, well-heeled, and horny young man, aged 18-34, who would, month after month—but only if she chose right—buy the magazine and take it home to scrutinize in silent, one-handed solitude. Quim Queen, indeed.

And the telephone rang again.

"Yes, Lynn."

"Sorry, but it's Suzi Steiger again," Lynn told her. "She wants to know if you're out of that meeting yet. She's pretty insistent, and since she's a friend of yours, I said I'd check."

Megan and Suzi had been roommates at Bennington. They got together about once a month, although Megan had a hard time taking seriously any woman who spelled her name with a cute little "i" at the end. Suzi worked at some vaguely defined but high-paying job in the programming department at ABC-TV—not WABC, the local station, she was always careful to specify, but ABC-TV itself—and Megan could picture her now, crisp, elegant, expensively dressed. Suzi was one of those women whose overflow of energy and high spirits could exhaust those around them. On the other hand, she was always lively and interesting. And distracting.

Megan cradled the phone against her shoulder, slid lower in the chair, and recklessly lifted her feet to the corner of her desk. "I'll talk to her," she told Lynn. She pushed down the lighted button on the phone. "Hi, Suzi."

Suzi's familiar voice bubbled out at her. "Honey!" she cried. "God, I've been trying to get you all day! Hello there, how are you?"

It wasn't really a question—it seldom was with Suzi— and Megan, instead of replying as she was sorely tempted to, settled for saying, "Okay," and letting Suzi get on with it.

"Listen! I have the most marvelous news," Suzi rushed on. "God, it's so wonderful, you're not going to believe it. I swear, you won't believe it."

"You're pregnant," Megan said drily.

"Oh, God forbid!" Suzi gasped. "Megan, don't be gross and disgusting. No, no, no, nothing like that. But, listen, I want to tell you my news."

"What is it, Suzi?" Megan dutifully inquired.

"Megan, do you remember how we used to talk about making all our dreams come true back at Bennington? Well, I've done it. I've fulfilled my lifelong ambition!"

Megan grinned weakly, remembering. "You mean you've slept with three hundred men already? And before your thirtieth birthday? What happened? Did you get ahead of schedule or something?"

"Megan, you can be so crude sometimes."

"Okay, never mind. So tell me. I'm listening."

"Remember how I used to tell you about my childhood and all that crap?"

"Sure, you sounded just like Holden Caulfield."

"Who? Oh, never mind. Well, you remember how I always said I lived in apartments all my life, with my parents, and then of course we were at school, and then after college I've lived in the city, of course . . . ."

"Of course," Megan sighed, remembering the beautiful apartments Suzi's wealthy parents had always lived in, first on Central Park South, later on Beekman Place.

". . . and for a while there it looked like I'd live in the city absolutely all my life? Do you remember?"

"Sure."

"Well, I've done it!" Suzi cried triumphantly. "You are now talking to the proud owner of my own personal *real estate!* Can you imagine? I mean, I actually own land, *dirt*, for God's sake, real, honest-to-God dirt. With a house and trees, the whole bit. God, I feel just like Scarlett O'Hara!"

Megan remembered visiting Suzi at her parents' beach house in the Hamptons one summer. Suzi had been bored by the place. "That's great, Suzi," she said. "Congratulations. Where is it?"

"Ah ha! That, for the moment, is a secret. *And* a surprise. So you'll just have to come to my party tomorrow night to find out all about it. Derek and I are calling everybody today. Megan, of course you'll come, you and Jack."

"Well—"

"Oh, Megan, don't say you can't make it. You just have to be there. It wouldn't be the same without you. I mean, you've known how much I've wanted this longer than anybody in the world, right? Just be there, both of you."

"Okay," Megan said resignedly, and a moment later Suzi's voice had bubbled away.

A party was not exactly what she'd had in mind for Friday night. Insofar as she had any plans at all, they consisted of going to bed early and not waking up until Saturday afternoon.

Suzi lived in a large loft in SoHo, its space divided into different areas by Japanese screens. When she threw a party, the whole space could be opened up, and Megan had seen as many as two hundred people there at one time, with room left over for a live band. The live band, of course, played only the very latest kind of music. When punk rock was hot, they played punk rock. Currently it was New Wave. Suzi's taste in music changed only a little less often than her taste in men.

So the latest boyfriend was named Derek. Megan leaned forward and cautiously pulled a memo pad from the clutter on her desk, then printed the name in large letters, reminding herself to make Jack memorize it. Every time he saw Suzi and her latest, he called the boyfriend by the wrong name.

Megan smiled at the thought. Then she realized that she should call Jack right away at his office to tell him about the party before he made any other plans. And maybe the party would be fun. If the band was good, maybe they could just dance themselves into a coma and sleep the weekend away. She reached for the phone and punched Jack's number.

When she got his office, his assistant said he was on his way to an editorial meeting but she could still catch him if it was important. Megan, feeling a little better now, said it was important. A minute later, she could tell from Jack's tone of voice that he wasn't in his office; he was probably standing beside his assistant's desk, using her phone.

"Hi, babe," he said. But then added instantly, "Listen, I can't talk now, I'm due at a meeting." It wasn't unusual for him to be in a hurry, but his impatient tone now dispelled the momentary pleasure she had felt.

"It's not that important," she said.

"Well, just tell me quick, okay? This place is a looney bin. The production department lost the corrected galleys for three of my books this morning. That was for openers. And I'm already late for this meeting. Is it something urgent?"

"No, not really," Megan said, knowing she was keeping him even later but wanting to hear his voice a few seconds longer. "I just wanted to tell you we're going to a party tomorrow night."

"Oh, no."

"What's wrong? Did you plan something else?"

She heard him sigh. "Nothing that can't be changed," he said. "Tell me about it at dinner, okay? Let's eat out. Can you meet me at Angelo's at six-thirty?"

"Okay."

"See you then. I really have to go, babe. Love ya."

"Love you too," Megan said. "See you later."

No matter how rushed he was, Jack always reminded her that he loved her. And didn't care who heard him say it. She was glad to hear the familiar words, glad of the familiar habit, but it did little to ease the trials of the afternoon ahead as she hung up the phone.

And, right on cue, there was Dave standing at her desk.

"I couldn't find any," he said when she looked up. "I don't think we have the sort of thing you're looking for."

Megan looked into his face for a second, then lowered her gaze.

"Okay," she said softly. "Okay. Then start calling the agencies and see what we can get quick. We need another good set by Tuesday."

"I'll do my best," Dave said.

"Right," Megan said, and closed her eyes. After a moment, Dave moved away from her desk.

"Right," Megan said again to herself.

"Do you come here often?"

Megan looked up from the book she was reading and saw Jack standing over her. Even in the dim light of Angelo's, she could see the tiredness in his face. He was smiling but the muscles around his mouth looked strained. He leaned over and kissed her, then pulled out a chair and sat down as Megan slipped a bookmark into the paperback and pushed it aside.

"What are you reading?" he said, tilting his head to read the title. The cover showed a young girl in a filmy nightgown, running down the lawn from an old mansion where a solitary light burned in an upper window. "Good God," he said when he made it out. "Your taste is getting as low as mine."

Megan shrugged. "That job is driving me crazy," she said, and managed to keep her tone very matter-of-fact.

"Yes, I know," Jack said gently. He glanced down at the table. "Have you looked at the menu yet?"

"No."

Jack picked up the bright red menu, studied it briefly, and when the waiter came ordered for both of them, including a full bottle of Bolla Chianti. Then he looked back at Megan.

"Okay—" he started, but she wouldn't let him go on.

"Jack, look, I'm sorry. I know I'm in a lousy mood, but you look like you had a rotten day too, and I haven't even asked."

Jack looked as tired as Megan felt, but he reached across the table and took her hand. "As a matter of fact," he said, "I had a *thoroughly* rotten day. But you go first. C'mon, tell me about it." He held on to her hand.

So Megan told him. She went on and on, each item in

her list of annoyances reminding her of three more. The waiter delivered bread and salads and the wine, but Megan ignored him and just kept talking. She was only winding down when he finally returned with their dinners. They both kept silent while he set the food in front of them and hoped they enjoyed their meal.

Jack lifted his wine glass. "To better days," he said.

"Yeah," Megan said listlessly, but she raised her own glass and sipped from it. Then she set it down and said, "Tell me about *your* rotten day."

"About like yours," Jack said, "only translated into the paperback business." He related quickly how the production department had lost the corrected galleys of three books, and he'd had to call the authors and tell them they'd have to correct the proofs again, on short notice, so the books could stay on schedule. The day had ended with an editorial meeting at which the powers-that-be had expressed "grave reservations" over a book, soon to be published, that Jack thought was the best and most commercial novel he'd bought since going to the house as an editor. Oh, and the middle of the day was taken up by a two-hour lunch with a bestselling author who drank too much and talked too long and too loud. Jack couldn't stand him and, worse, thought his writing might, if he worked at it, improve someday to the point of mere illiteracy. The editorial director, his myopic gaze fixed firmly on the bottom line of the profit-and-loss sheets, refused to let Jack "tamper" with the writer's "unique and highly individual style."

"Sounds lovely," Megan said when he finished.

Jack smiled thinly, the expression barely moving the corners of his mouth. "Hey, that's publishing for you. Everybody knows it's a mug's game."

This time Megan managed a genuine smile in return.

"Eat your dinner," she said. "Your food's getting cold."

They ate in silence for a few minutes. Then he looked across at Megan. "So tell me about this party we're going to."

"It's some sort of surprise thing Suzi Steiger's giving," Megan said. She repeated as much as she could remember of the conversation. "And next thing I knew, I'd said we'd be there."

Jack shrugged. "Okay," he said. "I just had something else in mind." He hesitated, then put down his fork. "Actually, I was thinking this morning that we should get away for a couple of days. So I called that motel, the place with the cabins down by the creek, that we stayed in one time in Woodstock. I made a reservation for the weekend. Figured we'd spend the time in intellectual pursuits like browsing through the candle shop or climbing Lookout Mountain. It's nice there in May. I even called that club, Joyous Lake, to see who's appearing this weekend."

"I give up," Megan said. "Who?"

"Johnny Paycheck. I was all ready to join in a few choruses of 'Take this job and shove it.' "

"Jack—"

"It's all right, honey, we'll do it some other weekend."

"I could call Suzi and make some excuse."

Jack shook his head. "No, you said we'd be there, so we'll be there. Just tell me the current boyfriend's name so I don't get it wrong this time. Donald, isn't it?"

Megan smiled. "Donald was the last one. This one is Derek."

"Are you sure? I thought there was one back a bit who was Derek."

"No, you just *called* him Derek."

Jack sighed. "So this one is Derek."

"Right."

"So this time, if I call him Derek, I'll be right?"

"Right," Megan said. "Unless, of course, Donald is reinstated between now and nine o'clock tomorrow night."

Jack shook his head. "Promise to keep me posted?"

"Promise."

"Let's hope that surprise is something totally terrific."

"Well, with Suzi, things are never less than interesting. Maybe it'll turn out great."

Jack raised his wine glass. "I'll drink to that," he said.

Megan rapped her knuckles on the table. "Knock on wood," she said, and raised her glass to join him.

2

Megan knew a woman who had discarded lovers because the two of them didn't "look right" together; Jack declared that the guys just didn't match the woman's outfits. Had Megan cared about such things, she would have said that Jack suited her to a T.

At thirty-two, he was tall, broad across the shoulders, and moved with a purposeful confidence. His mouth could be grim—it had been a lot harder until Megan's presence in his life had softened him up—but the tightness was usually ready to turn into a broad smile at a moment's notice. When relaxed, he was easy-going and often quiet. When irritated, he could be impatient, and when angry, could be a truly threatening figure. If suitably provoked, he could be the most devastatingly sarcastic person Megan had ever heard. Even so, his treatment of her suggested that he had spent all his life until then looking for someone to be nice to and, in Megan, had finally found her.

On bad days, Jack was inclined to put down his success as an editor to the fact that he wore the right sort

of tweed jackets. Megan sometimes teased him about
the sameness of his outfits: the tweed jacket, open shirt,
and jeans (the only designer name he really trusted was
Levi's). "People know natural talent when they see it,"
he would answer. "They can tell by the natural fibres.
I'm like a walking health food, that's why people love
me. One look, and they know I'm good for them."

Whether or not the jacket had anything to do with it,
Jack was making a good career in publishing. Among
his recent accomplishments were two new lines of series
books, one of which was doing extremely well already
and had earned him several flattering mentions in
Publishers Weekly and *Magazine and Bookseller*. He
had also been responsible for bringing into the house a
number of authors who would be generating enough
revenue to pay the company's rent for years to come.
He knew what would work in a book, what would make
it a commercial success without bastardizing it. And
unless something terrible happened—a sale of the company to a different conglomerate, a merger with another
house, or a "consolidation of staff," as publishers liked
to call wholesale firings—all of his colleagues expected
him to move further up the ladder.

But his list of frustrations was getting as long as
Megan's these days. When Jack had begun work on the
two new lines, one a men's action series, the other a new
twist on the old romance formula—both of them things
he was good at but that didn't really interest him—he
had asked for an additional assistant and been refused.
And when he reminded management that he was due for
a raise, especially with the increased work he was doing
now, to make no mention of the increased earnings his
books were bringing in, management hemmed and
hawed and stalled and, after a three-month delay, de-

clared that it might be possible to think about a raise "maybe in a few months."

And lying beneath the daily round of frustrations was a longer-lasting one. If Megan was irritated because her work left her no time for painting, Jack's work left him no time for the writing he wanted to do. He remembered reading somewhere that western writer Louis L'Amour said he could put his typewriter on his knees and write a novel in the middle of Sunset Boulevard. But Jack couldn't work like that; he needed time and a little peace of mind in order to concentrate.

The summer before, he and Megan had rented a small house, barely more than a one-room cottage with a porch, near Woodstock in the southern Catskills. The house was actually in nearby Mt. Tremper because they hadn't wanted to be too tempted by the bars and galleries and shops of Woodstock itself. They'd had the house for the whole summer and managed to spend three solid weeks there and several long weekends. Megan had painted happily on the sunny porch while Jack worked at the typewriter inside. By the end of the summer, he had finished three-quarters of the first draft of a novel. He didn't mind, afterward, putting it aside for a while to "cool off." What he did mind was that, since last summer, he hadn't been able to touch the manuscript at all. The sketches and paintings Megan had done were still stacked behind the couch. Jack's book—three-quarters of the first draft—was still in a gray box in the bottom drawer of a filing cabinet in the bedroom.

They talked sometimes, happily, about the house they'd rented, remembered with pleasure the good work they'd done during the days, the pleasant evenings when Megan cooked and Jack baked bread, the yard sales they'd gone to and all the junk they'd poked through and been tempted to buy, the friends they'd made. But they didn't talk about it very often or very long, because those conversations inevitably reminded them of the painting and the writing they had undertaken with such enthusiasm, and that had been left afterward to turn dim and yellowed and soiled, the initial inspiration that sparked it as faded as the paper itself.

There were just too many parties, too many lunches, dinners, drinks, too many phone calls to return, too many manuscripts to edit, too many sets of chromes to examine, too many deadlines, and too little time for all of it, too little time, hardly any time at all.

They usually shared a cab in the mornings as far as Megan's office and then Jack walked the rest of the way by himself. On Friday morning, the ride down Manhattan's east side was long and slow, the taxi barely creeping along in bumper-to-bumper traffic.

"Friday," Jack grumbled. When they'd emerged from the building into the bright May sunshine, he'd smiled at the day and drawn a deep lungful of the soft air. Now, in the taxi, he was scowling at the traffic crowding Lexington Avenue.

Megan reached over and took his hand. "Honey, we really don't have to go to this party tonight, you know."

"No, it's okay. It's really not that. It'll probably be a lot of fun. Actually, I was just thinking that it's May already and we haven't even thought about planning a vacation."

"Well, we did talk about it once—"

Jack turned to look at her. "Sure," he said. "Last winter. Before my two series started taking all my time and before you became the Quim Queen of Manhattan." Out of the corner of his eye, he saw the taxi driver turn his head slightly. "Never mind," he said. "We'll talk about it later."

They rode in silence while the taxi inched its way the length of one block.

"Jack," Megan said, frowning, "I just thought of something. God, I'm sorry, I forgot all about it. Isn't the A.B.A. convention in May? Aren't you going to that?"

The American Booksellers Association holds its annual enormous convention in a different city each year. It lasts the better part of a week and, in general, everybody who is anybody in the publishing business is there.

Jack's voice was calm when he answered. "I'm not going this year. It seems the economic squeeze has squeezed me out. I'm told it costs too much to be sending as many people as we've always sent before. My books will be well represented in displays, of course, but *I* won't be there. So the honchos go to San Francisco for a week and hobnob with the stars while the rest of us stay home and dust the bookshelves. Funny, you know, for a while there I was getting to think I was a honcho."

Megan was about to say something but the taxi driver beat her to it. "Hey, fella," he said over his shoulder, "lemme tell ya somethin. Bosses are all bastards. They'll do it to ya every time. Screw ya every chance they get."

Jack stared at the back of the man's head for a moment, then said quietly, "You know, you're quite right. But you're forgetting one thing. While I'm in this taxi, *I'm* the boss, so why don't you just shut the fuck up and mind your own business and keep hoping I remember to tip you.''

"Oh, Jack," Megan said softly.

They rode the rest of the way in silence.

By the time they arrived at Suzi Steiger's place in SoHo that evening, they were both in much better moods. They had treated themselves to a leisurely and elaborate dinner at their favorite Indian restaurant, the Kashmir on 46th Street, enjoying the food, the service, the attention of the hovering waiter, and watching the table gradually disappear beneath a dazzling array of exotic foods. They ordered coffee and lingered over several cups, talking quietly, easily, each of them careful to stay away from any topic that might turn the conversation in a depressing direction. Jack mentioned that he'd cancelled the Woodstock reservations, and neither of them referred to it again.

When the waiter finally brought the check, Jack pulled out his American Express card.

"This one goes on the expense account," he said. "You know, I've spent more money this week wining and dining people I can barely stand than I earned this week for doing my job. I think the least the company can do is treat us to dinner."

Megan laughed. "I couldn't agree more. Besides, it's really a legitimate business expense. I'm a potential author, after all."

"Oh, really?"

"Sure. I'm planning on writing my autobiography one of these days. I'm calling it—"

"Don't tell me—"

"Memoirs of a Quim Queen," they said together, and it was the first good long laugh they'd had in weeks.

As they rode down to SoHo in a taxi a few minutes

later, Jack put his arm around Megan and whispered in her ear, "You'll always be my Quim Queen."

"That's a perfectly disgusting thing to say," Megan whispered back. She snuggled closer. "Please say it again!"

Suzi's loft was on a street of trendy restaurants and fashionable art galleries. As soon as they got out of the cab, they could hear the music of the party coming from windows upstairs. They rang the bell at the street door and wondered if anyone could hear it above the roar of the stereo system. Jack was about to ring it again when the door was pulled open and they found themselves facing a girl done up in the latest of punk fashions. Her face was chalk white except for black mascara that outlined her eyes and made her look like a cartoon character. Her black hair was cut short and stood straight up on top. A patch above her right ear was dyed bright red. Above her left ear was a patch of bright green. She was wearing what appeared to be a man's suit that might have been stylish in the mid-50's. Between the vee of the lapels was an expanse of bare flat chest.

"C'mon up," the girl said. "My name's Candy. Who are you?"

"The Tsar and Tsarina of all the Russias," Jack replied.

"That's nice," said Candy. "Okay, listen, here's how it works. I was the last one in, see, so I had to answer the door. I mean the bell. So now you're the last one in, so you have to get the next one, right?"

"Right," Megan said quickly. "Gotcha."

"Yeah," Candy said, then turned and ran lightly up the stairs, her fanny twitching at them as she went.

"Now I know why the British call them birds," Jack muttered as they climbed the stairs.

Megan arranged her face to look stern. "Just see to it
that you behave yourself tonight or you'll get the spank-
ing of your life when we get home."

"Promises, promises," Jack muttered.

A moment later, the party swirled around them and
they were swallowed up.

The loft was a huge expanse of gleaming hardwood
floors, interrupted only by two rows of structural
pillars. The walls were painted white and an intricate
pattern of exposed pipes crisscrossed the ceiling. The
pipes were painted in bright poster colors, some of
which, Jack suspected, probably glowed in the dark,
making a kind of eerie roadmap. "Don't you just love
the pipes in those colors?" Suzi had asked him at the
first party she'd given in the loft. "Swell," Jack had
assured her. "Really, they're just swell." "They're like
that place in Paris," Suzi had said. "You know, that
museum or something, the one named after that guy?"
"Oh yeah," Jack had said, "you're right, it's *just* like
that. God, what a great idea." Later he had asked
Megan if she was sure it was *college* where she and Suzi
had been roommates. "Well," Megan had answered,
"it *was* Bennington, you know." "Ah ha," Jack had
said.

Now all the furniture had been pushed out of sight
behind screens at one end of the space, and the loft was
alive with moving bodies, the air throbbing with the
beat of the music coming from six speakers. The other
end of the loft was piled with untidy heaps of trunks,
amplifiers, and instrument cases where the band was
setting up. For the present, everyone seemed satisfied
with recorded music, which was being presided over by
a thickly bearded man in a tee-shirt who was leaning

lovingly over a soundboard, delicately adjusting knobs on the panels in front of him and keeping a wary eye on the two turntables at his side. Every few seconds he cocked his head and glared balefully at one of the speakers mounted on the wall. Then he'd lean lower over the board and, with the delicate fingers of a safe-cracker, make an even finer adjustment in the quality of the sound. When he straightened up for a moment, Jack was able to read the front of his tee-shirt. It said BABY and had a red arrow pointing down to his beer belly.

The crowd ignored his intense concentration. Those who were dancing responded only to the music. Those who were talking ignored the music entirely, only raising their voices when the volume of sound required it. Jack, who had gotten separated from Megan in the crowd at the top of the stairs, watched the sound man for a few minutes, then drifted on toward the bar. Suzi thought it was chic to serve only beer at parties and Jack silently blessed her for it. Of course, it wasn't just any beer, not for Suzi; each party featured a different imported brand. This time, he discovered with pleasure, it was Whitbread, imported from England. The bar consisted of six plastic barrels filled with ice and bottles of beer. Jack pulled one out, opened it, and took a long swallow.

He drifted slowly along the wall, keeping an eye out for Suzi. He caught a glimpse of Megan once, in the distance, laughing with a loud group. He recognized a few faces here and there, people he had seen at other parties, but no one whose name he could instantly recall. Then he saw Candy, the girl who had opened the door downstairs, and realized that neither he nor Megan had stayed near the stairs long enough to hear the bell ring again. He smiled, picturing a frustrated mob of partyers gathered on the street outside, unable to make themselves heard above the noise.

"What's funny?" Candy breathed at him. She seemed to be dancing and didn't stop moving while she spoke, but she had no partner and apparently needed none, using the wall behind her as a kind of base of operations. She would take a step away from the wall, then move back and press her bottom flat against it, then bend forward and jerk, as if the wall were humping her. Each time she bent forward, Jack could see her nipples beneath the suit jacket. They were painted black.

"Life in general," Jack told her in a confidential tone, and moved on.

As he started on his second beer, Suzi Steiger appeared out of the crowd.

"Jack, darling!" she cried as she grabbed his hand and presented her cheek for a kiss. "Come with me. I want you to meet some people I know. Are you having a good time? Good! C'mon! You'll love these people, they're all writers."

"Oh, good," Jack murmured, "I've been dying to meet some writers."

Suzi introduced him to the group. At once, a rather masculine-looking woman on his left, who had a hint of a moustache and said her name was Felicia, told him, "I write historical romances."

"Oh really," Jack said, "how interesting. Tell me all about them." He was already calculating how long it would be until he could excuse himself to go back for another beer.

"Well, the first one was set on a plantation in the south and the heroine . . . ," Felicia was saying as Jack turned off his mind.

Half an hour later, he and Megan managed a rendez-vous. They went halfway down the stairs so they could talk more comfortably.

"I've met a juggler, a porno actress, and a science fiction writer," Megan told him. "And that was only in the first ten minutes."

"Quite a haul," Jack said. "That makes it a typical Suzi Steiger party."

"Oh, and I met Derek."

"Lucky you. I haven't had the pleasure. I met an accountant who swears that if we're paying more than three hundred dollars a year in taxes, we're paying more than we should. And I've had two propositions from gays."

"It's your ass," Megan said. "They love your ass."

Then Suzi yelled down to Megan that there was somebody she absolutely had to meet, and a moment later the band started up with a crash of sound. Megan disappeared into the mob. Jack followed more slowly up the stairs, feeling the vibrations of the music in the floor.

"Wanna dance?"

Candy stood at his elbow, bouncing lightly on bare feet.

"Why not?" he said. "Black is my favorite color."

"You're weird, you know that?" Candy said as they started moving with the music.

A little while later, when Jack and Megan were dancing together, Jack was momentarily blinded by a brilliant light that swept over him. Megan explained that it was Steve, Suzi's younger brother. He was studying filmmaking and television at N.Y.U. Suzi had asked him to bring a portable video camera with him to tape everybody at the party—it also had something to do with the surprise that was yet to be announced—and then the videotapes would be shown for laughs at a future party. Steve was prowling everywhere throughout the loft, trying to get at least a few seconds of everyone on tape.

"Nifty," Jack said. "Ask Suzi if we can get a copy of it. Then we can relive this night over and over."

"Keep dancing," Megan told him.

The band played one set, rested for twenty minutes, then started the second set. When they moved into the last number of the set, Suzi Steiger detached herself from her dancing partner—a tall, expensive-looking man who *should* have been Derek, Jack thought, even if he wasn't—and went up to speak to the lead singer while the members of the band sailed off on instrumental variations. The number finally ended, and the singer, after mopping sweat from his forehead with the back of his hand, detached the microphone from the stand.

"Hey, thanks!" he growled into it in response to the applause. "Now I want to introduce the hostess of this great party. Here she is!" And without further ado, he handed the microphone to Suzi, who was greeted with more applause.

"Okay, okay!" she shouted into the mike. "I want to tell you my surprise! C'mon, pipe down, everybody, it's time!" When the noise level dropped a bit, she announced, her voice ricocheting around the walls, "We're moving the party!" She held up her hands to silence the outcry. "Now I know everybody's having a great time—at least I hope you are—but this is the surprise I promised you. We're moving the party from here"—she paused and swept her gaze dramatically around the room—"to my house. My house! *I just bought a house!*"

"Just tell us where it is, Suzi!" somebody shouted.

After a few minutes of general confusion, everyone quieted down to wait for more information.

"We're going to the Catskills!" Suzi shouted.

Talking quickly, she told them that she had just bought a house in the northern Catskills and she was so happy about it that she wanted everybody to celebrate with her. The house was ready and waiting for them right now, and there were two rented buses downstairs. They could all spend the weekend there and the buses would bring them back on Sunday evening. And absolutely everybody had to come!

"I don't think I believe this," Jack said quietly to Megan.

"Think about it a second," Megan replied. "You'll believe it."

"You know," Jack said slowly, "that's the really scary part. I think you're right. I actually believe it."

"Well?"

"Well, what?"

"Are we going?"

"You're not serious."

"I am." She paused, then said, "Yes, I am. What the hell, let's go. Oh, Jack, yes, let's go. You've been wanting to go to the mountains anyway. Come on, let's do it. It'll be fun. If we stay home, you know, we'll just wonder what's going on."

All around them, people were conferring, checking quickly to see which of their friends were going to go.

More seriously this time, Megan said, "At least it's a chance to get out in the country and see something different for a change. Let's do it, Jack."

"Well," he said slowly, "I suppose Mother Trailways can always bring us home if we get stuck."

Half an hour later, about fifty people, including Jack

and Megan, were seated in one of the two coaches. The other bus had been sent away, Suzi declaring, "Poo on the party poopers who wouldn't come!" The driver remained impassive, staring out the windshield at the dark street, waiting to be told he could start. When everyone was settled, Jack looked at his watch. It was two-thirty in the morning. The bus pulled away from the curb and everyone cheered loudly.

Megan slid down in her seat and cuddled up against Jack. "You realize, don't you," she said, "that if this turns out to be a disaster, I'll hold you personally responsible?"

"Funny," Jack said, "I was about to tell you the same thing."

A few minutes later, as the bus made its way around Washington Square Park, heading for Sixth Avenue and the west side, Suzi Steiger came up the aisle.

"There you are," she said, and settled precariously on the arm of Jack's seat. "This is probably the wildest thing I've ever done," she said. "But, Megan, you know how much I've always wanted to have a place like this. It's really a dairy farm. Of course, the cows are all gone now. I had this real estate agent looking around for me up there and he found this place. Some hayseed farmer decided he'd had enough of tilling the soil or whatever it is farmers do all day and he happened to go to this agent of mine. The place is just what I was looking for. Wait till you see it! The house is real old, I forget when it was built, and there's this huge barn and everything and, God, you just have to drive miles and miles off the main drag before you even get to the place. Oh, God, I just love it. I'm planning on hiding out there as often as I can."

"Suzi," Jack said, "I only have one question. You

never told us where it is. Where are we going?"

"Oh, God, I didn't even tell you? It's in the Catskills, in the northern Catskills. It's sort of between, wait, let me see if I can remember. Oneonta. Yes, there's a big school there or something, right? Between Oneonta and Cobleskill. Can you imagine such names? It's about a four-hour drive, so we'll be getting there around dawn. Oh, and wait till I tell you the name of the town. You'll love it, it's really creepy. The place is called Deacons Kill. Isn't that marvelously creepy?"

"Marvelous," Megan agreed.

Suzi laughed and said, "I knew you'd love it!" as the bus made another turn and headed north.

3

Jack stayed awake for a while after Suzi returned to her seat. Beside him, Megan curled up tighter; he could feel the rhythm of her breathing grow steady as she fell into a sound sleep. Without disturbing her, he turned his head and kissed her hair. Someone from the back of the bus came down the aisle, passing out more bottles of Whitbread. Jack took one and sipped it slowly.

Beneath the bus, the miles of road glided away, rolling backward in endless unmarked succession, leaving behind Manhattan, the Bronx, Yonkers, Tarrytown. The bus hummed through the long sweeping S-curve of the Tappan Zee Bridge, the dark waters of the Hudson River flowing silently beneath it. Then west for a few miles, past sleeping towns and villages and the silent white steeples of churches. Then north through rolling hills, the trees gradually giving way to open farmland, an occasional barn breaking the smooth line of a hill against the sky, its dark shape promising secrets within, but left behind almost instantly. The green and white signs, bearing the names of exits and towns and cities, flickered past the bus, carried away into the pool of darkness behind, as if living for only an instant in the sweeping, rushing, silent lights of the bus, then dying when it passed.

Then the signs grew sparser, the distances between exits longer. Finally, after two hours, the bus glided onto an exit ramp and hissed to a stop at a toll booth.

Jack opened his eyes and shifted in his seat. In the light from the toll booth, he saw that a few people had apparently changed places. Across the aisle, by herself, he saw Candy. She was curled into a tight fetal position sideways in the seat. Her knees were pulled up under her chin, her hands joined and cushioning her cheek against the seatback. The dim light and her position made her look like a child, Jack thought. He was wondering how old she really was when the bus began moving again, and the blue-white light of the toll booth fell away behind the bus, and darkness swallowed it again. He closed his eyes and drifted back to sleep.

Now the hills and the trees closed in tight around the bus. Several miles of smooth multi-lane highway gave way after some minutes to a single-lane route that twisted through the hills, finding its wandering way northwest from the Thruway. Now only an occasional light flickered in the darkness as the bus rolled past. Tiny towns and villages snapped into momentary life as the bus, a bright-eyed but silent monster, revealed them, then cast them instantly away and rolled on, always seeking another and another and another. Mailboxes stood on spindly legs, like bulky metal flowers, by the side of the road. Sometimes storefronts, sometimes houses, loomed for a sudden instant at the windows of the bus and were as quickly flicked away. And always there were trees, seeming to reach for the bus, the

was still sound asleep beside him. He looked at his watch and saw that it was a little after six-thirty. He looked around quickly, saw buildings, the green, a church, a faint streak of light in the sky. On his right, he saw a three-storied white building, its Victorian front elaborately decorated with carved wood, its ground floor elegant with a wide, columned porch. He was just in time to see a sign over the entrance, its lettering bright with gold paint.

CENTENNIAL HOTEL
Deacons Kill, N.Y.
1876

He wiped a hand across his face and felt the stubble of his beard. He sat up a little straighter and tried to ease the kinks out of cramped muscles. Gently he shook Megan's shoulder. She opened her eyes sleepily and stared at him for a long minute. Then she looked past him, out the window of the bus.

"Where are we?" she asked, her voice still husky with sleep.

Jack leaned over and kissed her. "Well," he said, "as near as I can figure, we're here. I saw a sign a minute ago that said Deacons Kill."

"Oh," Megan replied. "Does that mean I have to wake up?"

"I'm afraid so. For a while, anyway."

"I knew you were going to say that."

Jack saw Suzi standing at the front of the bus, leaning over the driver and pointing toward the road ahead, giving him directions. There was just enough light outside now for Jack to see plowed fields sloping up the sides of hills whose tops were crested with thick woods. The bus passed three isolated houses, their plots of land fenced

off from the fields that surrounded them on three sides.
Then there were two farmsteads, facing each other
across the road, tall red barns flanking each house.

There was no longer any pavement beneath the bus.
The steady rubbery hiss of the tires had changed now to
the crunching of gravel and shale. In spots, the gravel
disappeared and the bus bounced over rutted, hard-
packed dirt, then found itself again on the smoother
gravel surface. A single small house appeared on the left
side of the road, a red jeep and a battered pickup truck
standing in front of it. Then the road divided. The
driver, following Suzi's instructions, took the road uphill to the left and slowed down to accommodate the
rougher surface. A few minutes later, the road still
climbing, the trees on the right gave way to open fields,
one more isolated house, then fields again. The ground
here was rough, rocky, patchy with tough vegetation,
unsuitable for anything but the dairy cows that would
graze it all day. The road climbed steadily higher up the
hill, leveling off here and there, then climbing again.
Then it reached a flat section. Jack stretched to see if
there was anything beyond the high weeds that lined
both sides of the road. There were only rocky fields. On
the left the land sloped farther upward; on the right it
sloped down for a short distance, then climbed the side
of yet another hill, endlessly creased by the irregularities
of ancient mountains. Then a fence appeared on the
right, a wooden fence that replaced the rusted barbed
wire that had been there since the last house was passed.
Jack leaned forward in the cramped space to look ahead
through the windshield. All around him, people were
waking up, jolted by the lurching of the bus.

Then suddenly a white farmhouse and red barn, both
of them tinted faint gold in the light of dawn, appeared

on the right a little farther up the hill, more dark forest covering the hillside beyond them. The bus slowed, gravel crunching beneath it, and moved slowly through an open gateway in the fence. It bounced over the uneven dirt of the yard, then came to a stop in front of the house.

"Wake up, everybody!" Suzi shouted. "We're here!"

It was a venerable house, steady and patient through the passing of generations. Built in the middle of the nineteenth century, it had survived more changes of fortune than any man alive. It stood, solid but graceful, on its hillside, surveying its domain. Hard-working people had built and designed it generously, and the house had responded in kind. Its large rooms, broad windows, high ceilings, wide halls and encircling porch had sheltered an ever-changing family for more than a century and a quarter. It had held at bay the snow and the rain and the cold. Its stone fireplaces had warmed generations, as many as four at a time, from sun-wrinkled great-grandmothers to pink new infants. Its windows had stared unblinking at hundreds of changes of season, spring forever turning to summer, summer to fall, fall to winter, and winter again and again and again turning to spring. The wooden steps of the porch showed the wear of decades and decades, the soft wearing and rounding of useful years. Children had tripped on those steps, lovers had jumped up them, and friends had carried down them the remains of friends deceased. The lives and dreams of men and women had whirled through the house, filled its rooms, had cascaded down its steps, plodded across its porch, throbbed heartily all around it. The house itself did not change or move with

the tides of men. In some corners, the angles were no
longer true, in some of the floors narrow gaps had appeared between boards, and one corner of the porch
dipped slightly away from the house by a couple of
inches, but it remained one solid thing, whole and im-
movable, the signs of wear making no more substantial
difference than the deepening lines in a grandmother's
face. It seemed always to have stood there, solid, un-
shakeable, patient, infinitely patient.

"I love it," Megan said, and Jack nodded agreement.

Quietly, haltingly, its momentum interrupted, the
party resumed. Suzi had planned everything and, while
there weren't beds for everyone who had come, there
were dozens of blankets, still in their clear plastic
wrappers, stacked in a corner of the huge living room.
The freezer and refrigerator were filled with food. Cases
of beer—Genesee, this time—were piled in the kitchen.
The rooms were bare of furniture, but a litter of
cushions and lounging pillows in bright colors covered
the floors. A stereo system had already been set up. Suzi
had brought a suitcase filled with tapes so, while the
party might have lost its thrust, it wouldn't lack for
music to help it catch up. Within minutes, several
people were crouched on the floor, admiring the ampli-
fier and sorting through the tapes. Moments later, the
sound of the Plasmatics echoed through the house. A
few people groaned but continued their exploration
through the rooms. Others were already in the spacious,
old-fashioned kitchen, pawing through the food,
pulling pans from hooks on the walls, preparing to
make breakfast. One young man in white jeans and a
shiny red nylon jacket was promising to make "the
great-grandma of all omelets" if he could just find the

right sort of pan. Somebody else had found an
enormous coffee urn and was measuring out coffee
from a can.

The bus driver shook his head at the scene, collected a
cash advance from Suzi to cover the cost of his room
and meals at the Centennial Hotel, then climbed back in
the bus and drove away with instructions to return at
five o'clock on Sunday afternoon. No one remarked on
the departure of the bus, except Suzi's brother Steve,
who dutifully aimed his video camera at it as it rolled
away down the hill.

A few people were still poking through the house,
opening closet doors, climbing the stairs to the attic,
peering out windows on the second floor, while others
went off to explore the barn. A few couples strolled off
toward the thickly tangled woods that came to within a
couple of hundred feet of the back of the house, sloping
up and away from the cleared ground, climbing higher
up the hill.

Jack and Megan explored the house, going from
room to room, not missing anything, not saying much,
but each knowing what the other was thinking. Suzi accompanied them part of the way, chattering happily
about details of the house and land. She explained that
she only owned the farmstead itself and not the
meadows or whatever they were called that sloped away
beneath it. The farmer who owned it before was named
Ferrand; the real estate agent had warned her that his
family had owned it for years and years, and in the
minds of local people, it would always and forever be
"the Ferrand place." Nothing short of a century or so
of occupation would change that. All signs of the Ferrands were gone now from the house, the barn, the tool-
shed. The dairy herd that had been the livelihood of the

Ferrands had been sold to other local dairymen and the grazing land had been added to the acres of adjoining farms.

Finally, Jack couldn't restrain his curiosity any longer and asked Suzi if she'd mind giving them an idea of what the place had cost.

"Jack," she said, laughing, "if I told you, you'd accuse me of ripping off some innocent hayseed. But I'll tell you this much; it wasn't nearly as expensive as you might think. C'mon, let me show you the barn. *Cows* used to live in it, can you imagine?" And they were off to explore the barn.

Later, by themselves, they stood in the wide doorway of the barn, blinking in the bright morning sunshine. Across the yard, the house stood white and gleaming, and a bird sang in the woods.

"God, I'd love to have a place like this," Megan sighed.

"No, you wouldn't," Jack said. "You'd hate it here."

"Oh, yeah?"

"Sure. Do you really think you could live happily without all those nice familiar civilized things you're used to? You know, the taxis, the subways with all that nice graffiti, the winos, the air you can really sink your teeth into, the noise, the dirt, all that good stuff? Hell, I'll bet there hasn't been a decent garbage strike here in years."

"You know, maybe you've got a point there," Megan said thoughtfully. "It really would be pretty awful, wouldn't it? Gosh, I can picture it now. There'd be nothing to do, of course, so we'd have to spend all day, every day, just sitting on that porch. We'd have to get rocking chairs, I guess. I think they have a law or something up here that says you have to have rocking chairs. And with nothing to do, we'd have to find hobbies to fill our days. I know! I could take up painting! I'd have to sit on the porch all day, just painting, one picture after another. Just to fill the boring hours, of course. And you'd have to find a hobby too, maybe something like . . . whittling. No, maybe not whittling, I like you with fingers. Let's see. Maybe, oh, say, writing. You could—"

"I could work in that small room in the corner on the second floor, the one that faces the barn," Jack said quietly.

Megan looked at the ground. "It'd be just awful," she said.

"Awful," Jack agreed.

"I think I'm going to cry."

Jack put his arm around her shoulder. "C'mon," he said, "let's have something to eat, then find a place to get a few hours' sleep."

Megan slipped her arm around his waist and they walked slowly across the yard toward the house.

When they woke up at twelve-thirty, they waited their turn for one of the bathrooms and took a long hot shower together. Then they joined a group making sandwiches from piles of coldcuts in the kitchen. Ravenous appetites were the order of the day. The country air, they all agreed.

Megan went off to explore what looked like a vegetable garden near the woods in back of the house. Jack made another sandwich for himself and strolled off to eat it outside. On the porch, he found Candy stretched out flat on her back.

"Can I have a bite of your sandwich?" she asked.

Jack held it out to her. Candy propped herself up on her elbows and took a large bite from it.

"Yeah," she said by way of thanks.

"Any time," Jack said. "Let me know when you're hungry again." He went down the steps from the porch and took a bite from the sandwich himself.

"Okay," he heard Candy say behind him.

He walked toward the open gate, enjoying the air, the breeze, the view of the hills, the food, the feeling of having escaped to another world where everything was at peace. The day seemed to stretch endlessly beneath a blue sky, offering untold possibilities, none of them urgent.

He reached the gate and strolled out to the road. To his right, the road extended past the house, then gradually petered out into the woods that covered the rise of the hill. He could see how the vegetation on both sides closed in over it, narrowing it to a tunnel. On his left, the road offered a view of stony slopes covered with tough greenery and, farther away, more wooded hills. Gray slate gravel crunched satisfyingly beneath his feet as he turned left and strolled a little way down the road, finishing the sandwich as he walked. He was partway down the hill now, within sight of the last house he remembered seeing as the bus passed it earlier that morning. The house was surrounded by a low white fence that marked its smooth green lawn, edged with marigolds, from the rougher land around it. A man and woman stood in the yard at the side of the house—a vegetable garden, Jack thought it was—and looked steadily back at him. He could just make out their faces and thought he could see the man saying something to the woman. On an impulse, Jack raised his right arm and waved to them. They waved back.

For an instant, he remembered a train trip he had
once taken in Norway. Traveling north to Trondheim,
the train had rolled steadily for a day and a night,
passing through some of the wildest country Jack had
ever seen. It was an empty land, beautiful, but bleak
and unpromising. But every now and then, on the road
that ran parallel to the tracks on the other side of a
river, a car would stop, people would get out to watch
the train, and all of them, adults and children alike,
would wave at it until it was out of sight. The willing-
ness, perhaps the need, to greet another human being in
the empty landscape, had moved him then, and he remembered it suddenly, warmly, now. He raised his arm
and waved again in parting. The couple waved back,
and Jack turned and started up the road to the farmhouse.

Halfway back to the gate, his eye was caught by tiny
wildflowers growing among the weeds and nettles at the
side of the road. He stopped and crouched to look at
them. They were pretty and fragile-looking, and he
examined them closely, fascinated by their intricacy and
the thrust for life that motivated them to grow here in
the dry gravel. Selecting some of both the larger white
variety and the smaller purple ones, he gathered a small
bouquet to bring back to Megan.

He was about to stand up when he thought of Candy
lying on the porch and wondered if anyone had ever
brought flowers to her. He crouched to gather a second
bunch. As he set down the ones he'd picked, he noticed
for the first time the blue-gray color of the dusty gravel.
He scooped up a handful. It crumbled easily between his
fingers and one of the larger pieces split in half. He
dropped the rest and examined the piece that had come
apart. On the flat surface that had been inside and pro-

tected was the faint but clear impression of a seashell. Jack examined it with delight, then put it down carefully beside the flowers. Then, feeling like a kid, he sat cross-legged on the ground and began brushing his hand through the gravel, seeking the larger pieces.

He found several promising ones and carefully split them open along their natural lines to reveal the fossil impressions of seashells. Some were better preserved than others and, as near as he could tell, there were several different kinds of shells. He had been at it for quite a while, oblivious of the time, when he became conscious of someone standing behind him. He looked up quickly and saw Megan.

"Having fun digging in the dirt?" she asked.

"As a matter of fact, yes, I am," Jack said, his smile matching her own. "Sit down." He patted the ground. "I want to show you something."

As she sat beside him, he remembered the flowers he had picked. "Here," he said, handing them to her. "I picked these here posies for you. I'd dig my toe in the dirt but I think I'd hurt myself if I tried it in this position."

"Oh, Jack, they're so pretty," she said as she took the flowers. "Like you," she added and leaned over and kissed him.

"Look here," he said. He showed her three of the best fossils he had found. "These things must be millions of years old. These mountains were all under an ocean in prehistoric times. It's hard to believe they're still here. And the locals use them to surface the road. Boy, have we come a distance from East 80th Street!"

Megan examined the seashell fossils with the same pleasure Jack had felt when he found them. They sat awhile longer at the side of the road, searching for bigger specimens and showing each other their finds. Megan became so engrossed in what she was doing that Jack finally asked her if she was having fun digging in the dirt.

They laughed together and stood up, brushing dust from their jeans, then, holding hands, started back up the road.

"How did you know I was out here?" Jack asked.

"That gal on the porch told me, the one you were dancing with last night."

"Oh, wait a minute!" Jack said. "Now don't get jealous, but I was just going to pick some flowers for her too when I found the fossils." He stooped and quickly gathered a fresh handful of flowers.

"You know, you're pretty neat," Megan said as they reached the gate.

"Yeah, I know," he answered. "I think it has something to do with the company I keep. Either that, or all this fresh air is rotting my brain."

"Oh, it's definitely the company you keep," Megan said. "No question about it."

Jack looked at her. "I think we need another shower," he said. "We got really dirty back there. I think another shower would be the very thing we need."

"That," Megan said, "is the best offer I've had all day. Besides, the bathroom is the only place you can get a little privacy around here." She grinned at him.

"That, my lady, is precisely what I had in mind."

When they reached the porch, Candy was still lying where he had left her earlier. He leaned over and handed her the tiny bouquet. Her face blossomed into a broad smile, made incongruous by her black lipstick.

"Hey, thanks!" she cried. "Thanks a lot!"

As they crossed the living room, Megan said, "You're

getting to be positively almost nice. I don't know if I can stand it.''

"Actions speak louder than words," Jack said. "You can show me how much you love me in the shower.''

"Is that a proposition, sir?"

"You better believe it.''

"Thank God," Megan said, and sprinted for the stairs.

Jack finally met Derek late in the afternoon and talked briefly with him. Suzi's boyfriend-of-the-week ("I think she orders them from a service or a club, like exotic fruits," Jack whispered to Megan) turned out to be a handsome, pinkly clean man about forty, with the kind of healthy, ruddy complexion associated with sea air taken on yachts. He was in banking, he declared solemnly to Jack.

Megan got into a conversation with Candy and discovered that she was interested in art. The girl's appearance betrayed her, Megan quickly learned. Candy knew every painting in every major museum in New York and talked easily about them as if they were old personal friends. And she loved to draw, she told Megan. Pictures of animals were her favorites. Together they searched the house, finally locating in the kitchen a pad of looseleaf paper and three felt-tip pens. Candy happily and easily dashed off a drawing of a llama that looked as if it might lean right out of the paper at any second. Megan was delighted.

Steve, Suzi's brother, seemed to have become one with his video camera and went everywhere with it, like a newsman at a fire. If he heard laughter in the yard, he dashed out of the house to catch the source of the merriment on tape. He leaned over the shoulders of

Megan and Candy as they watched each other draw animals. His lens followed the flight of Frisbees through the sparkling sunshine. He took footage of the wildflowers in the road, and pictures of the barn from the house, and pictures of the house from the barn.

By nightfall, the party had moved back to the living room. Jack and Megan slipped away around midnight, planning to get up early in the morning to explore the town of Deacons Kill. They settled into the corner of an empty bedroom upstairs.

"Oh, I wish we had a place like this ourselves," Megan whispered as she settled her cheek against his shoulder.

Jack kissed her forehead. "Go to sleep," he said gently.

Throughout the night, the house stood strong and silent. A sigh whispered through it, a snore, the rustle of blankets. A cellophane bag rattled across the living room floor, plaything of a breeze. Half a hundred people slept within, and the stone and the wood of the house held them safe.

After some hours, the sky lightened once again: first blue, then gray, then pink, gold, white, and blue again. Sunlight rose above the silent hills, picked out the dew and moved the mist, slid across the yard and touched the porch.

In the woods behind the sleeping house, where the ground sloped upward toward the crest of Deacons Rise and sunlight pierced with arrow-sharp rays between the gently stirring leaves, a human voice screamed in terror and another shouted.

4

Catherine McBain was nineteen years old. Three days
after her sixteenth birthday she had boarded a bus in the
grimy depot in Youngstown, Ohio. When she arrived at
the Port Authority Bus Terminal in New York City a
dozen hours later, she had in her pocket $112.43. She
owned the clothes she was wearing—a pair of sneakers,
jeans, panties, a tee-shirt, and a yellow windbreaker—
plus a few odds and ends: a lipstick, a bony rabbit's
foot, a twisted paperclip she used to clean her nails, one
tampon, and a Harlequin romance she had found on the
floor of the bus. She didn't know about New York's
Minnesota Strip, a stretch of Eighth Avenue in the 40's,
filled with runaways and teenage prostitutes. She didn't
know either about the detail of cops that regularly
patrols the bus terminals, matching the faces of young
people passing through against the photos they have
memorized of youngsters missing from their homes in
Virginia and Ohio and Maryland and thought likely to
show up here. Either she looked sufficiently self-
possessed or her features matched none of those in the

photos, because no one spoke to her or stopped her. Unchallenged, she walked out into the streets of the city.

She told people her name was Candy—she had always, from the time she had been a little girl, wanted to be called Candy—and dropped her last name. "Candy," she would say. "That's enough, isn't it?" It always was. She told strangers any story about herself that she thought, unconsciously, they might be willing to hear. Before her first New York day had ended, she had gravitated toward Greenwich Village, Washington Square Park, and the environs of N.Y.U., drawn by instinct toward other young people. She slept that night, and for two months after, in the room of a newly made friend in Weinstein Hall, a dormitory on University Place. After those two months, she moved on. She still had little more than a hundred dollars in her pocket, but she needed nothing more. As with natural survivors everywhere, the things she needed came her way. People gave her things, bought her meals, offered their couches for her to sleep on. Some of the people were women, some men, and now and then a family, but she was never raped, never abused, and slept with a man only when she chose. The city tested her, challenged her, finally learned to respect her, and at last made her welcome.

She discovered the museums and became a familiar visitor. The paintings became friends and family, filling a need she wasn't aware she had. And she met people there, people with more money than the friends she'd had before, and now they too took her in and made her welcome. She was unschooled but intelligent and could talk interestingly with anyone, showing genuine curiosity about the subjects that excited them. She was, at the very least, tolerated wherever she went. She "borrowed" money on occasion, but never very much and there was always something concrete to show for it and the patient lenders were satisfied. Her friends brought her to parties, and if no one quite knew who she was or what she did or with whom she had come— "Who? Oh, that's Candy"—she asked very little, made no demands, and seemed always to belong in any setting.

The sky was already growing bright when she left the sleeping house that morning. She sat for a while on the steps of the porch, letting the sun gradually ease the kinks from her body. She was wearing a dark blue tee-shirt now—no one could have said where she got it— that said "Schaeffer Music Festival, Central Park, '76" across the front. She stretched her legs out straight before her, elbows braced on the floor of the porch. A breeze touched her and her small breasts made tiny points beneath the cloth. Birds chirped on the roof of the house, and in the distance, somewhere among the hills, she heard the lowing of a cow. She closed her eyes and drifted.

After a while, she stood up, then strolled slowly, hands deep in the pockets of her pants, around the corner of the house and back toward the woods. There might be animals in the woods, maybe even deer, and it would be nice to see some animals. She wished fleetingly that there were still cows in the barn, but maybe she'd see something in the woods. She came to the first of the trees and stepped into the darker air, moving slowly, aimlessly wandering. The moist earth was dappled by light and Candy thought it looked very pretty.

Steve Steiger had slept in the barn, on a bundle of blankets brought from the house. He took special care with the camera, wrapping two blankets around it to protect it from the damp. He only wrapped one around himself. It was, in fact, the camera that had made him sleep there. He was afraid that in the house someone might accidentally kick the camera during the night. He could have put it in a closet, out of harm's way, but he was reluctant to leave it out of sight and out of reach. The camera was almost a part of him and, besides, it was going to make his fortune one of these days. His view of the world had a frame; he saw through the lens of the camera, and automatically his mind edited, clipped, rearranged everything he saw.

He awoke early, and when he rolled over to look through the open doors of the barn, he saw the girl Candy stretched back on the steps of the porch. He watched her for a minute, judging distance, angles, light levels, then quietly crept back into the half-light of the barn and got the camera. He already had a full minute of Candy on the steps, including a closeup of her face and another of her pointy breasts when she stood up. A freak, he thought. That made her an especially good subject: odd, colorful, interesting. When she turned and walked toward the woods, Steve followed her.

Candy made her way slowly through the trees. The ground sloped upward before her, and she picked her way carefully over rough stones and twisted roots and damp patches of dirt. It was cool here in the shade, and her bare arms were covered with gooseflesh until she adjusted to it. Where the ground was clear for a little way, she walked with her arms folded beneath her breasts, hands clutching her upper arms and hugging them to her for warmth. But the chill felt good in its way and she moved deeper into the woods, higher up the hill.

She saw a robin pecking among the rotted leaves on the ground and stood still to watch until it fluttered away. She watched a squirrel stare back at her from a tree branch, its head cocked curiously to one side. She found a rock covered with bright green moss and she stooped to examine it. Lying on the moss were a couple of seed pods from the maple trees above. She picked one up and remembered that, if dropped the right way, the double structure of the pod would make it spin like a drunken helicopter. She tried it and it worked and she smiled. She picked up another from the rock and, using her nail, split open the pod itself to reveal the green sticky inside. Whirlies, she suddenly remembered they were called. Whirlies! And, her smile widening, she folded back the sides of the open pod and stuck it on the bridge of her nose as she had done when she was a kid.

Walking carefully now, so as not to dislodge the whirlie, she came to a patch of the hill where the ground was stony and the trees more sparse. She paused and glanced around to find a suitable spot, turning and facing down the hill for better balance. Then she opened her pants, pushed them down to her knees, and squatted to urinate. Her thin white buttocks hovered a few inches above the ground as the stream hissed into the gravel. With one hand, she fixed the whirlie more firmly on her nose. Still squatting, she raised her head and saw, below her on the hill, the reflection of sunlight on glass.

"Hey!" she shouted. "Creep!"

Steve Steiger had stayed at a safe distance but kept her always in sight as she made her way slowly up the hill. When she stopped, he held his ground and made no attempt to get closer. He didn't know where she was heading or what she had in mind, but he had a feeling that something would come of it, maybe just a couple of seconds of usable tape, but something. She was such a weirdo, maybe she'd take off her clothes and run naked through the woods, or lie on the ground and play with herself. He hoped so. He'd caught more than a few glimpses of her black-painted nipples this weekend and already had several minutes of tape that would be edited into his own personal record of the weekend. What was she doing now? Stopping. Looking around. She looked like she was taking her pants off. Holy shit! Then he realized. Of course, she was going to take a piss! Well, Suzi and the others would never see this bit of tape, but he was going to record it for posterity. He checked the ground around him, then moved quickly to his right, seeking a clear line of sight through the moving branches of the trees above him. He was in position, camera rolling, by the time the girl squatted, and he saw, in his viewframe, the stream shooting from between her legs. Then she raised her head and her eyes looked straight into his own.

"Hey!" she shouted. "Creep!"

She waited the few seconds it took to finish urinating, then stood and automatically stepped to the side, away from the wet spot on the ground. She didn't hurry but deliberately began pulling her pants up toward her hips.

"Creep!" she shouted again. "You should—"

Something hard, rough, rocklike, crashed against her shoulders and knocked her sprawling in the gravel. She slid a little way down the hill before coming to a stop. Her hands and face were bleeding where the jagged stones had scraped them raw. The world was colored red with the blood that filled her eyes.

"Wha—"

Aching, hands bleeding, she pulled herself up on the uneven ground, trying to get her feet beneath her. She turned her head and looked up the hill to see who had hit her. There was no one there. Just above her, a section of gravel shifted, as if pressed down by some monstrous but invisible weight. Near that spot, another patch moved also, the stones crushed together. Then she heard the harsh dry breathing. It came from above her, uphill from her, as if something were standing, looming, over her. She blinked the blood from her eyes, tried to clear her vision, but still there was nothing to see. The breathing grew louder, harsher. In front of her, the gravel shifted again.

Candy pushed with her bleeding hands and made herself slide a little lower down the slope. She still couldn't see anything but she knew she had to get away. Amazingly, one part of her mind remarked on how well her senses were functioning. What was it? If she knew what had attacked her, she'd know better how to get away. *What was it?*

She couldn't see anything, but she could hear even more clearly now the sound of heavy breathing, like the sound of some terrible animal. Sharp stones dug deep into her knees as she inched backward, away from the thing she could only hear. That was the worst of it, the breathing, a sound almost too rough, too raw, to be made by anything alive. Above her, loose gravel was dislodged and a few larger stones tumbled toward her. Something crunched, crunched again, on the gravel. The breathing was louder, closer. She scrambled to her feet, hardly aware that she was moving, just trying to get away, get away, *get away!* The breathing was all around her, fast, rough, a sound like sand on stones, sand on gravel, sand on . . .

She screamed, a long loud wail.

Something smashed into the side of her face, snapping her head back. The world was red again. A thick salty taste filled her mouth and she gagged on it.

The thing that sounded like stones moving against each other was right over her, *right there!* She felt something like a stone column, but moving *moving!* brush against the side of her face. The sound of gravel being crushed filled her mind, engulfed her as if the stones of the mountain had been rent apart purposely to swallow her. Gravel again, a crunching sound, close to her ear, and loud, so loud. She made one last instinctive effort to get away, but her knotted muscles and the pants that were still around her legs held her in place. As she dimly realized that her legs would not move to help her, she felt something like sandpaper scrape across the soft skin of her stomach. Her body cried out to protect herself, to cover her crotch and her breasts and her face, but she could no longer move. Her skin was torn and bleeding across her stomach, and still she couldn't move. Then she felt herself grasped, held, squeezed tight around the middle, lifted into the air. She was carried a short distance, her body limp, then dropped roughly to the ground. She was almost unconscious when something like a stone club crushed her skull. The last sound she heard was the breathing above her, a sound like sand being sucked in and out of a cave, and then the world was gone.

A moment later, gravel crunched beside her lifeless body, crunched again, then again, and then was still.

Farther down the hillside, Steve Steiger beat his way through the undergrowth, stumbling, clutching at trees to keep his balance, leaping over exposed roots, ignoring the branches that whipped his face, plunging headlong down the hill to the farmhouse below.

After a few minutes more, the gravel stirred again beside Candy's body. Then the breathing and the gritty crunching sounds moved slowly up the hill.

5

It was no accident and John Chard knew it.

He stood in the roadway, watching the van that carried the body of the girl named Candy disappear down the hill. A tall man with short sandy hair, he carried his fifty-seven years easily and comfortably, despite the arthritis that caused him more pain than he readily admitted. Most of the stiffness was in his fingers, and he had long ago developed the habit of keeping his hands in his pockets. When the need arose, he could use his hands as necessary and could shoot the gun he wore with deadly accuracy; it was as if, in those moments, the arthritis receded, unstiffened the fingers, and responded to his call. At other times, the three outer fingers on each hand remained barely flexible, moving as a single unit. He stood with his hands in his pockets now and waited until the light cloud of dust had settled back to the road. Then he turned and walked slowly through the open gateway toward the house.

Chard had been sheriff of Deacons Kill for a quarter of a century, and a deputy before that, and the scene in the yard was familiar. Six cars were parked at haphazard angles, wherever they had bounced to a stop. Two of them were blue and yellow New York State Police cruisers, their doors flung open and left that way. The big green Chevy belonged to the two detectives who had arrived from Oneonta. The blue Ford had brought the two forensic technicians, both of them businesslike and impatient, obviously annoyed with the call and eager to get back to Sunday dinner with their families. The one who was wearing a cowboy hat was leaning on the roof of the dusty car, scribbling on a clipboard. The other sat in the front seat, writing in a notebook. They'd be gone in a couple of minutes, the whole scene efficiently committed to forms and reports and erased completely from their minds. The two detectives would go with them. Chard had listened as they questioned the people at the house, hearing the same useless stories he had heard himself before they arrived. So the techs would go, and the detectives, and the two young troopers. He looked at the two of them, tall, straight, broad in the shoulders, with their neat uniforms, neat haircuts, tinted sunglasses. One stood on the far side of the cars, his arms folded, looking regal. The other was counting the names on a list he carried on a clipboard: the list of all the people at the Ferrand place when the death had taken place. Names, occupations, addresses, telephone numbers, useless information, all of it useless. The only purpose served by having the technicians and detectives and troopers come by on a case like this was that it would keep them out of his hair later on. As long as they had enough paperwork, they'd be happy. Deacons Kill lay on the border between Otsego and Schoharie counties, and Chard was frequently at great pains to let all the adjacent police authorities get their fill of paperwork. Then he'd be rid of them and could get down to the serious business of protecting Deacons Kill himself.

And despite all the questions asked and answered, no one but that kid, Steve, knew anything at all. There were other state troopers watching the roads in the area now, especially those in the vicinity of Deacons Rise, but he doubted they'd turn up anything of value. There had been murders before this in Deacons Kill, and unusual deaths aplenty, some never accounted for, but if a stranger happened to wander through the hills, just passing through, and commit a murder in his progress, there was nothing to do to prevent it and, as happened sometimes, little to do to catch him. So the troopers now scouring the roads with his deputies would most likely turn up nothing. And Chard hated it.

But that kid knew something, Steve, the brother of that Suzi Steiger who owned the Ferrand place now. It's a good thing Martin Ferrand is miles away, Chard thought, and can't see his front door steps and his yard at this minute.

The other cars were his own, a white Buick LeSabre, and a fire-engine red Mustang that belonged to Doc Warren. The Mustang was new and Chard almost smiled, remembering the day three weeks ago when the old doctor had swung it, tires screeching and spitting gravel, into his driveway. The gray-haired doctor had exulted over the car like a teenager with his first wheels. Chard saw him on the porch now, handing a sheet of white paper, a pink copy attached to it, to one of the detectives. So that was that. The girl Candy, no last name, was officially dead.

Chard glanced around the yard one more time, and thought again of Martin Ferrand, and the family he had raised in this yard and this house. It's just as well you're far away from here, Martin, he thought. Chard, for all his years in office, hated these scenes, all of them he had ever witnessed, and this one had taken place on his own hill, just up his own road, almost within sight of his own house. He carefully rearranged his face to wipe all expression from it, then, hands still in his pockets, stepped onto the porch.

Chaos had invaded the sleeping house when Steve Steiger shouted his news at the door. The people in the living room had awakened first, some thinking for an instant that Suzi's dumb kid brother was playing some stupid practical joke. Several voices told him to fuck off and let them get some sleep. But others heard the sobs that threatened to choke off his words and reacted quickly. Four of the men went up the hill in the half-light toward where Steve was pointing—he flatly refused to go himself—and, after a few minutes of cautious searching, found the battered body of the girl. They knew enough to see that she was certainly dead, and knew enough too not to touch her or make any unnecessary tracks near the body. They returned to the house, where everyone else was awake by now, and, voices unsteady, told the others what they had seen.

"Is she really dead? I mean, *really?*"

"But what happened to her?"

"We should get out of here!"

Suzi Steiger was on the porch, holding her brother, alternately crushing his head against her shoulder and shaking him to make him repeat his choking story more slowly and more clearly, but after the first announcement, Steve wasn't able to say much of anything. There was a yellow wall phone in the kitchen but the line hadn't been connected yet. While people debated about the proper procedure—Who do you notify? Can you dial 911? What the fuck do people *do* out here in the sticks?—Jack Casey remembered the house a little way down the road. He pulled his shoes on, told Megan where he was going, and ran.

As he neared the house, the owner's white LeSabre was just coming up the hill and slowing, preparing to turn in at the driveway. Jack could see in the front seat the couple who had waved to him the previous afternoon. A young girl, about nineteen or twenty, was in the back. They looked as if they were returning from church and Jack remembered it was Sunday. The man at the wheel stopped the car without pulling into the driveway. He leaned out as Jack reached him and said quickly that he had to call the police. The man ducked his head inside, said something quickly to the woman and the girl, and they jumped out of the car. "My name is John Chard," he told Jack. "I'm sheriff in Deacons Kill." The woman had left the passenger door open and Jack hurried around and climbed in. As the car started to move, he heard her saying, "John, be careful."

The car leaped up the gravel road as Jack gave Chard the basic information, as much as he knew. Chard had a police radio in the car, and he was on the air, calling a doctor, before they squealed through the gate and lurched to a halt at the porch.

It took only seconds to gather everyone outside. He recognized Suzi Steiger at once as the new owner of the house. He had seen her before, once or twice driving past on Deacons Road and several times in town. The woman's brother, he learned, was the one who had found the body. After questioning him briefly, Chard returned to his car and called for additional personnel.

Then he immediately started up the hill in the direction the men pointed out. It took several minutes to find the body. Chard stayed only long enough to determine that the girl was dead. It didn't take long.

Back at the house, he asked more questions and quickly determined that there wasn't much to learn. Then he went back up the hill.

He stared a long time at the corpse. His eyes traveled up and down the girl's body and swept all around her, memorizing details. He touched nothing. The scene told him as much as there was to know. The body lay on its side and he could see where the front of the skull had been crushed. He noted the pants twisted around the legs. The angle of one arm was odd, suggesting it had been broken at the shoulder, possibly when she fell. The hand that lay palm up was scratched and bloody, like the face, the arm, the stomach. Slowly, his eyes swept the area again, seeking information. Gravel, he thought. No tracks. His gaze searched higher up the hillside, above the body. More gravel, scattered rocks, dead tree stumps among the living, only scattered patches of stony soil, nothing to hold a footprint, nothing but the silent mountain that kept its secrets so well, nothing but the crest of Deacons Rise. Chard looked again at the body. He guessed the girl was about the same age as Nancy, his daughter. He turned away and walked carefully down the hill.

By the time he reached the house, the others were arriving, first Doc Warren in his shiny red Mustang, then the State Police cruisers and, a little later, the detectives and technicians. The mortician's van was summoned from Deacons Kill and arrived shortly after. All the personnel on the scene fell quickly into the familiar routines and procedures, quick, efficient, orderly, im-

personal. Chard let the others do their jobs and stayed
in the background until all the forms were filled out.
When they were done, he could get to work himself in
this, his own territory.

Shortly after the mortician's van drove away with the
body, the others finished their jobs and followed it. The
troopers assured Chard they'd be joining in the watch
on the roads, and then they were gone. Only Doc
Warren stayed behind. Now the only cars left were his
own white one and the doctor's red one. The yard
looked suddenly very empty and the cars unusually
bright in the sunshine.

The crowd on the porch followed Chard's every step
as he walked over to Doc Warren. "Let's take a stroll by
ourselves," he said, and together they stepped off the
porch and walked toward the barn.

Conscious of the eyes on their backs, they halted in
the shade just inside the doorway. They stood in silence
for a moment, each easily imagining the other's
thoughts. They had been friends for most of their lives,
both of them lifelong residents of Deacons Kill, their
thinking and attitudes shaped by a common experience.
Through the years there had been more than a few times
when their areas of professional knowledge had
touched, and neither ever hesitated to contact the other
for advice. Doc Warren was a dozen years older than
Chard. He didn't look like a man nearing seventy but, if
it seemed appropriate, he could make himself appear
even older than his years, downright patriarchal, if he
thought it would accomplish something worth accom-
plishing. He seldom used the trick on Chard; the
years of friendship had evened out their ages, brought
them level. Neither had a closer friend.

Chard looked back toward the house and the uneasy

group that stood and sat on the porch. He saw the boy, Steve, peering across the yard into the darkness of the barn. Chard pushed his hands into his pockets, leaned back against a wooden stall, and faced his friend.

"I don't like these people," he said. "That's not a nice thing to be saying, I know, but it's the truth. Look at them. They're rich, most of them, and all they can think to do is play. That Suzi Steiger, the one who owns the place now. There's the difference all spelled out. What do you think this place will be like when she's done playing with it?"

"You just miss Martin," the doctor said, and raised his eyebrows.

Chard was silent for a few seconds, looking out at the house and seeing it as it had been in other times. "I do," he said.

"Odd," the doctor said, as if they were both parceling out the words. "Not hearing from him all this while." It was a familiar topic for them in recent weeks, one that neither would dwell on but that they both felt compelled to mention from time to time.

Chard nodded. "And look at it now," he said. Old friends could fill in the gaps in a friend's conversation.

"Well, times change, John."

"They don't change that fast in a place like the Kill."

Another silence hovered in the still air between them.

"You know, I keep thinking of Carla Helbig," Chard said at last. "I don't like it when somebody, especially a child, just disappears like that, and I can't figure out what's going on. And for some reason, this business today reminds me of Carla Helbig. And that girl who died up there." He nodded in the direction of the Rise. "We've had deaths before, and murders, but this just doesn't look right somehow. The whole scene didn't look right. Everything looked too . . . normal, too natural, if that makes any sense.''

"Very peculiar marks on her body," Doc Warren said quietly. "Very peculiar. On her stomach, for example. Skin looked like she'd been scraped with sandpaper.''

Chard shook his head. "These people," he said. "Girl didn't even have a last name.''

The doctor looked him in the eye. "Neither did Dagmar. Or Liberace.''

"They're not my kind of people, either," Chard said. "That boy, the one who found the body." He tilted his chin slightly in the direction of the porch. "He knows more than he's telling.''

"I know," Doc Warren said.

"I didn't kill her," Steve said, his voice hoarse and shaky.

"I didn't say you did.''

"I didn't!''

"I agree. So far. I believe you.''

"Then why—''

"Because you're not telling me everything you know," Chard said.

They were in the barn, the empty structure standing very still around them. At the house, Doc Warren was seeing to it that no one interrupted them.

"What . . . ? What do you mean?''

"I mean just what I said." Chard's voice suggested infinite patience, suggested that it was only a matter of time before Steve told him everything he wanted to know anyway, so he might as well just tell him and be done with it. "What did you really see?''

The boy was silent. He twisted away so that his back

was toward Chard.

The warm silence of the barn held them.

"What did you see?" Chard asked again. In the end, he knew, the boy would be glad to unload the weight. "What did you see?"

"Nothing." The boy's head moved from side to side. "Nothing," he said again.

Chard waited.

"She was just up there," Steve said. "She was just up on the hill, above me, and she was . . . she was looking at me and then . . . ."

"And then?" Chard's voice was soft, gentle, patient.

"She . . . fell forward, fell down." Steve turned suddenly to face the older man, his eyes pleading and frightened. "Honest to God, she looked like somebody shoved her or hit her or something but, I swear, there was nobody near her, I swear it!"

"There was nobody near her," Chard said, his voice toneless.

"No," Steve said. "Nothing, nobody. I swear to God. I saw the whole thing. She was alone. She was just . . . sort of standing there, and then all of a sudden she just went flying, just went sprawling in the dirt. Look, if I was trying to cover up, I'd tell you I saw somebody, right? Wouldn't I? But this was crazy. Weird. It was like . . . It was like something invisible just knocked her flat. Hey, I'm not making this up!"

Chard shoved his hands in his pants pockets and leaned against the dusty wooden slats of a stall, making himself appear easy and relaxed, interested.

"Start at the beginning," he said. "Just tell me what happened. Don't leave anything out."

Steve looked down and spoke slowly, deliberately, holding his nervous breath in check, anxious for Chard to know that he was very carefully recalling each and every detail of the experience. He said he's seen the girl start up the hill and he had followed.

"Why?"

"I . . . I just wanted to see where she was going."

Chard shook his head and made it look like a kindly gesture. "Not good enough," he said.

"I was going to . . . take some pictures of her," Steve said after a moment. Chard noted that the boy's face was suddenly flushed.

"Where's the camera?"

"Here. In the barn. I put it in here before I woke everybody up."

"Did she know you were taking pictures of her?"

Steve shook his head.

Hands still in his pockets, Chard shifted his position, put one foot back against the slats of the stall. "C'mon, son, just tell me the story."

Steve told him: about the video camera, about the purpose of the tapes he'd been taking all weekend, about how he'd already taken some footage of Candy without her knowing, about following her up the hill.

"So you were filming her when she was attacked?"

"Yeah. I forgot to turn on the sound."

"What was she doing?"

Steve didn't answer.

"Why were her pants around her legs?"

Steve's eyes were pleading with him to ease off. Chard was thinking how little he liked this kid.

"Okay," he said. "You followed the girl up the hill. You saw her stop. You watched her pull her pants down and, uh, relieve herself. While she was doing that, she was attacked by something or somebody you couldn't see. Is that right?"

"Something like that, yeah," Steve muttered.

"When she was attacked, were you watching through the camera?"

"Yeah."

"What did you do?"

"What did I do? I was so surprised, I didn't do anything. I nearly dropped the camera."

"But you kept watching?"

"Yeah. I lost my balance and slid on the dirt but I kept looking."

"Did you have a clear view?" Chard's voice was slow and steady.

"Sort of. Not really. I did at the beginning but then I slipped. There were a lot of branches. And I was surprised, like I said." He hesitated, then shrugged. "And I was scared."

"But since you had the camera going all the time, you got the whole thing on film, right?"

"On tape, yeah."

"On tape."

"Yeah."

"And since the tape proves you're innocent, you won't object to giving it to me, right?"

Steve looked into Chard's unblinking eyes, then quickly dropped his gaze. "Right," he said quietly.

Chard held out his hand.

As Chard walked slowly across the yard from the barn to the house, with Steve Steiger a few paces behind him, his eyes swept over the anxious group watching from the porch. They suddenly looked like a school outing group whose chaperones have mysteriously vanished: aimless, frightened, at a loss about what to do next. Suzi Steiger broke the tableau by running down the steps and throwing her arms around her brother, who tried halfheartedly to shake her off. Still holding him, Suzi asked the sheriff if they were free to go. Chard said yes and the group looked relieved. Someone suggested they call the hotel in Deacons Kill and have the driver bring the bus up right away. Chard quietly offered to make the call from his own home since the phone here wasn't connected.

"But I think it would be a good idea," he added, "if somebody from your . . . group . . . maybe stayed in the Kill overnight. In case there are more questions. Something might come up that needed a quick answer."

The group shifted as one, faces blending together, and looked back at him in silence.

Chard let his eyes come to rest on Jack. He recognized him as the one who had come running to report the death of the girl. At least he had a head on his shoulders. But it wasn't so much the memory of Jack's quick thinking that drew Chard's gaze. He was remembering the day before when he and Martha had been in the garden and looked up the hill to see the man standing in the road. He had waved to them, twice, and Chard had been impressed enough, even if it was an impulsive gesture, to think that just possibly this one wasn't like the others. He certainly couldn't picture any of the rest waving across a distance to greet strangers. "How about you?" he said to Jack.

"We can stay," Megan Todd said.

Chard switched his gaze to her and saw that her arm was around the man's waist.

"We don't have to be at work tomorrow, so we can stay," she said. She looked quickly up at Jack.

"Sure," Jack said. "We can stay."

Half an hour later, they were alone in the house. Chard had called the Centennial Hotel immediately and had no trouble locating the driver. Suzi Steiger acted like a mother hen as she bundled her silent brother and the other guests into the bus.

Jack and Megan stood silent on the porch as the loaded bus backed slowly into the road, straightened out, and started down the hill. A few seconds later the only signs of its existence were the distant and diminishing roar of its engine among the hills and the light cloud of dust that hung in the air above the road. Jack sat on the porch steps and Megan sat close against him. He put his arm around her and rubbed her back for a minute, then balanced his elbows on his knees and looked at the worn wooden step between his dusty shoes.

"For a while there, it was really nice," he said.

All around them, the Sunday afternoon air was getting warm. Somewhere in the woods behind the house, a bird chirped noisily and another answered. Across the yard, some tiny thing scuttled through the grass beside the barn.

"I'd give anything to own a place like this," Megan said. "I really would."

Jack glanced sideways at her. "Even after this morning?"

"Even after this morning," she answered instantly. "That had nothing to do with the house or the farm or even any place in particular. It has nothing to do with here, or a place *like* here. I saw a woman hit by a bus on Madison Avenue one time but I still cross at that same corner."

She slid her foot across the step until the side of her shoe touched Jack's. A fly buzzed around them briefly, then flew away.

"I wanted to stay," Megan said, "because I didn't want to be on that bus with those people for four hours, all the way back to the city."

Jack nodded. "Okay," he said. "But we're not staying *here*. This house is old and quaint and beautiful and other good stuff like that, but somebody was murdered—or something—almost within sight of it this morning."

Megan was silent a moment, then reluctantly admitted that he was right.

"That Centennial Hotel in Deacons Kill looked perfectly fine when we passed it yesterday," he said. "We can walk down to Chard's house and call for a taxi from there. Okay?"

"Okay."

But neither of them moved. They sat awhile longer on the steps, each of them reluctant, despite the memory of recent death, to forsake the soft green smell of the air and the warm embrace of the house around them.

The decision to move was finally made for them when they heard a car coming up the hill. Over the tall weeds and nettles that lined the road, they could see the fresh trail of dust it was raising. A moment later, a silver Pinto turned in through the gate. Jack recognized the driver as Chard's daughter.

"Hi!" she called, and waved without getting out of the car. "My father said you were still here. He said he doesn't want you staying in the house. Sheriff's orders. I'm supposed to bring you down to our house. C'mon, my mother's making chicken for dinner."

They spent most of the afternoon with Martha Chard and her daughter Nancy. Mrs. Chard, a solid woman who was more at home in her kitchen than her living

room, fed them huge quantities of fried chicken and
kept urging them to eat more, at the same time for-
bidding any mention of the morning's events. Nancy
was twenty and going to be a senior at Cobleskill Ag
Tech in September. She was hoping, she told them, to
get a good office job somewhere in the vicinity when she
graduated next year, but this summer she was going to
take advantage of her parents—she glanced at her
mother who was busy at the refrigerator—and just take
the summer off, since this would probably be the last
three-month vacation of her life.

Martha Chard invited them to stay overnight. "You
can't be staying at the Ferrand place, not tonight," she
said, "and where's the point in handing out good
money to stay at the Centennial when the spare bedroom is going to waste upstairs?" But Jack and Megan
flatly refused to take advantage of the Chards' kindness
any further, and asked only that Nancy drive them
down to Deacons Kill and drop them off at the hotel.

As soon as they saw the lobby of the Centennial
Hotel, Jack declared it "a veritable outpost of
progress." Antique wood paneling gleamed everywhere,
set off by polished bronze sconces, now converted to
hold lightbulbs in the shape of candle flames. The light
was just enough to accent the high carved ceiling. At
one side of the lobby, a pleasant restaurant—called,
simply enough, The Dining Room—promised a more
than decent meal later if they were still hungry after
Martha Chard's chicken. Attached to it was a very in-
viting lounge, done in dark wood and leather, with high-
backed booths and slowly revolving ceiling fans. Simul-
taneously, Jack and Megan breathed an exaggerated
sigh of relief. Jack paid at the desk and a few minutes
later they were settled into a room that glowed with late

afternoon sunshine on the knobbly white bedspread.

"Civilization," Jack said.

"That restaurant and lounge looked nice," Megan said. "I'll bet this is the late night place to be for miles around."

"I'll bet," Jack said. He was looking out through one of the two small-paned windows and holding aside the white lace curtains.

"You make a lovely bride," Megan said, and sat on the edge of the bed.

Jack dropped the curtain and turned to look at her. His face was serious. "That was very upsetting this morning."

Megan lay back on the bed and stretched her arms out for him.

It was dark when John Chard swung his car into the driveway of Steve Whitmore's house. Steve and his wife Jackie owned Whitmore's Appliances on School Street in the Kill, and Chard had known them both all their lives. When Steve opened the door, he knew instantly from the look on Chard's face that this was business. Chard refused his offer to come in and told Steve only that he needed the key to the store and no questions asked. Steve stood in the doorway for a moment, regarding his friend, then wiped a hand across his mouth and went back inside for the keys. He returned a moment later and handed them over, telling Chard they were duplicates and he could drop them off tomorrow. Chard thanked him and a moment later was gone.

Whitmore's Appliances was around the corner from the Centennial Hotel. The street was quiet, empty, as Chard pulled into the alleyway that led to the customer parking area in the rear. He turned the car around so that the headlights shone on the rear door for a moment, then cut the motor and sat waiting for his eyes to adjust to the dark. Steve Steiger's videocassette lay beside him on the seat.

He had to try several keys before he found the right one for the door. He almost dropped his flashlight in the process. Not like you, Chard, he told himself, not like you at all.

Inside, the store was a silent mausoleum of appliances. He didn't want to turn on the lights and possibly attract attention, so everything would have to be done in the dark. The beam of the flashlight, almost a solid thing as it cut through the blackness, swept over shelves filled with radios, electric mixers, clocks, hair dryers, compact stereo systems. A pile of air conditioners still in their cartons rose in a dark pyramid at the junction of two aisles. The skin at the back of Chard's neck tightened as he made his way carefully to the display of television sets and videorecorders. The two rows of blank TV screens stared down at him blindly from the shelves. He played the flashlight slowly over the area to orient himself, then pulled the cassette from the pocket of his jacket.

It took some minutes of fumbling before he found the right kind of machine for the cassette, located the instruction brochure behind it, and finally managed to get the thing loaded into the machine. By that time, he was noticing how stuffy the store was; he was sweating when he stood up straight at last to ease his back. The shadows around him shifted every time he moved the flashlight and the once-familiar shapes of household appliances loomed like living monsters in the dark. Chard grunted and leaned forward, one finger extended to press the start button.

He had to wait while the tape played through scenes

from Friday night's party and all day Saturday. The
flashlight, held loosely in his left hand, made a pool of
light at his feet but left the rest of the store in darkness.
Only the television set in front of him glowed with life.

Finally he saw what he wanted. An outdoor scene, a
hillside, the girl climbing the hill, unaware of the
camera. The picture jerked violently for a few seconds,
dipped suddenly toward the ground, then steadied as it
aimed up the hill through tree branches and came to rest
on its subject, the girl Candy. Chard shifted his feet,
planted them firmly, as he thought ahead to what he
was about to see.

Candy was climbing the hill slowly. She seemed aimless, wandering, as if at any moment she might decide
she'd climbed far enough and would turn to descend the
hill. The camera followed her, stopping every few
seconds, then moving unsteadily uphill and stopping
again. Then Candy reached a clearer space where the
hillside was covered with gravel. Tree branches moved
in front of the lens, hiding the girl for a moment, then
the camera moved a little closer and to the side, away
from the branches, where the line of sight was clearer.
Candy stood still for a moment, then turned around,
almost looking into the camera as she faced down the
hill. She was opening her pants and pushing them down
over her hips. Chard could see the green whirlie on her
nose and he thought, Oh, poor child. Her slender legs
looked very fragile and white against the gravel. Then
she squatted and urinated. Chard shifted his weight
from one foot to the other.

The scene appeared to last an eternity. Then the girl
raised her head and, almost as if she knew it was there,
watching her, looked directly down the hill at the
camera. Her lips moved, spoke a couple of words.
Chard, wishing the tape had sound as well as pictures,

thought she didn't look so much angry as disgusted.

Candy finished urinating and stood up. She started to pull her pants up but still kept her eyes on the camera. She yelled another word down the hill. The camera moved quickly to the side and a leafy branch snapped in front of the lens. The pictures shook for an instant, steadied, moved to the side, away from the girl, then found her again, partially obscured by trembling leaves. Chard frowned. He could just make out the figure of the girl standing half-dressed on the hillside above. Then suddenly she was sprawling face down in the gravel. A spasm shook the camera but in an instant it found her again as she lay on the ground. A branch was in front of the lens and Chard thought he could see a hand trying to move the leaves aside. Then the camera seemed to be moving unsteadily backwards down the hill, catching only intermittent glimpses of Candy. She shook her head and climbed painfully to hands and knees, then raised her head, apparently looking around to find her attacker. The camera jerked again, steadied for an instant, swept away in a wide unsteady arc, then came back to the girl. There was only Candy on the hillside, nothing near her, nothing at all.

Between the shivering leaves that partially hid her from view, Chard could see the girl on her knees, turning to look up the hill. Then, somehow, her head snapped away and Chard thought he could see a red flash of blood on the side of her face. Almost in the same instant, the camera whirled away, swung dizzyingly up toward a sky mottled by branches, then there was a blur of trees and leaves whipping past, then nothing.

It was a long moment before Chard leaned forward to turn off the machine. He stood for a moment, breathing heavily. The pool of light at his feet trembled like water in a wind. He clutched the flashlight tighter to keep it from shaking.

At a little after nine-thirty, Jack and Megan were the last customers in the Centennial Dining Room, Jack finishing a banana split and Megan working her way through an imposingly large dish of fresh fruit. The waitress, a plump and friendly woman who had announced herself as Peggy, had just refilled their coffee cups when John Chard appeared in the lobby door of the restaurant. He looked around, spotted them, and made his way across the room to their table. He was still wearing the same gray suit, white shirt and blue tie he'd had on earlier, although he looked a lot more rumpled now than he had before. Jack, watching him approach, realized for the first time what a big man he was, big the way city people imagine country lawmen being big, as if the size of their territory demanded men of a similar scale.

They greeted each other, and as Chard took a seat opposite him, Jack asked, "Is it Mr. Chard or Sheriff?"

Chard's eyes met his for an instant. "It's John," he said.

At the same moment, the waitress appeared. Without waiting to be asked, she set a cup and saucer in front of Chard, and with the other hand filled it with coffee from a steaming pot. "Just coffee for you, John, or can I get you something to eat?"

"Just coffee, Peggy, thanks," Chard said.

"How you folks doing?" she asked Jack. "Can I get you something else?"

"We're fine, thanks," Jack answered.

Chard waited until the woman had left before he

spoke. "We covered the whole area all day," he said. "Didn't find a thing." Briefly, he outlined the search he and his deputies, aided by four state troopers, had conducted of Deacons Rise and the surrounding hills. When he finished, he sipped carefully at the hot coffee, three stiff fingers extended away from the cup. He kept his eyes turned down into the steam. "To tell the truth," he said, "you're both supposed to be at work in the city in the morning, aren't you?"

"Actually, yes," Jack admitted. "We'll have to call our offices in the morning."

Chard glanced at both of them and merely nodded, but it was enough. "I need another favor," he said. "Did you know that Steve Steiger was taking television movies of the girl when she died?"

"We knew he had a camera," Jack said slowly. "Nobody could escape the damn thing all weekend. I guess none of us thought of it in all the confusion."

"That would be evidence, wouldn't it?" Megan said.

"It might be," Chard answered. "But I'm hoping nobody else thinks of it and I'm asking you to forget it." His eyes were steady as he looked from one face to the other.

Megan glanced quickly at Jack, then looked back at Chard. The sheriff's meaning, whatever the reason for it, was clear.

"I don't remember any tape," Jack said steadily.

"Neither do I," Megan added.

Chard toyed with his coffee for a few seconds, then quickly finished it off, and stood up. Jack and Megan stood with him, and they all walked toward the lobby. Jack was reaching for his wallet to pay the bill when he heard Chard telling the waitress he'd take care of it. She said, "Sure thing, John," and glanced more curiously at the couple with him. "You folks have a nice evening now," she called after them.

They stood on the porch together, looking out over the sleeping square of Deacons Kill. When Chard spoke, his voice seemed almost part of the breeze that rustled branches in the square.

"It's a good place," he said. "It's a small town, and it's got all the good points and all the bad points of being a small town, but it's a good place. Good country here. Good people. I've lived here all my life. These hills. . . ." His voice trailed off and they heard only the breeze.

A moment later, Chard stepped down from the porch and walked away, disappearing from view around the corner of the hotel. Almost instantly, his footsteps were gone. Jack and Megan stood a few minutes longer on the hotel porch and the dark of the Kill closed in silently around them.

At a quarter to seven the next morning, John Chard left his house for work, but instead of turning left, downhill, he swung the car to the right, up toward the Ferrand place. When he reached the driveway, he stopped the car and sat there, looking at the house, thinking of all the hours he had spent on that porch with Martin Ferrand. The house, patient as ever, stood passive before him, as settled in its place here as the wooded hills themselves.

Chard swung his gaze upward, up the slope of Deacons Rise, and sought through the trees the place where the girl Candy, no last name, had met her death. He couldn't find the place and saw instead only the slope of the darkly wooded hill.

He sat for several minutes, his eyes taking in the sweep of the hill and the shadows the early sun cast across it. Then he pulled the car into the driveway, backed it into the road, and drove slowly down the hill.

The Trailways bus arrived one minute ahead of schedule and hissed to a stop at the entrance of the Centennial Hotel. Jack and Megan climbed aboard, handed over their tickets to the driver, and settled into the front seat on the right side. There were only five other people on the bus.

The driver closed the door and eased the bus away from the curb. As it swung around the square, heading back to Route 7, Megan craned her neck to see as much of the town in the daylight as she could. Only when the town was left behind and the woods closed in did she sit back comfortably in her seat.

"I really do want to come back," she said to Jack.

The bus driver, a young fellow, glanced over his shoulder at them, then looked back at the twisting road. "Nice place here," he said. "Nice little town, I can tell you that much."

Megan reached for Jack's hand and squeezed it.

And on the slope of Deacons Rise, something moved slowly downhill. It drifted across the shadows cast by the early morning sun, although it cast no shadow itself. Beneath it there was only soft ground and rotting leaves, but the thing moved with a sandy gritty sound, a slight sound, almost a part of the hill itself. Unseen, the thing yet could see. Suddenly, in front of it, a gray squirrel sat upright on a rock. Without warning, the squirrel was snatched into the air. It had no time to chatter in angry protest, because instantly its head was twisted, its neck broken. And again there was the gritty crunching sound as something slit open the squirrel's belly and began to eat.

PART TWO

6

It was three weeks later, very close to the end of an unusually hot and sticky June, before Megan finally listened to Jack's advice and took a day off from work by calling in sick. It was a Monday, and the thought of going into the office and facing those awful mountains of papers and proofs was, for the first time in her life, more than she could bear. Not after this weekend.

On Saturday, she and Jack had decided, with uneasy bravado, to chuck the work they had each brought home and spend the day in Central Park. If they got there early enough, they could get a good place in line for free tickets to Joe Papp's Shakespeare in the Park production of *Timon of Athens* at the Delacorte Theatre. "I saw it once in London," Jack said, "at the outdoor theatre in Regent's Park. Had to be the worst production of Shakespeare I've ever seen. How bad could this one be?"

They left the apartment around ten and strolled west toward Fifth Avenue. When they got that far, they decided on impulse to go into the Metropolitan Museum of Art for a while; there would still be time afterward to get on line in the park for tickets. They hurried past the crowds of tourists and vendors and street entertainers on the steps, and headed immediately for the rooms of Impressionist paintings. They weren't there five minutes before a chattering tour group arrived, shepherded by a uniformed and imperious white-haired woman. The group took over the room and the tour leader began telling her captive audience about how wonderful the paintings were. Jack and Megan gave up and went downstairs to the costume exhibit. There, five teenage girls, armed with notebooks for some end-of-year high school assignment, giggled their way from room to room, laughing and calling to each other to look at something even sillier than the costumes they had just seen. Jack and Megan lasted only a few minutes before fleeing the costume exhibit too.

Outside on Fifth Avenue again, they discovered that somehow an hour had gone by and now they were hungry. Jack declared that they deserved a treat. They hurried across Fifth Avenue to the Terrace Café of the Stanhope Hotel. The lunch itself was about as nice as the price would buy, but there were no more outside tables on the street, and they had to content themselves with one far to the rear inside. And they had to be patient, because the overworked waiters really were doing the best they could with the Saturday crowd.

When finally they had finished lunch and crossed Fifth Avenue into the park, the line for free tickets at the Delacorte stretched out of sight to the north and around the far end of the baseball fields. They trudged the distance anyway, making a rough count of people as they went. It was hard to tell for sure, but they thought they'd still be close enough to get tickets. When they

reached the end of the ragged line, the theatre seemed
very far away. Like everyone ahead of them, and those
that were already joining the line behind them, they
settled down on the dusty grass and prepared to wait
until six o'clock when the tickets were distributed. Each
of them was careful to say nothing discouraging to the
other; the outlook for the day already seemed pretty
fragile.

Their place in line was unsheltered by any trees, and
Megan settled herself at an angle to avoid the direct rays
of the sun. Not a single breeze seemed to be stirring anywhere in the park. The vast open space of the playing
fields swallowed up the shouts of the baseball players
and the music from portable radios, blending all the
noise into a distant blur of sound in the heat of the
afternoon. Megan opened the paperback she had
brought, slipped the bookmark into the pages near the
end, and started reading. She had read only two
sentences when, with a sickening thud, a baseball
slammed into the ground two inches from her knee.

"Hey!" she and Jack shouted at the same time, looking around for the player who had thrown, or missed,
the ball. Almost in the same instant, a little boy who
couldn't have been more than eight or nine, but whose
face was almost that of an adult, swooped off the
nearby path, snatched up the ball, and hightailed it off
into the distance. One of the baseball players came
running and leaped over Jack and Megan as if they were
a hurdle and he a highjumper, the yells of people in the
line trailing away in his wake. He returned empty-
handed a few minutes later and ignored the catcalls of
those in line.

The hot sun seemed determined to bake them, and
both Jack and Megan regretted not bringing long-

sleeved shirts to protect them from sunburn. But, except for when a pigeon dropped a green-and-white load on the magazine Jack was reading, the rest of the afternoon was uneventful. Finally, at a little after six o'clock, people ahead of them began stirring and the line slowly wound its way around the field toward the theatre. And, when there were only about twenty people left ahead of them, there were no more tickets and everyone else was turned away.

By then, they were both so hot and sweaty that nothing else appealed to them. They walked home, ate a slow dinner in a nearby coffee shop, and spent the rest of the evening watching a movie on television that they had both seen before.

That was Saturday in the big city.

Over Sunday breakfast, Jack, after mumbling something about falling off a horse, suggested that they try again. Reluctantly, Megan agreed. This time they prepared better, brought sandwiches and fruit and long-sleeved shirts, and waited until they could get a place in line that was in the shade of a tree. They were close enough to the front this time to be certain of getting tickets, and the afternoon passed pleasantly enough. Then, at five-thirty, the heavens opened and dumped a fierce summer storm on them that turned the field into a vast expanse of mud. Along with other people from the line, they huddled beneath the shelter of their tree, Jack all the while predicting imminent electrocution for all. After fifteen minutes, the storm eased off to a steady drizzle that showed no signs of letting up. At six-fifteen, word was passed down the wet and bedraggled line that the evening's performance was cancelled.

That was the weekend in the big city.

And on Monday morning Megan thought, the hell
with it, and called in sick.

As it turned out, she needn't have bothered.

When she arrived in the office on Tuesday morning,
she had a splitting headache, caused by not wanting to
be there, annoyance with herself for feeling that way,
and guilt over the whole thing. But understanding the
reasons for it did nothing to kill the pain, and the three
Excedrin she'd taken showed no signs of having any
effect at all.

The first thing she saw in the office was an untidy pile
of mail and paperwork that had accumulated on her
desk in one day, *one single day*. The next was the note
from Harvey Mendel taped to her telephone. "See me!"
it said in block letters, and suddenly she was fourteen
again and her math teacher had written "See me!" on
the bottom of a test paper beneath a failing grade. Oh,
Christ! What now?

Harvey was all smiles when she presented herself at
his office. The smiles invariably meant trouble, and
Megan's insides knotted as she sat down across the desk
from him.

"Hope you're feeling better," he said. His tone was
perfectly casual, no implications in it, but Megan
couldn't stop herself from feeling guilty about taking
the day off yesterday. She assumed he knew she'd been
faking. And a Monday, at that, the worst day in the
world to call in sick. She tried to smile, failed, and
nodded silently instead.

Harvey straightened a pile of folders on his desk—
prolonging the torture, Megan thought, and could have
kicked herself for feeling this way—then sat back com-

fortably in his chair. "Well," he said, "I wanted to share some news with you before the rest of the staff is told."

When Harvey used the words, "the staff," the news was always bad.

After mentioning lightly that he had "discussed" this with some of the editors yesterday, he began talking about increased costs and decreased profits, increased overhead and decreased revenue, increased salaries and decreased capital. Bad times for business. Bad times for the whole publishing industry. Bad times for magazines, very bad times. Cash flow problems. Dunwoodie's bright outlook if they could weather the current storms. Cutbacks. Cutbacks were the answer. She was losing two people from the art department staff.

"What? What are you talking about?" The words escaped her before she could stop them.

Harvey pretended not to hear and rehashed what he had already said. The gist of it was the same: she'd have the same amount of work and responsibility, but now she'd have to do more of it herself.

"You're crazy," she told him, and shocked herself more than she shocked him. "There's no way—"

"I'm afraid there's something else," Harvey added, his casual tone more ominous still. "This cash flow problem," he said, and Megan saw it coming. The problem, temporary though it was, had been causing all sorts of difficulties in the accounting department. Harvey was very sorry, and it was only this week, of course, but he was afraid that paychecks would be a little late this time. He had "mentioned" this to "some of the other people" in the office, and everyone was very patient and very deeply committed to Dunwoodie's happy future and their own investment in it. It was only a temporary situation, he wanted her to understand that, just a matter of this week alone, until the accounting department could get some matters straightened out. So this Friday's checks wouldn't be "coming through" until next week, probably on Tuesday. Wednesday, for sure, at the latest. He knew he could count on her, she was one of the most important people in the entire organization. He could count on her, right?

"Right," Megan said, and left his office without another word. On the way back to her desk, she stopped and fixed herself a cup of coffee, then sat drinking it in a silence so obvious that Dave stayed far away from her. Twice she reached for the phone to call Jack but each time she decided not to. This was one she'd have to solve for herself. Finally, when she couldn't put it off any longer, she tossed away the empty cardboard cup she'd been crushing and walked back to Harvey's office.

"Tell me this is a very bad joke," she said from his doorway.

Harvey spread his hands helplessly. "Megan," he said, "I've explained to you—"

"Am I getting my check on Friday?" she asked, her voice tight. "Because if I'm not, I'm walking out of here this minute."

"Megan, please, I've told you—"

"Am I?"

"Well, no, but—"

"Then I quit."

"But you just promised—" Harvey said quickly as he stood up from his desk.

"I lied," Megan said, the muscles around her mouth

bunching tightly. She kept the palms of her hands pressed flat against her thighs to conceal their trembling.

Grim-faced, she walked back to her desk and spent about three minutes clearing out of it anything that could reasonably be identified as her own. She dumped the things into a red-and-white Paperback Booksmith shopping bag she found in the bottom drawer, then walked directly to the elevators without saying a word to anyone. Mercifully, an elevator came at once. Megan stepped in quickly, stabbed at a button, and waited until the doors slid shut before turning around. She didn't want the receptionist to see her crying.

"No calls," Jack told Karen, his assistant, as he closed the door of his office. "I'm working on a manuscript."

But he wasn't. The gray manuscript box sat unopened in the center of his desk, the rubber band still around it. Jack sat down and looked at it for a few seconds, his face expressionless. He was thinking of his father.

Matthew Casey had come to the United States from the old country with nothing more than a brother and a few scattered cousins here to help him learn the ways of America. With him he brought only the equivalent of about ten dollars—all his family could spare to arm him for the unknown future—and no skills at all other than how to work in the fields and the bogs of the farm at home. But there were no fields or bogs in New York, no farms where he could work the cows or plant the rows. He did the next best thing, with the help of one of the cousins and a priest in his brother's parish who was distantly related to another cousin back home in Ireland. He took a job as a gravedigger. It was work he could do and, God knows, he had the back for it, didn't he? It was honest work, it was, there was no denying that, and times were always hard for a greenhorn newly arrived in the land of promise. And it was outdoor work, too, after all, and, in its way, the Lord's work, after a fashion. He did it all his life and relieved the tedium with the bottle, which, he would tell the missus when she took a notion to be complaining of it, was no more nor less than his own father, God rest his soul, had done himself and a man had to be having some relaxation in his life, now didn't he?

He had worked for a time at St. Raymond's Cemetery in the Bronx, and Jack had vague memories of his father bringing him there sometimes before he was quite old enough to understand the meaning of the crosses and stones. But he could still recall the swagger and strut of his father's gait as he walked the green fields of his domain. He remembered too the single word whose sound always epitomized for him his father's voice.

"Land!" his father would say and sweep his arm in a grand wide arc across the fields. "We come from the land and we go back to the land, son," he thought he remembered him adding, but memory was untrustworthy that far, and those words may have been added by Jack's own imagination. But the sense of it was always there when his father spoke that one magical word. "Land!" And the sweep of the arm.

Remembering, Jack smiled and wondered how much that part of his father's living memory was actually him and how much was Scarlett O'Hara's father in *Gone with the Wind*. Funny sometimes how our dreams mix with reality.

But for his father, dreams and reality had never mixed, and the land he touched was always someone else's, always that of the dead and never his own, not a foot of it, not an inch, until he was dead himself.

Jack reached for the phone and pushed a button. "Karen," he said, "I need a number upstate. I don't know the area code. A place called Deacons Kill. I want the sheriff's office."

He pushed the manuscript box aside and waited.

Megan had long since forgotten why she'd bought the can of red enamel paint that she found in a kitchen cabinet. But she was home from the office—for the last time and, oh God, what was she going to do *now?* She had decided on the way home in the bus that she wasn't going to call Jack and ruin his day too; there'd be plenty of time for that when he got home this evening. She had stalked from bedroom to living room and back and forth and back and forth until she lost patience with herself, and then she'd decided she had to do *something* and she'd started to empty the cabinet to take out all the good plates and give them the good washing they needed and there was the can of red enamel paint. And, the instant her eye fell on it, she knew what she wanted to do.

She put away all the dishes and the serving bowls and the gravy boat that she'd already taken out. Then she cleared everything off the kitchen table and removed the tablecloth and replaced it with a triple layer of pages from the Business section of the Sunday *New York Times.* No need for *that*, she thought, and toyed for a second with the idea of using the Classified section instead. Then she was prying open the can and admiring the brilliant red of the paint, thick and bright and glowing. It took a few minutes of hunting before she turned up a new brush that was thick enough to hold the heavy paint. Then she set to work.

John Chard wasn't there when Jack's call went through and Jack reminded himself that he shouldn't have expected the sheriff to be sitting there waiting to answer the phone. Jack left his office number and asked if the sheriff could call him back when he came in. Now that he had actually done something about getting in touch, Jack found that he could concentrate on his work. To his own surprise, he was actually able to finish going through the last hundred pages of the manuscript before his call was returned.

All morning, his mind had been filled with thoughts of his father and his father's voice saying "Land!" It was filled too with thoughts of Deacons Kill and the house, that wonderful house, and thoughts of Candy and thoughts of John Chard.

He had told Karen that Chard's was the only call he would take, and he jumped for the phone when it rang.

"Hello. Is this Jack Casey?" Chard's voice. Strange and familiar at the same time.

"Yes. Hello, sheriff."

There was an awkward hesitation at both ends of the line and Jack suddenly wondered if Chard could be feeling the startlingly odd sensation of closeness and friendship and common concerns that he felt himself. He cleared his throat.

"Sheriff, I'm sorry to bother you but—"

"No bother."

"—I was wondering how that case turned out. Candy. The girl who was killed. I've been meaning to get in touch, you know, since we weren't hearing from you. Not that *you* should be calling *us*, of course. But I've been wondering.'' Jack shook his head at the stupidity of his own words and blessed the phone for hiding him. How could he tell John Chard, nearly a stranger, that the death on Deacons Rise of a girl he barely knew somehow mattered to him? Or did Chard understand that without being told? Jack remembered the way the sheriff had looked at Megan and him, and spoken to them that night in the Centennial Hotel's Dining Room, and he wondered. He was going to say something else, something that might explain, but he closed his mouth instead.

There was a heavy silence from Chard's end of the line, two hundred miles away. Jack imagined he could see the look on the sheriff's face as he weighed the situation and chose his words.

"Well," Chard said at last, "I'm glad you called. I've been hoping you would, to tell the truth. But I'm afraid I don't have any news about the case. At least, nothing I can tell you right now."

"Yes, of course, I understand," he said quickly. "But Megan and I have been thinking a lot about Deacons Kill and we were curious, that's all."

"I can understand that," Chard said, and Jack believed him and felt himself very close to this man who lived in such a different world and so far away, so much farther than the two hundred miles of road.

"Truth is," Chard said, his voice perfectly level, revealing nothing more than the words themselves, "we've pursued every path we have here and turned up nothing. The boys in Oneonta did their part and came up empty-handed. For the matter of that, I even sent some samples and such to Albany for further medical examination"—Jack could see Doc Warren standing beside Chard on the porch of the Ferrand place—"but they didn't give us anything useful either. Likewise the troopers, so the case remains as open as the day it happened."

"You've ruled out anything medical, I guess."

"Yes," Chard said. "Yes, we have."

"It's a shame, the girl dying like that."

"It is," Chard said, and Jack could see him nodding.

"Yes," Jack said and the silence, closer this time, hung between them.

"Have you talked with those people at all?" Chard asked after a moment.

Jack caught the significance of "those people." Chard's opinion of Suzi Steiger and people like her was apparently the one thing he wasn't good at concealing.

"No, we haven't. It's possible Megan may have spoken with her on the phone but I doubt it. She would have mentioned it. We haven't heard from her either. Of course, she could be in California. You know, she works—"

"I know," Chard said. "I've spoken to her. By the way, I don't think she'll be in the Kill very often anymore."

"Oh?"

"Lost interest, I'd say."

"It's understandable, I guess, after what happened."

"For someone like her," Chard said flatly.

"Yes."

Another pause, briefer than the others, but long enough for both of them to hear it.

"Well, you know you have an invitation here," Chard said, and again Jack could see the man's face across the table in the Dining Room. "You're welcome any time."

And before he realized what he was saying, before he realized what he was thinking, Jack was telling Chard, "Well, actually, one of the reasons I called was because Megan and I were thinking of coming up next weekend and we were hoping we could get together for dinner. We owe you folks a meal."

"That would be very nice," Chard said. "We'd be glad to see you."

And Jack said maybe they could all have dinner on Saturday night, and Doc Warren too. Chard agreed that that sounded fine with him and, since they were both on the brink of embarrassment, the conversation ended there. A moment later Jack was staring at the telephone and feeling ridiculously well pleased with himself, as if he had pulled off a monumental coup.

The feeling of well-being flickered for an instant when he realized the time and saw that he would have to hurry to meet the author he was lunching with. But the feeling returned at once. This was a lunch he'd been looking forward to since that manuscript box had arrived on his desk the week before.

He spent the time it took to reach the restaurant preparing what he had to say. If Bob Brockden was agreeable and things worked out right, then truly, in the words of Bob Dylan, "the times they are a-changin."

He was still a block away from the restaurant when he realized two things. The first was that he hadn't called Megan to tell her about the weekend. Too late now; he'd call her this afternoon. The other was that, in talking to Chard, he'd said they were thinking of "coming" up next weekend rather than "going" up. Point of view can make a world of difference, he thought, and he was smiling when he entered the cool, dark interior of the restaurant, ready for another step in what now could honestly be called a *plan*.

Megan had to thin out the paint after a while to make it last, but it was okay now and it would get her another good distance across the expanse of kitchen wall. But an hour after she began, she thought she remembered having a can of green enamel paint as well as the can of red. She had no idea why or even when she had bought it, but, yes, she thought there was green somewhere too. Maybe something to do with Christmas, but she didn't care why or when, only where, and there it was, in the cabinet under the kitchen sink. Perfect.

The kitchen wall was turning into a mural that pleased her immensely and would have horrified the owner of the building. It started in the top left corner of the wall; she'd had to stand on a chair to reach that high. With no plan and no design, she had just started painting, drawing, letting her hand and fingers and brush go where they would, however they would. She drew the outline of a face, a female face, added a touch and made it a child, and from the child's neck grew a vine and the vine swooped across the wall, curving up to the ceiling and then, for a couple of loops, *onto* the ceiling and she loved it, loved the effect, and then her concentration on the task was complete. The vine ended in a tangle of leaves halfway across the wall from the corner of the room to the refrigerator and she would get back to that later. As if she had planned every detail in advance, the mural took shape before her eyes. A nameless creature, half horse, half bullock, something borrowed from Marc Chagall, peered benignly over the vine as if glancing curiously over a hedge. A swirl of stars appeared. A maze. A bouquet of flowers, a sailboat, a dribble of teardrops and a Valentine heart that turned into the exposed heart of a weeping clown, and she painted and painted. And now the painting jumped to even more vivid life as the vine grew spots of green and the clown's cheek was dotted with puffs of green and a Christmas tree sprouted, all green with red decorations, and a bright red barn grew up in a field of green and the wall swept in a brilliant array from the top left near the ceiling to the bottom right beside the refrigerator, images jumping from the wall, and she wiped the sweat out of her eyes with the back of her arm and the afternoon passed.

"Bob, it's great!" Jack said as soon as they were seated at a table, and the two of them grinned at each other. A waiter took their order for drinks, a Bloody Mary for Bob Brockden and a Miller for Jack, and presented them with menus. They studied the list briefly and made their decisions. Before the waiter returned with the drinks, Jack had already said, "Let's get right to business," and Brockden had happily agreed.

Robert Brockden was the author of a novel called *Gestures*, which Jack had edited and which the house had published ten months ago. It had done much better than Brockden himself thought he had any right to hope for, and had actually touched the bottom of the *Publishers Weekly* paperback bestseller list for all of one week. Brockden had been elated at his good luck, but Jack had insisted to him, as their friendship grew over several months, that the book merited its healthy sales.

"It's good," Jack had told him, "and it's selling because it's good and because word goes around about good books."

They spent many lunches together, many hours on the phone, and Jack worked closely with Brockden as the second novel took shape. It was, Jack was convinced, even better than the first. And for once the editorial director and the powers-that-be, the ones who decided which books got "the push," were in agreement. *Multiple Exposures*, a July release, was being shipped from the warehouse this week, in time to catch the summer book-buyers. It was everything that Jack had hoped for, that rarest of commodities that he'd never stopped believing in: a commercial novel, with obvious broad appeal, told in a way that was uniquely the author's, and with the unmistakeable feeling of truth woven magically into its fabric.

Minutes before his phone rang with that call from Deacons Kill, Jack had finished reading the first draft of Brockden's next book. It needed work—needed the same careful editorial guidance that Jack had given the others and that Brockden was eager to have—but it was even better than the others.

"Bob," Jack said when they were halfway through the meal and had discussed the book in general terms, "I want to talk seriously with you about something else, but it's something that's related to the book."

"Sure," Brockden said agreeably.

Jack took a deep breath and put his plan into motion.

John Chard swung the police cruiser out of the shopping center parking lot and into the light stream of traffic heading west on Route 7.

It was a wonderful day. The heat that had been

attacking the mountains for nearly a week had finally evaporated and rewarded the area with a day of crystal air, sharp and clean and bright. The slopes of the hills looked close enough to touch, close enough for a man to count the needles on the firs from across the valley. You could inhale it deeply, fill your lungs with it and hold it and *taste* it, sweet and dry and good. If you were lucky, there might be half a dozen days in a year that were as fine as this, a couple in the spring, one or two in summer, a few in the fall, but their fewness made them better and you thanked God for the goodness of them. A man could feel on top of the world on a day like this, able to conquer anything, thrilled to be alive.

Chard had felt the glory of the day this morning, and when he'd hit the road himself—any officer of the law worthy of the job covered his domain every day—he had rolled open the windows and headed for the back roads, the winding ribbons of asphalt and flint and gravel and sometimes just dirt that only local people knew. On those roads, you could come to a sign that announced, say, "Smithville," and a few hundred feet past the sign there would be a big old Victorian house, with a barn and outbuildings behind it, and cows on the hillside, and the name on the mailbox at the side of the road was "Smith." Only a stranger, if one ever came here, would smile. He passed hamlets consisting of five houses, aging but clean and repaired and neat out front, with laundry flapping on lines in the back, and there might be a tiny church that a hopeful congregation had started a generation or two back, and possibly a general store with a porch and a soda machine beside the door and a gas pump out by the road, shined and polished and brighter than the ones down on the Thruway.

And you passed people on the road, too, an old man sitting on a porch and enjoying his years, a woman in the yard, a man in the doorway of the barn, all of them with eyes on the road because not too many cars passed here back among the hills and it was probably someone you knew. Besides, in the country quiet, you could hear a car approaching for some while before it passed. And the oldtimer and the woman and the man raised a hand in greeting as the car rolled by, and John Chard knew every last one of them by name.

Coming out onto Route 7, he turned toward Danny's Diner for a mid-morning cup of coffee. Danny Lester was an old friend, and Chard always welcomed the sight of him standing at his griddle, baseball cap pushed far back from his pink forehead. Chard always sat on one of the red plastic stools at the counter, opposite the griddle and Danny's sandwich board, so they could talk while Danny worked. He sipped his coffee and talked about the weather, and Danny talked about his daughter and the price of food these days. When Chard finished his coffee, he dutifully left change in payment on the counter. As he slid off the stool, they wished each other a good day and Chard nodded to the other people in the diner as he left.

Then he was back in the car again, driving the familiar, comfortable roads. He drove for another hour, then decided that any more and he'd only be indulging himself, so he went back to the Kill and his office and the paperwork on his desk and the message about the call from Jack Casey.

And the brightness and purity of the morning flickered and faded and slid away to a distance that was separate from himself, part of another world entirely, and all he could see was the desk and the office and the scenes that had haunted his thoughts for nearly a month.

The conversation with Jack was good, and he was glad the man had called. Very glad. Chard had been thinking about him and Megan off and on, and wondering if they'd ever be in touch. There were some people you could like instinctively. But the odd pleasure he felt at the thought of having a meal with them on Saturday night—at having too an occasion to take Martha out of her kitchen for a dinner cooked by someone else, something she agreed to only with reluctance but enjoyed nonetheless—was not enough to lighten his mood and let him enjoy the day, the breeze and the air, as he left the office and turned the car out of town and up the Rise toward home.

Martha and Nancy were shopping in Albany for the day, and Chard stood just inside the door and hesitated. No, he decided, he didn't want to eat beforehand, he'd eat after, and he opened the door to the cellar and went downstairs.

Steve Whitmore had insisted, absolutely insisted, that the new color TV and the videocassette recorder were on loan to him indefinitely, "on a trial basis," he said, and at last Chard had agreed. All Whitmore knew was that Chard had come to the house for the store keys three more times after that first time, giving no reason, and Whitmore had known better than to ask. But Chard needed the equipment, and Whitmore had insisted, so there it was in what he called his "den" in the corner of the finished basement, the one spot in the house that belonged to him alone and where his wife and daughter never went.

Against one wall of the den was an old battered desk,

one leg shorter than the others—and how that could be, he'd never understand—with a piece of shirt cardboard folded and wedged beneath it to keep it steady. He opened the bottom drawer on the right and took out the videocassette and held it in his hand, weighing it: wanting it, needing it, but at the same time—and this he *did* understand—fearing and hating it too. At the desk was an old straight-backed chair, banished years before from Martha's kitchen and then from her sewing room and now happily come to rest here. Chard pulled it out and sat down.

He hated this thing in his hand. He didn't even like touching it. He leaned to his side and set the switches on the machine and slipped in the cassette, then turned the TV on, and a second later he was living through it again for the . . . How many times? He'd lost track.

There were the trees and there was the girl, Candy. He knew her last name now, McBain, and he knew about Youngstown, Ohio, and the mother who drank and the father who only came around on rare occasions but was known nonetheless among the neighbors for his terrible temper. He knew a lot of other things too, things he didn't need to know and didn't want to know, and all of it, every last scrap of it, totally useless. And there was the girl herself, her pants around her ankles, half naked, unprotected and unguarded, unsuspecting of death. And then, seconds later, there she was again, and incredibly she was dead and for the life of him, *for the life of him*, if he sat here looking at the thing until his eyesight dimmed to darkness, Chard could swear that nothing touched her.

His stomach was in knots, muscles clenched, his back aching and his fingers stiff. Eyes aimed at the now blank screen but no longer seeing it, he kneaded the fingers together to loosen the muscles.

Perhaps five times in the course of a year, Chard indulged himself by swearing. He swore now, and reached out an angry hand, and flipped a switch and turned the damned thing off.

Jack's conversation with Brockden turned out exactly as he'd planned. The book was wonderful but, like the previous ones, it needed work. And because it was even better than the others, the revisions would have to be all the better this time. Brockden agreed, and said all the points Jack had so far made about the book touched on the elements that he himself had been uncertain about. As before, Brockden would respect Jack's judgment. Besides, he admitted ruefully, he had more confidence in Jack's editing than he had in his own writing. Bullshit, Jack said, and they both laughed.

Then Jack delivered the kicker. He was planning, he told Brockden, to leave the company. Before Brockden could do more than look panicky, Jack hurried on to say he wasn't abandoning him and his book. He'd work on it with him just the same as before, whether he did it officially or not and whether he got paid for doing it or not. He'd promise that. But this was what he wanted: he wanted Brockden to insist that they hire him, Jack, and nobody else, to edit the book on a freelance basis.

"Will they agree?" Brockden asked.

"It's not an unusual situation at all," Jack told him. "Editors who want to take a stab at writing themselves very often keep the tuna casserole on the table by doing freelance editing. And it's in everybody's best interests, at this point, to keep the continuity for your work and also for the house to keep you happy and merrily typing away. A happy author is a productive author, we always say!''

"You mean they really think it's important to keep me happy?''

"Indeed,'' Jack said solemnly. He was feeling great now. "Yes, indeed, they do.''

"Well, how about that?'' Brockden mused, a tentative smile on his lips.

They sipped coffee in silence for a minute. They liked and trusted each other, but these were big decisions and careers were at stake, and it took a minute for each of them to admit what they were doing. Then Brockden put down his cup and broke the silence.

"If I had an agent, what would he say about this?''

"If you had an agent, as I told you long ago you should,'' Jack said, "in the first place, he'd be a she. It's women who run publishing . . . as is true of everything else, I might add. But I think that if you had . . . .''

He raised his eyes and met Brockden's gaze. This time the other man looked very sure of himself indeed.

"Are you thinking what I think you're thinking?'' Jack said slowly.

"What do you think I'm thinking?'' Brockden said, and now he allowed himself another smile.

"Have you finally decided that you should have an agent to protect you from the wolves in the woods?''

"I have,'' Brockden said.

"Have you decided on who that should be?''

Brockden looked deeply thoughtful. "Well, you know,'' he said, "I've given this a great deal of thought, and it occurs to me that, if I'm going to hire an agent, it should be somebody who's enthusiastic about my work.

Actually, I've had a couple of offers. Three, to be exact, so I really have been thinking about it.''

"And?"

"And I've thought too that I'd want an agent who is, shall we say . . . hungry. Not somebody who's old and tired and just going through the motions. I'd want somebody who's—"

"Desperate for the money and willing to work his ass off to earn it?"

"I couldn't have put it better myself."

"Let's see," Jack said slowly, "ten per cent of everything you make from now on should come to about . . . ."

"My point exactly," Brockden said.

"You know," Jack said, "you have a very low and devious mind."

"Why, thank you."

"I admire that in a client."

And they grinned and shook hands and ordered another round of drinks.

Jack had an editorial meeting at three o'clock, and when he got back to the office he only had time for one quick phone call, the one call he still had to make to complete the day. With the way things were going, it seemed only fitting and proper that Suzi Steiger was in her office and free to take his call. He had to listen to five minutes' worth of all her latest tribulations, balanced by an equal number of perfectly marvelous accomplishments, all of which were sure to revolutionize the television industry, before he could mention Deacons Kill.

"Oh, God," Suzi said, "don't remind me! Really, Jack, I just don't want to think about it. That whole scene was awful, just awful. And, do you know, that sheriff or marshall or whatever he is up there, the one who thinks he's Matt Dillon or something, for God's sake, he's been calling me I don't know how many times and asking questions about that brother of mine and, I swear, the whole thing is just driving me crazy.''

Jack let her rattle on until she ran out of steam. When there was an opening, he said, ''Megan and I were thinking of going up there this weekend and I was wondering—''

''My God, whatever for?'' Suzi cried.

''Oh, just to get away for a bit. Someplace remote, you know.''

''Well, if it's remote you want, that hayseed burg fills the bill. Jesus, I never should have listened to Derek. Remind me never to take investment advice from anyone named Derek as long as I live, which, at these rates, won't be a hell of a lot longer. Honest to God, I don't know what possessed me. The very thought of that place and what . . . what happened. . . . Well, it just gives me the creeps, it really does.''

Jack said quickly, ''I thought you might like us to take a look at the house for you, just sort of check it out. You know.'' Suzi was the kind of person you could say ''You know'' to all the time because she always thought she did.

''Christ, Jack, you can *stay* in the damned thing if you want. Yes, actually, that's a good idea. Always protect a worthless investment, right? Hey, Derek would approve! Sure, that'd be good, check it out for me. In fact, listen, you guys can use it anytime you want. I won't be around much through the summer, anyway.'' And she launched into an excited account of how her responsibilities were growing by leaps and bounds, and how the network practically depended solely on her for its very survival and she was going to be spending a lot of time, really *a lot* of time on the coast "getting things in shape," and so on and so on.

Jack signaled Karen to ring his other phone. When it rang, he told Suzi he'd have to go but quickly offered to send over a messenger to pick up the keys. Yes, he could wait a second while Suzi checked to see if she had them with her, although why she was carrying them around, she had no idea at all. But she did have them, and Jack told her the messenger would be there by five o'clock and assured her he'd give her love to Megan.

There was one other thing to do before the meeting. Do it now, a voice shouted in his head, before you lose your nerve! Go in there and tell him. Jack marched down the hall to the office of the editorial director, and ten minutes later returned a free man, snapping his fingers with excitement.

He told Karen his decision, and that he'd be there until Friday, and that he'd recommended she be promoted to take over at least some of his responsibilities on her own. He also asked her to send a messenger to ABC for Suzi's keys.

He sat through the meeting and only offered his opinion twice, carefully ignoring the curious looks of the other editors. His thoughts were not on the meeting. He had already decided to save all the news until tonight as a surprise for Megan. And there was a lot of news: his decision to leave the company, his arrangement with Bob Brockden, and the weekend. Finally things were coming together. At some point, you have to take control. He and Megan had been letting things drift for too long. And he was worried about her. That job was getting to her. He could have—*should* have—called her before he actually quit, but he thought too that presenting

her—and himself, for that matter—with a *fait accompli*
would give her the nerve to look for another position
herself. He had done some careful calculations and
figured that, even at their present level of expenses, they
could get by for maybe eight months if not another cent
came into the kitty. It they were careful, they might last
a year. And that was if neither one of them was
working. And, after all, they were two bright, talented,
resourceful people who, when forced to live by their
wits, would surely make their way very nicely, thank
you, and *oh shit!* he hoped he had done the right thing.

When Megan had finished painting the mural on the
kitchen wall—and she had only declared it finished because there was no more wall left to paint and no more
paint left either—she stood back and admired her
handiwork with grim pride. Then the tiredness hit her
with a force that weakened her legs. She sat on one of
the kitchen chairs she had pulled to the other side of the
room. She was still looking at the mural, her gaze
sweeping over the details, but then she realized she
wasn't really seeing it because her vision was blurred
and her eyes were filled with tears.

Then she grew angry with herself for crying, so she
marched off to the bathroom and took a long shower
and washed her hair. She felt better afterward and,
while her hair was still drying, sat at the desk in the
bedroom, pulled a yellow pad in front of her, and
started writing down the names of every single person in
the business who should know that she had left Dunwoodie and was "available." Go to it, my girl, she told
herself, and when she ran out of names, she got up and
paced back and forth, and went through all her friends
and acquaintances very methodically. She came up with

still more names and added them to the list. Then she re-arranged the list into what seemed the best order of priority to call people. It was a pretty good list, she decided, and she started feeling a little better. She'd begin making calls in the morning.

She brushed her hair and dressed and went out to the kitchen to put things back where they belonged. She was drinking a glass of orange juice and studying the mural rather more critically than she had earlier when she heard a key in the front door. She realized she'd had no idea how late it was.

She met Jack at the door.

"What are you doing home so—" they said together.

Then, out of the corner of his eye, Jack got a glimpse of the kitchen wall.

"Oh, my God," he said, "we've been attacked by the evil spirit of Pablo Picasso." He looked at her questioningly, but she said nothing and only followed him into the kitchen.

He studied the mural for a minute, then looked at her. "This took a long time to do," he said, "and unless I'm going nutso, which I wouldn't rule out as a possibility, this wasn't here when I left this morning. You've been home all day?"

She looked him in the eye and said, "I quit my job."

They stared at each other for a long time, standing there in front of the red and green mural, until Jack said at last, "Oh, brother, have I got news for you."

Later, in bed, in the dark, they clasped each other very tight.

"Jack?" she whispered against his shoulder.

"Hmm."

"Are we going to be all right?" She sounded very tiny.

"We'll be all right."

"Do you promise?"

"I promise."

He pulled the sheet up to settle it more snugly around the back of her neck. She touched his face with her fingers.

"What I did today was really stupid," he said.

"No," she said. "Or at least, it was no more stupid than what I did." She kissed his chest. "I love you."

"I love you," he murmured into her hair.

Steve Steiger had the dream again that night and he awoke in darkness to find the pillow soaked with sweat.

He dreamed of a television movie, replete with special effects of his own devising, based on the death of Candy McBain and using actual footage he had shot on the scene himself. He was famous, and Steven Spielberg announced to *Variety* that he would make no new movies without the aid of Steve Steiger, special effects genius and whiz kid of the industry.

At first, in the days following the trip to Deacons Kill, the events in the mountains had had little effect on him. He cursed himself for letting the sheriff confiscate the tape. If only he'd known what to say, he could have held on to it. That tape was easily the best thing he had ever shot. The best. With the right kind of editing, he could have really turned it into something. Probably could have made his name with it. That scene could have been duped and slowed and speeded up, and if he could get into a real studio and use the new Mirage machine, there was no end to the things he could do with it.

Damn that sheriff! Everything was always screwed up. People were always screwing him up!

He punched half-heartedly at the pillow and tried to settle back into sleep again.

But he didn't have the nightmare yet. That came later.

7

The nice weather lingered in Deacons Kill all that week, and Thursday was as bright and clear as Monday had been. Beautiful days, and the marigolds that lined driveways in the Kill called for the eye to see them. Crisp evenings, and residents ate their dinners on porches and in yards and appetites were hearty. Cool nights, and you could sleep with a sheet over you and be cozy.

John Chard had not been sleeping well at all. He felt the same way he'd felt in that first week after the death of the girl on Deacons Rise, almost within sight of his own home that sheltered his wife and his daughter. Disgust. Frustration. Fury. Was any place filled with human beings ever safe from murder? As pathology turned up nothing, and the special forensics team from Albany turned up nothing, and the extensive search of the area by his own deputies and by the New York State Police turned up nothing, that thought had returned more and more often. Only human beings murder. He thought over the other mysterious deaths in the Kill that he had faced as sheriff. There were a few for which the files were marked "Circumstances Unknown, Pending Police Investigation." In plain English, that meant the crime was never solved. A couple of them went back fifteen and twenty years. But always in the file there was at least something, a clue, a bit of evidence, a hint of an answer. In this case there was nothing.

Only human beings murder. The thought would not leave him in peace. Only human beings murder. Animals kill but they never commit murder. Could it have been an animal, he asked himself again and again, and hoped every time he could tell himself yes, it must have been an animal. But he never could. He had been over the ground several times. There were no tracks, no hint of anything out of the ordinary. And what could it be? A bear? Not at this time of year. What, then? What?

And of course there was the tape, always the tape, with its distant and blurred and obscured pictures of the girl as she met her death. And the tape showed nothing, nothing you could use, nothing you could make sense of, nothing you could follow up on, nothing you could even *understand*. There she was alive, and there she was dead, and nothing more.

The marks on her body. No answers there either. He had read the autopsy report and the medical terminology that told him what he had already seen for himself about the marks on her skin, and that he had asked Doc Warren about so many times that they both now hated and dreaded the subject. No leads there.

And Steve Steiger, that spoiled little rich kid playing with expensive toys, there he was too, in the barn with Chard, and he was talking and what he was saying did not make sense, simply did not make sense at all.

And as Chard lay in bed these summer nights with his sleeping wife beside him, and his daughter safely asleep elsewhere in the house, he could hear what Steve was saying and, the later and darker it got, the easier the words were to believe, though part of him said they were madness and could be nothing else.

Disgust. Frustration. Fury. And, added to them: fear.

And a further thing too.

Carla Helbig.

Nine years old. Missing. Or dead. Gone since April. Two months now. Gone for two months and not a trace. Somewhere in these nearby hills, that much at least seemed certain. But where does a child like that get to? How does a child disappear without a clue? Who does things to a child? Who?

Or what?

He thought of Jacob Helbig, Carla's father, and how little help he had been.

Chard shifted in the bed, carefully so as not to wake Martha, and stared again at the dark.

Since the unexplained disappearance of his daughter, Jacob Helbig's life had changed only in small ways. He brought home less food now—no need to buy those damned breakfast cereals with the damned stupid names anymore.

Christ, kids could be hard to put up with! Well, hell, life was simpler now anyway. No need to put up with all the shit a kid gives you, not no more. Goddamn kids rule the house nowadays, wantin this and wantin that and never satisfied no matter what the hell you do for them. Christ Almighty, what you have to put up with from kids. That goddamn cereal, for instance. Wouldn't never eat nothin else. Jesus!

No cryin and screamin in the house, neither. And no more needin this and needin that for school, for another thing. Goddamn schools today, they think a man has nothin better to do with his hard-earned money. Don't care what they make you spend these days. Don't give a shit. And what in the hell do you get for all your trouble? There you are one day and you got a kid, and never mind for a minute how much trouble and expense they put you to, she's your *kid*, she's *yours*, and then, Christ Almighty, the kid's up and gone. Just like that. Ran away from home and there's the thanks you get for all the shit and bother. No life for a man, no fuckin life at all. First the wife dies on you, no warnin or nothin, and leaves you with a kid that don't want to raise a hand to help her old man nohow after all he done for her, and then the goddamn kid up and disappears too, just like the mother almost. Jesus H. Almighty Fuckin Christ!

John Chard came to visit Helbig on Thursday afternoon, Helbig's day off from the Agway that week.

He was a bear of a man, tall, barrel-chested, barrel-bellied, meaty in the shoulders, with hands like hams. He walked with a limp—a "lurch" they called it in the Kill and shook their heads behind his back as they grieved for his dead wife and his undoubtedly dead daughter—because he was missing two toes from his right foot and three from his left. Gangrene rotted them away because he was diabetic and he drank, and when he was drinking, which was often, very often, he forgot to shoot the insulin into his leg, and forgot sometimes too when he was sober. Each time the gangrene attacked a toe he nursed the pain, drowning himself in beer to drive it away, and ending up roaring until the neighbors finally called the sheriff or the hospital and he had to be carried off. He was partially deaf, so he roared as a matter of course, but the roaring that went with the pain

was more than a person could bear. They took him
away each time to Fox Memorial Hospital in Oneonta,
and the doctors cut off the toe and sent him home until
the next time.

But he still worked, hauling sacks and cartons at the
Agway market in Cobleskill. He could heft a hundred-
pound sack of feed or fertilizer the way a strong man
might lift a toy, roaring his complaints all the while
about the fuckin this and the goddamn that. At first,
when the wife was alive, the manager of the market had
kept him on out of pity for her. Later, when she died—
he just wore her down, people said in the Kill, just
roared her and scared her to death—he kept him on out
of habit, and also because there was still the child, little
Carla. Even if no one liked or cared about Helbig, Lord
knows, the child still had to eat.

"Thought we might talk about Carla, if you don't
mind," Chard said and walked in before Helbig could
turn him away.

"Aw, Jesus," Helbig growled. "Won't you people
ever leave me the hell alone? Man can't even get any
peace in his own home these days."

He slammed the screen door and turned heavily to
face Chard. "What is it now? Haven't you people tortured me enough?"

Chard selected the one straight-backed chair in the
living room. The sofa had an old yellowed sheet tangled
across one end of it. He guessed that Helbig had been
sleeping there. An open beer bottle stood on the floor
beside it.

For a moment, Chard wondered if he had done the
right thing in sitting down. A man like Helbig, for all his
mental limitations, exulted unconsciously in his size,
and he loomed now over the sheriff. But, as Chard had

expected, Helbig yielded to his own unmoving presence
in the room and, sighing heavily, sat down on the couch
and placed his hands on his wide-apart knees. Men like
this, Chard thought, have no easiness in their bodies.

"Sometimes," Chard said, his voice level and his gaze
steady on Helbig's face, "it's good to go back to something after some time has gone by. Sometimes you can
see it more clearly, get a better look, sort of, from a
distance."

"Ahh," Helbig sneered, and wiped the idea away
with a sweep of one meaty paw. "It's all dead and done.
I'm tellin ya, it's all dead and done."

"The case is still open," Chard said.

"Christ, don't you people know nothin?" Helbig's
voice boomed through the house. "No wonder cops
these days don't never catch nobody. Jesus Christ, ya
don't got no sense. Two months later and you think
you're gonna catch them now?"

"Catch who?" Chard asked.

Helbig shook his head in frustration at the idiocy of
the world. "The bastards who got her or killed her or
whatever the hell they done to her."

"Do you think she was killed or do you think she ran
away?"

"What the hell am I supposed to think?" Helbig
snapped back. "You people can't tell me nothin, I
learned that a long time ago."

Helbig wore oil-smeared khaki slacks and a once-
white tee-shirt that now had food stains in long streaks
down the front and curving wider over his belly. On his
feet were battered cloth slippers with the front parts cut
off. He had reddish-blond hair, short on top but long
and swept back and greasy on the sides. His face was
pale, puffy, unhealthy looking. There were three angry

pimples on his chin. Chard didn't like being in the same room with him.

"Tell me what she was wearing," he said.

"Ah, for . . . ." Helbig looked around the room for relief. "All right, if it'll get you to leave me alone, I'll tell you again." He held out his left hand with the fingers extended and placed his right index finger on the tip of the left thumb, ticking off the items. "Sneakers, red and white sneakers, just like I told you." He moved to the next finger. "Sweatshirt."

"What color?"

"Green, green, green, like the color they make 'em!" Next finger. "Corduroy pants."

"What—"

"*Brown*. Eight fuckin dollars at the Jamesway."

This was all in the record. Chard had it memorized.

"Could she have been on her way to visit somebody? A friend, maybe?"

"Who the fuck knows where a kid could be goin, the way they run around?"

"Had she mentioned she wanted to see anybody in particular that week? Anybody at all whose name she might have mentioned?"

"No."

"Nobody at all?"

"No!"

Careful now, Chard thought. "Do you think she was attacked by somebody or do you think she just ran away?"

Helbig glared at him, eyes intense. "I ain't answerin no more questions. Look it up in your nice cushy office." He planted his hands on his knees again, stolid and sullen.

Outside in his car, Chard knew that Helbig had

lumbered to the door and would watch until he drove off. He eased the car away from the curb and headed toward the office.

Again, he thought, nothing. Less than nothing, in fact. Chard had hoped for two months now that there would be some evidence to suggest a murder—what a way you had to think!—because if it was not a murder, then the child had just wandered away or, more likely, run away from her terrible father. The one sneaker had been found on the hillside, near the Rise, half buried in mud. No way even to tell which direction the child had been going. The hills had been searched for miles around the area. If the body was there—and Chard was certain it was—the searchers had missed it through the merest happenstance. If his best conjecture held up, it meant the child had run away from home in a torrential spring rainstorm, had run or wandered through the wooded hills, no way of telling how far or how long a child could travel under those circumstances, and while she was in the woods . . . something happened to her.

Something.

The vagueness of the word punched at the hard knot in his stomach.

It was a little after six o'clock on Friday evening when Jack and Megan arrived at the Centennial Hotel. By six-thirty they had unpacked and come downstairs. They strolled out to the porch and stood there, taking in the view of the square.

Jack shook his head suddenly and laughed. "Either we have actually made the big jump," he said, "and taken charge of our lives, as I believe the current expression goes, or else we have wigged out completely. As the other expression goes."

Megan took hold of his arm. "You look sane enough to me. Nervous, but sane."

"Of course I'm nervous here. This is an alien environment. It's disorienting. This odd smell, for example. What do you suppose it is?"

Megan sniffed. "Fresh air?"

"Hmm. Could be. We'll have to check it out, make sure it's safe to breathe."

"Yeah."

"Yeah. And where is everybody? Where's the blaring traffic, where are the eager, hurrying crowds, where's the friendly neighborhood mugger, the panhandler, the bag lady? All the familiar faces that make a place seem like home, where are they?"

"Yeah," Megan said. "The clatter of the subway trains, the rattle of the taxis."

"Yeah."

"Yeah."

They both fell silent, thinking of the conversations they'd had this week about what they were going to do now, and about the possibility of moving out of the city. Maybe moving upstate. Maybe to Deacons Kill.

"I hope we like it here," Megan said now, quietly. "I hope we're not being foolish even thinking like this."

"Well," Jack said, "the way I see it is, given the circumstances in which we find ourselves, which any right-minded person would regard as a golden opportunity, the only recourse we have, in all actuality, is to rely on that oldest and truest of methods of procedure, handed down to us from the ancients and burnished with the golden patina of old wisdom."

"What's that?" she asked, smiling.

"When in doubt," Jack said solemnly, "fake it."

They ate dinner in the hotel's Dining Room, and the waitress they remembered from the other time was still there. She recognized them, smiled, and asked if they were visiting or just passing through.

"Lots of folks do that in summer," she said. "They spend a couple of weeks going all around this part of the state, staying a night here and a night there. Come up to see Howe Caverns over in Cobleskill, then usually pass this way going up to Cooperstown." She laughed. "By the time they get here, folks are glad to find a real hotel. Been written up in some books and everything."

By the time their meal arrived, the room was almost filled with diners and three more waitresses were on duty. For the most part, the diners looked like the businessmen and professionals of the area, lawyers, doctors perhaps, insurance agents, bankers, college administrators from Cobleskill and Oneonta, county officials, and their handsome wives. Many of them greeted each other as they entered the room and were shown to tables. And among them were a few who looked like farmers, or perhaps local store owners, husband and wife and children, dressed as well as the others but looking "dressed up" for their evening out to dinner. And there were tourists in wash-and-wear slacks and print blouses, here for the one night only. Jack and Megan wondered where they themselves fit in and how they looked to the others.

Once, when Jack was looking around for the waitress to ask for another drink, his eyes met those of a man at a table nearby. The man smiled and nodded and said, "How do?" Jack returned the greeting.

"Who was that?" Megan asked.

"A stranger," Jack said. "A total stranger."

"Don't let it bother you," she said. "It's good for the digestion."

The dinners—prime ribs for Jack, trout "almondine" for Megan—were prepared and served to perfection. When they finished, they lingered a long time over the excellent coffee. No one came to hurry them away from the table and the coffee cups were never more than half empty before the waitress was there to refill them. When they finally asked for the check, it came to a little less than thirty dollars. "Let's not enlighten these people," Jack said, and Megan agreed. He left a generous tip on the table.

After dinner, outside on the porch, with the last of the daylight fading away from the town, Megan said, "Since you've bought me dinner, does that mean I have to go to bed with you?"

"Hey, what kind of a guy do you think I am?" Jack said.

"That much, at least, we've established," she said. She took his hand and they walked down the wooden steps to the street. "The way I look at it, now that you don't have a job to support me, it's a lucky thing you're such a good lay."

"Women," Jack said, and shook his head, and they crossed the street to the tree-shadowed park that formed the center of Deacons Kill.

The darkening town was old, and a quick glance at the buildings that lined the square and the streets leading out from it suggested a peak around the turn of the century. Easily the grandest thing in town was the Centennial Hotel, its broad white front almost glowing in the half-light of late evening, dominating the north side of the square. An equally white clapboard church rose narrow and tall, its spire extending the line toward the heavens, on the south side. The east and west sides were lined with shops: pharmacy, stationery store, jeweler, insurance office, superette, an eatery called The Feedbag, a real estate agent's office, a dry cleaner, a launderette, a barber shop, two beauty parlors three doors away from each other, a Sears catalog order office, and an antique ice cream parlor complete with tiled floors, marble tables, bent-wire chairs, polished wooden counter and slow-turning fans overhead. A sign, hand-lettered on a piece of cardboard and taped to the inside of the door, announced that shirts and shoes were absolutely required in this establishment at all times. Prisco's Pizza was conveniently located right beside the movie theatre on the northwest corner of the square. The theatre's art-deco marquee announced that showings would be "Fri 7:30 Sat 7 & 9:30." The marquee lights were turned off now but, as they looked through the porthole windows of the doors, they could see a dim light burning at the back of the lobby and a skinny woman in a housedress dozing on a folding metal chair. Beside her was a card table with a display of candy. A tall wood-framed popcorn machine stood in darkness on her other side.

"Somewhere in this town," Jack said as they moved away from the theatre and into one of the streets leading out of the square, "I'll just bet you there's a pinball machine."

"Keep searching," Megan said.

The side streets were the same, lined with two-story buildings, most of them brick but a few made of wood. Some of the shops here were larger than those on the square, Whitmore's Appliances, for example, and an

A&P, and a dusty-looking discount store that reminded them of an odd-lot store in the city. There was a big empty place with a FOR RENT sign pasted to the window, partially obscuring a fly-specked neon sign that spelled BINGO.

"Bet the churches put a stop to that," Megan said, "especially if there are any Catholics in the woods."

"You're very disrespectful, did you know that?" Jack said.

"It's part of my charm," Megan answered.

They strolled a little way along each of the streets that led out of the square. The one heading north from the western end of the Centennial Hotel was called Hill Street, and a fine old brick building there, facing the side of the hotel, had "TOWN OFFICES" carved into the stone above the door. There were lights on in the windows and two police cruisers angled in at the curb in front of it. Hill Street, they knew already, became Deacons Road once it got out of town and climbed up the hill to the farm. At the eastern end of the hotel, School Street branched away from the square, and they walked far enough along it to see another white church a little farther along before they turned back.

The south end of the square had a big Arco gas station and, next to it, a municipal parking lot "for shoppers only." That side of the square was bisected by the main road that brought traffic up from Route 7. Jack and Megan walked along it a little way, crossed Railroad Street, then came to Depot Street, and stopped to look at the shadowy shapes of an old, old station and a huge warehouse that stood alongside the track beyond it. An immense open field bordered the other side of the tracks. At first they thought the railroad line was abandoned, but then they saw moonlight gleaming in a narrow ribbon along the center of the otherwise rusted tracks.

They walked back up the slight hill to the center of town and then across the square, beneath the gently rustling leaves of the trees and past the war memorial in the center of the park. Its polished brass plaque with the names of the town's heroic dead shone golden in the moonlight.

"I feel like we've come about a million miles," Megan said softly.

"We have," Jack said, his voice as quiet as her own in the still night.

They reached the curb across from the hotel.

"Want to come up to my room and fool around?" Jack said.

"Collecting on dinner, huh? Well, I guess I'll just have to grin and bear it."

"The grinning part is optional."

"I'll grin anyway," she said.

"Hey!" Jack stooped suddenly and picked up something from the sidewalk. "A penny," he said and showed it to her. "That's good luck. I knew this trip would mean good luck."

"Was it heads or tails?"

"I didn't notice."

Megan cast her eyes heavenward, then looked at Jack with mock seriousness. "You know," she said, "sometimes I think I have to tell you everything. If you find a penny heads up, *that's* good luck. If it's tails, you have to turn it over first, *then* pick it up."

"My God," Jack said, matching her tone, "I take you out of the city for a couple of hours and already you're going soft in the brain department."

"You can joke about it if you want, but this is impor- tant stuff. You just mark my words, Jack Casey, and hope it was heads."

"Well, we'll have to wait and see what kind of luck we have, then, won't we?"

"Precisely," said Megan, but she was starting to smile.

They crossed the silent street and went into the hotel and upstairs to bed.

"We were up there today," Megan was telling Doc Warren over dinner in the Dining Room on Saturday night. They had run into John Chard over breakfast that morning and he had offered them a lift to the Fer- rand place. They had swept up the remaining litter from the party and brought in some groceries, simple things that could be prepared without elaborate utensils. Chard had helped them and assured them that Martha would be glad to loan them anything they needed. They were staying at the hotel tonight and going up to the house tomorrow.

"How long are you planning to stay?" the doctor asked.

Jack said, "We don't really know." Briefly, he told the doctor and Mrs. Chard about what had happened during the week; they had told Chard himself that morning. "To be perfectly honest," he finished, "we're really not at all that certain what we'll be doing. Megan will be painting and trying to get assignments. I'll be doing some agenting and, I hope, some freelance edit- ing. And some writing, maybe. As for staying here, I think Suzi wouldn't give it a second thought if we prac- tically moved into the house. We were figuring on just staying for the weekend, or possibly stretching it a few

days. But we do have to be going back. The work we do
is in the city. This is just sort of a vacation for us." He
wondered why he was telling these people so much.

"You can paint a picture or write a book anywhere,"
Doc Warren said lightly.

"That's what I've been telling him," Megan said.

Martha looked worried for them and said, "I'm sure
you'll do just fine," then dropped her gaze to her plate.

"How's that suped-up car of yours doing, Doc?"
Chard said across the table.

Doc Warren put down his fork and said, "I know
you're just asking to change the subject, John, but since
you ask, I'm going to tell you." And he did, at great
length and with great enthusiasm.

Later, over dessert, Megan blushed and told the
Chards and the doctor, "Jack and I appreciate your
being so nice to us. We only just happened to come here
to the Kill in the first place, purely by chance. And now
we're here again and we already have friends here."

"And apparently we're already calling it the Kill, just
like natives," Jack said, looking at her.

"Oh, I did, didn't I?" Megan said, and all five of
them laughed.

And after dinner, when the Chards and Doc Warren
were leaving, Jack and Megan walked out with them to
the porch of the hotel and waited while they got into
their cars and drove away. Martha Chard waved as the
car turned right at the corner and disappeared into Hill
Street. John Chard had promised to pick them up in the
morning and drive them up to the Ferrand place.

"It was really a nice evening, wasn't it?" Megan said.

"It was," Jack agreed.

Neither of them referred to the one awkward
moment.

John Chard had been talking about how most families in the Kill had been there a long time, some as long as a couple of hundred years, and Jack had asked why the farmer, Martin Ferrand, had sold his property. Chard had hesitated, and it was Doc Warren who answered.

"Farming's not what it was years ago," he said. "Years ago a man could make a good living on a small farm and be proud of the work he did. It's different today. Today a man breaks his back all day long and gets nothing in return, especially on a small place, and Ferrand's was on the small side as dairy farms go." He had talked more about the economics of dairy farming, and the conversation had drifted to other topics.

But Jack had noted Chard's hesitation and had seen him look across the table at the doctor. He had seen their eyes meet for a second and had known, when Doc Warren answered, that the answer was a lie.

In the hour after midnight, while his wife slept in their bed, John Chard silently rose and, pulling a light robe around his shoulders, went out into the hall. He walked softly through the house, stopping for a moment outside his daughter's room. He had heard her come in about half an hour after they had gone to bed. Her light was out; she was asleep now.

The floor creaked a little as he crossed the living room and went to the door of the basement. He was careful with that door, opening it slowly so the latch wouldn't snap and make a noise. He went through the doorway and down two steps, then pulled the door closed behind him before switching on the light.

In his private den in the basement, he sat on the discarded kitchen chair, kneading his stiff fingers. Then he pushed the chair back from the desk and got out the tape, and switched on the television set and the video-cassette deck. He closed his tired eyes for a moment, then opened them and pushed the switch. And there were the images moving in front of him again, the images that taunted him and told him nothing of what he needed to know. Told him, at least, nothing that made sense.

He watched the tape three times and by then his eyes were aching.

In the hour after midnight, Elbert Warren, M.D., sat at the old rolltop desk in the dining room of his house on School Street. The desk was a twin of the one in his office, and he sometimes thought that the sight of that old desk did more to instill confidence in his patients than all the nostrums of modern medical science. When he had something important to do at home, a decision to make or a problem to solve, he liked to sit at this one in the dining room. It helped him think.

He was thinking now of the conversation at dinner and Jack's question about Martin Ferrand. Why were they acting like this, he demanded of himself, he and Chard? They had acted as if they were ashamed of what Martin had done, selling out like that and moving away. No, not "ashamed," he corrected himself. More like "embarrassed," that was closer to the truth.

Warren's people had never been farmers. His father had been a doctor, and his father before him had been a doctor, and together the three of them had nursed the people of the Kill through more than a century of sickness and pain. And if God was willing, his son Andy, now a resident at Montefiore Hospital in the Bronx down in the city, would one day return to the Kill, live in this house and work in that office himself, and another, younger Doc Warren would serve the town. And he too, though not a farmer, would understand what it meant to be one. And what it meant was: you loved the land and you didn't quit it. The land was your life. You loved it and respected it—maybe that was the major thing, respecting it—and you didn't walk away from it.

But Martin Ferrand had walked away from it, and neither Elbert Warren nor John Chard, Martin's closest friends, knew the reason why. Nor did they understand his haste, his silence, his avoidance of questions or, for the matter of that, his avoidance of the two of them. The farm had been sold, and Martin and his wife had departed before the sale was even settled. He hadn't even gone to a real estate agent in the Kill to make the sale, but to Tom Vogel in Cobleskill instead: almost a stranger.

The doctor sighed and reached into one of the compartments at the right side of his desk. He took out his address book and opened it. He stared a long time at Martin Ferrand's name. Martin lived now in Cambridge, Massachusetts, where his son taught at Harvard. Doc Warren had written to him once and had no reply. John Chard, he knew, had also written to Martin once and likewise had no reply. In fact, they only had the address because Martin's wife, Edith, had written to Martha Chard. Her one letter was brief: they were settled now, and she was glad to be near her son, and Martha shouldn't worry about her. Martha had written back immediately, but so far she'd had no answer.

The doctor stared at Martin's new address and wondered why a man like Martin, who loved and respected the land, would abandon it as he had. Jack's question at dinner had triggered all of this. That young couple was going up to stay in Martin's house, in Martin's *home*. To make no mention of that woman who owned the place now. Lord only knew what would become of it. And suddenly he realized what John Chard was up to. Chard, though never a farmer, loved these hills and fields and roads and houses, these *homes*, with a passion, and protected them fiercely. He was protecting Martin's home now, protecting it from the woman who owned it. If he weren't so upset, the doctor would have smiled. Chard, given his way, and his way counted for a lot, would have that couple moved in and settled in that house because Chard thought they were decent people.

And thoughts of Martin Ferrand's house brought up thoughts of what had happened on the Rise, and that poor girl's battered body, and the unpretty spiral of thought turned another turn, and suddenly he was thinking of Carla Helbig and wondering all over again what had happened to her, and whether she could have been on the Rise itself, after all, when it happened.

He reached into another compartment of the desk and brought out an envelope and carefully copied Martin Ferrand's address. Then he took out a sheet of letter paper and, using the fountain pen that he reserved for special occasions, dated it and slowly began.

"Dear friend," he wrote. "I barely know how to begin this letter. . . ."

In the hour after midnight, Jacob Helbig lay sprawled on the sodden couch. He had fallen asleep with a bottle of beer in his hand and the contents had spilled out, soaking the cushion. When he woke up, he cursed the wetness beneath him but did not get up at once. His toes were aching again, those toes that remained to him. He cursed the beer, and then he cursed the toes, and then the gangrene and the diabetes and the needles and the pain, and then he remembered Chard's visit on Thursday or whenever the hell it was, and he cursed him too, and then he cursed the kid for bringing all this trouble on him and cursed her again for good measure.

Where the hell had she gotten to? Where? Goddamn kid.

Goddamn kid did nothin but run away. Nothin you do for them is good enough nowadays, nothin. No gratitude in kids. Break your fuckin back hauling crap all day every day and where's the thanks you get? And all the shit. Take all the shit those bastards at the Agway hand out and where's the thanks. A man can barely live on what they pay you, and the kid wantin this and wantin that, every goddamn thing them other kids got. Never give a man no peace. And then ups and runs away. What's it all for? What's the good of it? Ups and runs away!

He was muttering aloud by now, filling the house with the sound of his own voice. He moved heavily, balancing first on one elbow, then got himself upright on the edge of the wet cushion.

"Goddamn kid," he said out loud. "Done nothin but run away and leave her old man alone. Oughta get her back and tan her hide."

He stared sullenly at the silent empty room.

In the hour after midnight, Jack and Megan made love again, slow and easy this time, gentle and warm, and afterward, breathing steadied now, they lay side by side in the bed, hips touching. Jack stroked her thigh with slow fingers.

"Do you think we got enough food?" she asked after a while, her voice low and dreamy.

"For a couple of days," Jack said and settled himself more comfortably, his right hand beneath his head. "If we stay any longer, we'll need more."

"Do you think we should?"

"Stay longer?"

"Hmm."

"If we stay past, say, Tuesday, we should call you-know-who and tell her."

"Your hand feels nice," she said. "Would you want to stay longer than that?"

"Can't make any money staying up here. Can't make those big bucks sitting on our asses. Gotta hustle. The wolves are at the door, you know."

"Maybe we could see if we could . . . get used to it. Staying up here. Just for a while, during the summer."

"I guess. We could think about it. Keep it in the back of our minds."

"We have enough money to coast for a while. A little while, anyway. If we get some freelance work, we could do it up here."

"I know."

"I like it up here," she said.

"Me too."

She rolled over and settled her cheek against his shoulder. With her left hand, she reached down and took hold of him, stroking him gently.

"When we make love," she whispered, "I don't feel so frightened."

"I love you, sweetie," he said.

"I love you too."

He put his arm around her shoulder and held her close and warm against him and together they dozed off to sleep.

In the hour after midnight, something moved slowly downhill through the woods of Deacons Rise. It moved with caution through the thick undergrowth of the hill-side, the only sign of its passing a branch pushed aside and a sound like sliding sand.

Suddenly it stopped. The trees ended here, and just beyond the last of them was a shallow ditch, and beyond the ditch . . . something different. A flat surface, black as the night. And new smells. Confusing smells, acrid and threatening. It had never seen such a thing or smelled such a thing. It stayed well back beyond the ditch for a long time, back among the trees—though there was nothing to see it, and nothing to be seen—watching and waiting. Nothing happened. But the thing was a hunter, with infinite patience, eternal patience, and it waited and waited and watched. And nothing happened.

Eventually, curious, it moved out from among the trees to the edge of the ditch, then, slowly, across the ditch to the flat black surface and, wondering, ready to attack and worried at being in the open, stepped onto it. Nothing happened. After a few safe moments, it moved farther out, to the middle of the flat area, and looked around quickly. The flat surface stretched in two directions and curved out of sight around the hills both ways. And still nothing happened. The thing sniffed the air, breathing in the strange smells.

Then it heard the growling. It sprang for the edge of the black surface and the ditch and the safety of the trees, then abruptly it stopped, crouched, swung around to challenge the night, angry breath hissing in its throat. The growling was so strange, so never-heard-before, that the thing could not tell from which direction it was coming. The sound seemed to swell and bellow among

the hills, from here, from there. The thing, no longer
startled, crouched at the edge of the ditch, ready to
attack, and waited.

The beast roared at it out of the night with a sudden-
ness and speed that brought terror. The thing froze
where it was. It had never seen such a monster, never
seen such a shape, never heard such a roaring, *never
seen such eyes*.

And suddenly the monster was past it and rushing
away and the thing saw a second pair of eyes, smaller
than the others and rushing away but red this time and
dazzling in the dark, and then suddenly it was gone and
the roaring died out to silence.

The thing stood, still and silent as a boulder. It waited
until the only sound in the hills was that of the woods at
night. And then at last it moved again, back among the
trees, slow and cautious, making a gritty sound as it
went that might have been the sound of the mountain
itself shifting in its sleep.

Here it knew the way and knew what to expect, and as
it climbed higher up the Rise it moved faster, favoring
gravel and rock that held no trace of its passing.

And at the top it stopped. Another open space here,
but this surface stony and familiar, a slab of solid rock.
The thing stood, breathing misty air into the clear light
of the swelling moon. Then it moved again, across the
open space. It was at the top of the hill but there was
still more climbing to reach its place of safety. And,
swaying, it started up the winding course of its final
climb with a sound of rough stone grating on wood.

8

Martin Ferrand and his wife lived in Cambridge, Massachusetts, in a comfortable old house on Trowbridge Street, midway between Kirkland Street and Cambridge Street, a ten-minute walk from Harvard Square, the Coop, the shops and the subway to Boston. The two-story house had a large master bedroom, a guest room, a large dining room designed to serve the social needs of another era, and a front room that Edith said she liked very much. There was a small stained-glass window above the front door and a small porch. The street was rather narrow, lined with great dark trees, and very quiet, though sometimes Martin could hear music being played on a guitar from somewhere up toward Kirkland. There was a cobblestone driveway at the side of the house and a garage in the back for the station wagon. The garage was big enough for two cars, and Martin figured that one of these days he would set up some of his tools back there in the other half and build himself a little work area so he could maybe do some repairs and occupy his time. All in all, he supposed, it was a very nice house and it would do, yes, it would do, but he really did not like it.

Of course it was nice being near Ramsey (that was Edith's family name before they married) and Susan and the two grandchildren but, if you had to tell the truth, it wasn't all that much. Ramsey had found the house for them and helped them move into it, and Susan had taken Edith around for two days and showed her where the best shops were. Edith had come home marveling more at the prices than the selection of goods to be had. But Susan was busy herself and didn't have all that much time, really, and after the beginning Edith had to find her own way. And Ramsey had a summer session course to teach on Spenser (he taught Chaucer during the year), and in the time left free from that, he was working on a book. He brought the manuscript over one day and they saw that his name on the title page was R. L. Ferrand. Edith was a little hurt and Martin saw it, but nothing was said and it didn't come up again.

On the first Sunday they were there, and still not completely settled in their new home, they had dinner with Ramsey and Susan and the children. Robert, thirteen, and Melanie, eleven, were both fine children with excellent manners. It was a pleasant day, a reunion. Two weeks later, Edith made dinner in the house on Trowbridge Street. Melanie excused herself and had to leave before dessert because she had promised to go skating with her friends, and somebody's mother was picking her up. Robert did not come at all. It's so hard, Susan said, with everyone so busy and the children getting older, to catch them all in the same place at the same time. And that, Martin had thought, is that.

Edith busied herself in the house, dividing her time

between the kitchen and the sewing room, where she was making new drapes and slipcovers. She did not complain.

Martin, alone, went for long walks through the streets of Cambridge and calculated that, in the past month, he had walked more miles on paved sidewalks than he'd done in all his life before.

And as he walked, he thought: What have I done?

On Tuesday morning, Jack and Megan decided to stay until Saturday at the Ferrand place. Megan walked down the hill to ask Martha if she could use the phone. Suzi was at a meeting when she called and Megan left a message asking her to call back at this number. Mrs. Chard insisted that Megan have some lunch while she waited.

Suzi called back an hour later and said that, when she got the message and saw the area code, she thought the damned house might have burned down or something, but since it hadn't, sure, of course, they were welcome to stay there as long as they wanted, no problem. Megan took a deep breath and said she and Jack would be glad to rent the place for the summer, say, until Labor Day. Suzi said she thought they had gone stark raving out of their minds but, yeah, okay, that sounded fine to her because she'd have to be on the coast so much from now on and probably wouldn't get up there anyway. And, hey, why not get together for dinner or something next week if they were in town—she was pretty sure she'd be in town herself but, of course, you never knew—and they could work out the details or whatever. Hey, swell idea, Megan told her. When she hung up the phone, her heart was pounding.

"I wrote to Martin," Doc Warren said.

It was Wednesday, lunchtime, and he and Chard sat at a table in The Feedbag, finishing their meals. In the background, the restaurant's music system was playing an Andy Williams record. The two men ate lunch together several times a week, and the doctor was a frequent dinner guest at the Chard house. It's no good for a man to be living alone, Martha always said, they never take care of themselves properly. And on the days when the two men lunched together, she always asked John what the doctor had eaten.

On the days when they planned lunch and then couldn't make it, it was usually the sheriff's work that kept them from it. Doc Warren had office hours from nine to twelve-thirty and from two to five, although residents of the Kill knew they could usually count on finding him in the office between eight in the morning and seven or eight in the evening. And if he wasn't there, somebody always knew where he was. But about lunch he was absolutely firm. He left the office at twelve-thirty, and he returned at two o'clock and that was that. "If they're strong enough to make it to the office," he would say, "they're strong enough to sit up and wait." But at two o'clock, as regular as religion, he was back.

That was why he had saved his comment about Martin Ferrand for the end of the meal. The clock over the restaurant's door said a quarter to two, and Chard would know that left a maximum of ten minutes for them to talk.

The sheriff slowly pushed away the plates from in front on him, as if clearing the decks for action. Then he nodded slowly and said, "I suppose it's time."

They looked at each other for a few seconds, until

Doc Warren said, "John, I have to be getting back to the office."

Chard made a point of glancing over at the clock. A brief smile flickered faintly across his face, then as quickly disappeared.

"I knew we'd have to talk about it sooner or later," he said. Suddenly, and it showed in his face, he was both very tired and very excited. "Come to dinner tonight," he said. "After dinner, I have something to show you. Don't say anything to Martha. And watch your speed coming up the hill in that Mustang or I'll slap you with a summons. And be careful turning into the driveway. Last time you almost got the marigolds."

But neither of them smiled.

That week Jacob Helbig had Wednesday off from Agway.

He owned a rattly flatbed pickup truck and occasionally rented out it and himself to local people who needed some hauling done. Today he was carrying a load of fencing slats from a dealer in Cooperstown to another in the Kill. He was on his way back now, the pickup rattling wearily through Main Street in Oneonta and through the little hamlets that poked up along Route 7. He had not loaded the slats very solidly in the truck, and the bundles were jouncing around, adding to the noise. He debated briefly whether he should stop and get them settled back there. If they were damaged, that son-of-a-bitch would probably argue with him about the money. Then he thought, Ah, fuck it, and did not stop. Goddamn it, a man had to work on his day off too just to make ends meet.

The truck rolled through Schenevus and Worcester and East Worcester and then left at the turnoff for the last few miles north to the Kill. A minute later, the road curved sharply right, and as Helbig swung the heavy wheel, he was looking at a broad field in front of him on the other side of the road. And that was when he saw the figure way out there in the distance, almost back among the trees, and he tromped down on the brake pedal and the pickup shuddered violently and slid to a lurching, bucking halt in the middle of the road just past the turn.

He was out of it in a second, ignoring the screaming pain in his feet and toes, and limping halfway across the road, bellowing, "Hey! Hey!" and flailing one arm above his head. A car that had been following him up the road screeched to a halt six inches from the rear of the truck. A van coming down the hill had to swerve onto the gravel shoulder to avoid running him down.

"Hey, what are you doing, stopping like that?" somebody shouted.

"What's going on?" someone else yelled. "Somebody get hurt?"

Helbig stood panting in the road, sweat running out of his hair and down his temples, hands on his thighs as he leaned forward and squinted out across the field. Eyes narrowed, he stared through the shimmer of heat, lifting and lowering his head like an animal, trying to make certain of what he had seen.

"Get that heap out of the road!" someone yelled.

Goddamn it to fuckin hell, Helbig thought excitedly, the breath rasping loud in his throat, his barrel chest heaving, all this goddamn time and there she is right over there. He took a limping step toward the field and then, in the distance, over near the trees, the cow that he'd thought was his missing daughter Carla climbed slowly to its feet and stood up.

"Come downstairs with me," Chard said, and he and Doc Warren stood up from the table.

"What are you two up to?" Martha asked.

"Down to, you mean," the doctor said.

"Don't be smart with me, Doc," she said. "I know your tricks."

"Ah, Martha, you promised you'd never tell," he said, and they laughed, and he followed Chard down the stairs.

Chard pulled a dusty milk crate, one of the good heavy wooden ones, from under the steps and carried it into the den. He made Doc Warren sit on the chair and settled himself on the crate with his back to the wall. They looked at each other.

"I'm an old man," the doctor said. "Go easy on me, officer."

"Why do you think Martin left?" Chard asked and let the question hang in the air a minute before continuing. "His family built that house, back before the Civil War, I think. At any rate, a long time ago. His own family. And the farm was good. He wasn't a wealthy man but I never heard him complain, not about any money problems serious enough to make him sell out. And it's not just that. And you know it's not. He went so sudden. Just all of a sudden up and went and sold the place and stayed away from everybody and would hardly talk even to you and me. And, Doc, it's been killing me not to know why."

Doc Warren was staring at the television set and the videocassette recorder.

The basement was a little damp and it made Chard's fingers ache slightly, just enough to notice. He rubbed them for a minute, not saying anything. Doc Warren would wait for him. He could hear Martha's footsteps overhead as she went out to the kitchen to wash the coffee cups and dessert plates.

"Very little happens in the Kill that I don't know about," he said abruptly, and more harshly than he meant. "Very little. I don't say that with wrongful pride, and I think you know that, Doc, but I do mean it. Very little. But in the last three months I can think of three things. One," he said and held out the thumb of his right hand.

Doc Warren was looking at him now.

"Martin Ferrand, who has lived all his life on that farm up this very road suddenly sells it and won't tell his closest friends why. Not his closest, and he was close like you and me are close. Made excuses to walk away when you'd meet him, I remember that so clear. No reason, no explanation, nothing, and that's the worst part of it." He stopped and looked at the floor. Then he held up another finger and said, "Two."

"Would you fellows like some more coffee?" Martha called from the top of the stairs. "There's enough left here. I could bring you some down."

"No, thanks," Doc Warren called back. "It would only keep me up all night."

"Two," Chard said again, his voice lower, thumb and forefinger still extended. "Carla Helbig. Doc, we've had kids do all sorts of things here, and all sorts of things have happened to them. Some of them we've brought back okay, and some of them you've put back together again yourself, and the rest you've written the certificates for. But we've never had one just disappear like that. Never." His breath was coming short now and he paused again.

"We searched," Doc said.

"Searched," Chard said. "We searched every square

inch of the Rise and every hill around it, and then we searched some more and we still didn't find her.''

"The rain, remember."

"I remember," Chard said bitterly.

"The boys could have missed her."

"All right, say we missed her; that still doesn't tell us what happened to her."

"No," Doc said. "No, it doesn't."

"Three," Chard said. He held out the next finger and the remaining two came with it, stiff, as if the three of them were splinted together. "That girl, the one who was killed. What happened to her? All the tests and the questions and roadblocks and lab reports, and all we know is that she's dead. Nothing else."

"You think they fit together," Doc said.

"Somehow," Chard answered, and they sat together in silence for a while. Then, "Somehow," Chard said again.

Doc Warren waved a hand at the TV equipment. "You have that kid's television tape, and you've been looking at it on this," he said.

"Yes."

The doctor watched his friend for a minute and then said quietly, "Well, let's see."

Chard got the cassette out of the desk drawer and snapped it into place, ready to begin.

"Maybe the reason you never told me about it is something like the reason Martin wouldn't talk to us," Doc said.

Chard stared at him a long time and felt a chilly sweat break out on the back of his neck. Then finally he turned his face away and pushed the button and started the tape.

"Watch," he said. "Just watch."

On Thursday morning, Martin Ferrand sat on the
porch of his house on Trowbridge Street in Cambridge
and read Doc Warren's letter. He had to concentrate
to make his hands steady enough to hold it still.

"Dear friend," it began, "I barely know how to
begin this letter. I suppose in a way you will say
that I have no right to be writing it at all, that this
is, when you come down to it, none of my business. And you are right. But, Martin, you know
that every opinion has a contrary and every expert
someone to say him nay. Things have happened
here in the Kill since you left that you don't know
about, and those things make me think that you
might be able to help us in understanding them. I
hope and trust that you will.

"When I say us, of course, I mean John and
myself. John does not know I am writing you this
letter, but I know that he feels as I do. Friendship
compels us to leave you to go your own way and
think no less of you for it and assume that you
have your reasons. But we have, all three of us,
been friends for these many years, and we are hoping that even now you still feel the closeness of
those years.

"Martin, please see that this letter, which in so
many ways I do not enjoy writing, is in place of
the telephone call that would be so much quicker.
There is no emergency here as far as we know, it is
not that sort of thing, but there is a puzzle. I hope
that you will think about this letter and that you
will be in touch with either of us. Then at the least
we will not have lost contact completely.

"My love to Edith and to you.

"Please think about this, Martin."

Ferrand read the letter three times, trying to hear the words in Doc's voice, a voice that had once been so familiar and that now, after a period of time that was still short enough to measure in weeks, was not as easy to recall as he expected it would be.

He was sixty-one years old and suddenly felt a hundred. As the thought came into his mind, it spurred others into vivid but unwilling action, thoughts of the years in the house, a house that bore his own family's name, as if it lived there too on the land, proud of its century and more of existence. Fingers awkward and fumbling, he folded the letter in thirds and pushed it into the pocket of his shirt and buttoned the flap over it. Then he stepped down off the porch and went out to walk these streets where he did not belong.

He walked the streets, heading away from Harvard Square because he wasn't comfortable with all the people there, especially the younger people (this was a young people's place), and he thought about that day in the woods on the Rise, and of that day in the field, and he kept on walking. He thought of Doc Warren and of John Chard, and he wondered what they had thought when he'd avoided them and evaded their gentle and puzzled questions. He wondered about the farm and the house and the Kill itself. And he thought about Edith forever sitting up in that sewing room making drapes they didn't need. He remembered the note that had come for her from Martha Chard and how Edith had tried to hide it from him because he had asked her not to write in the first place.

What possessed me? he demanded of himself. Why didn't I act differently? What in the name of God possessed me?

And then there was the other thought that came so

often to his mind, especially at night.

They'll know one day why I ran, and then it'll be all
the worse. I'll have to tell them I knew, or thought I
knew, all along and they'll ask why I let it happen, why I
couldn't have told them before and prevented whatever
will happen today or tomorrow or the day after that.
What is starting to happen now, he thought, already, or
else Doc would not have written as he did. "Things have
happened here since you left." What? *What?*

And somewhere in his walk he had turned a couple of
corners and was heading back to Trowbridge Street.
Hardly noting his steps, he reached the house, and Edith
was still upstairs in the sewing room. He rummaged
quickly in the breakfront in the dining room and found
a pad and took it out to the porch. He could sit there,
over at the side away from the door, but with the door
open, so that if Edith came downstairs looking for him
he would hear her and he could drop the pad off the end
of the porch and get it back when she was gone. And, oh
sweet Jesus, look at all the sneaking around and the
secrets. He had to go back inside to look for a pencil.
He found one in the kitchen and hurried back to the
porch to get started before he lost his nerve.

"Dear Doc," he wrote.

But that was all.

"Well, we're in touch with the world again," Jack
said on Thursday afternoon. "Hooray. I think."

"You can't fool me," Megan said. "You've been
champing at the bit for days."

The telephone had been connected that morning, and
they both had long lists of people to call. Megan was
going to hit up every friend she had in the book and
magazine fields to see if she could get an illustration

assignment. Jack had to call his own contacts. There were a few writers he knew who didn't have agents and might be persuaded to come along with him. And he knew a few editors here and there who occasionally got swamped and relied on freelance editors to handle the overload. They had sat and sprawled on the porch, making the lists and notes and reminding each other of people they could try. The lists looked promising.

The plan was this. They were enjoying staying here at the house and would stay until Sunday. It was like camping out, living in the house with no furniture except the blankets and cushions and a few kitchen utensils. It was fun. And meanwhile they were already working, or would be, as soon as they began making their calls.

Then next week, back in the city, they could really go at it, calling people they missed now, seeing others. They didn't know yet how long they would stay at the apartment—"our city residence," Megan was already calling it and smiling every time she said it—but they would stay as long as necessary to turn up some chance for work. And of course they would have to see Suzi.

There were so many things to think about. A car, for example, they would have to have a car. They couldn't go on catching rides with Martha and Nancy Chard if they were going to be here all summer. Apart from not wanting to impose like that, they needed the freedom to come and go as they pleased. And they wanted to explore. The minute things began to feel solid under their feet, they would buy an old used car and make it do for a while. No more renting cars the way they used to, not on their budget now.

And furniture, at least basic necessities, like a bed and a table and something to sit on. Martha had told them about the yard sales and auctions they could try, and the sorts of things they could find at them, and the sorts of prices they could expect to pay. "Macy's will never look the same," Megan told her. She could hardly wait to start.

"You go ahead and use the phone first," Jack said. "I think I'll just sit out on the porch a while longer and whittle or something."

"Whittle me a desk, will ya?" Megan called back to him.

Three hours later, Megan had six appointments for the following week, three of which looked promising. Jack had talked to two of the authors he had in mind and they both sounded interested in having him represent them. They would get together and talk while he was in the city. He had also found one editor friend who thought he could give Jack something next week, and two who said they'd keep him in mind.

Not a bad start, they agreed.

"Now what's for dinner?" Jack asked.

"Rice."

"That's good for the Chinaman in my soul. What else?"

"That's it. Rice. We both forgot to shop."

They went to the kitchen and searched through the cabinets to see what could be added to the rice. Just as they were deciding that dry pancake mix (they were almost out of milk) was not the answer, the telephone rang. They both jumped at the sound.

It was Martha Chard and she was pleased to know that she was the first to call. She wanted them to come for dinner.

"The first call on your new phone should be an invitation," she said. Then she said, more slowly, "I guess you don't know, of course, but the number is still the same as when Martin and Edith lived there. Funny to be calling that number and getting somebody else. It just feels strange. But I'm glad it's the two of you and we're glad to have you for neighbors. Now why don't you come on down around six-thirty? John will be home about seven and we'll be eating then. And tomorrow you can come grocery shopping with me. You kids must be pretty near out of supplies by now."

When Megan hung up the phone, there was a lump in her throat. They stood in the kitchen and she told Jack what Martha had said.

Then she said, "Oh, Jack, I really want to stay here. I want to fix things so we can stay here and live here. I really do."

He put his hands on her waist, and she came close to him and joined hers behind his neck. "Are you absolutely sure about that?" he asked. "This is no joking around. It'll be the second biggest decision we've had to make."

"I am," she said. "I really am. Except for the business part of it, I'm not even looking forward to going home in a couple of days. I just wish we were settled and could just stay here now. And we have enough money to cover us for a while. And if we can make some, we'll have more, which would mean it's working out, which would mean—"

"We could give up the apartment in the city and become pioneers in the country."

"Well, something like that. And it's only about four hours to the city. We could still get there when we needed to."

"As soon as we buy a car."

"We'll get a clunker."

"As soon as we find a permanent place to live up here. We can't count on staying in this house past Labor Day."

"We haven't worked it out with Suzi yet," Megan reminded him. She was talking faster than normal now. "Maybe we can get a lease from her for a year. Or two years. She doesn't want anything to do with this place, Jack, I know it. It's just a toy for her. We can bring up just what we need to get by so we don't have to spend too much money, then later on, when it's absolutely definite, we'll already have our furniture from the apartment."

"There's something else," Jack said.

"What?"

"There's the matter of what happened when we were here. Candy."

"I've thought about that. And it has nothing to do with us, not in any practical way. I hate to talk this way about . . . well, about somebody's death, but the truth is, it could happen anywhere. There was a break-in in our own building six months ago, Jack. And two others on the block last March. No, it doesn't frighten me."

"Okay, but you know something, if we were actually going to move into this house for keeps, I'd be curious to know why this Ferrand sold out the old homestead so quickly. I get the feeling there's something odd about that."

"I'm sure the Chards could tell us, if you really think it matters."

"I'm not too sure about that. I asked them at dinner that night, last Saturday, and I got the impression that both John and the doctor evaded the question. On the other hand, it's all academic at the moment, and you know how I hate anything academic. There's just one—''

"Jack, wait a minute. I know you want to be sure I really want this. And I do. But do *you* really want it? Do you?''

"I do," he said. "For one thing, circumstances have conspired, as they say, to bring us to this place at this time. It looks right, it feels right, and we both like it. And it's important to you, which makes it important to me, for another thing. And besides, I guess I've reached the age of do or die. Take the big risk now or forever hold your peace. And all that. Yes, I really want it.''

Megan hugged him.

"But there's still one other thing," Jack said. "Do you really want Suzi Steiger for a landlady?''

Megan laughed. "I hadn't thought of that.''

"And, besides," he said more seriously, "you know what Suzi's like. She could sell this place right out from under us, remember.''

Megan shrugged. "You'll just have to talk her out of it, that's all. At least, until we're ready to buy it ourselves.''

"What do you mean, *you'll* have to talk her out of it?''

"Well, you're the agent around here.''

"Oh yeah," Jack said. "I forgot. You'll have to keep reminding me. Well, then, it's done, settled, and agreed. Zap! You're a pioneer!''

"It takes one to know one!" Megan said, and then they were laughing and hugging each other and making terrible jokes about pioneers.

On Saturday evening, Jack and Megan had the

Chards, their daughter Nancy and a friend of hers from school, and Doc Warren to the house for dinner. They had found three barbecue grills and two picnic tables, complete with benches, stored in the barn and dragged them all out and scrubbed them clean. When they'd gone shopping with Martha the day before, they'd bought a large supply of charcoal and hamburger and all the fixings. And they were as excited as teenagers giving their first party when the guests arrived at the door.

A little while later, when everyone was seated at the tables in the yard just in front of the porch, Doc saw Jack kneeling by the grills and reading the instructions on the charcoal bag.

"Looks like we're in danger," he announced. "I am reminded of the time I saw a surgeon with a scalpel in one hand and an instruction book in the other. Time for the pros to take over," he said with mock weariness and went to help Jack.

The hamburgers turned out fine.

Later still, when the light was fading rapidly from the sky, Jack switched on the porch lights. With the yellow lamps illuminating the yard, and the evening air sweet and cool, they all sat outside talking quietly and easily. Jack and Megan told their guests they'd be staying for the summer, and the others showed genuine pleasure at the news.

John assured them that he knew an honest used-car dealer. Martha and Nancy and her friend wanted to see Megan's paintings and drawings as soon as she brought them up from the city. Doc Warren said he'd like to read Jack's book as soon as he was finished with it. They sat talking so long that Jack had to cook another round of hamburgers, and it was a little after midnight, late for them, when the Chards finally said they should be going.

No one had mentioned the Ferrands. Jack and Megan thought that plain old hamburgers had never tasted so good in all their lives.

Late that same Saturday evening, Jacob Helbig went out to drink.

He always did his outside drinking at a joint called Eddie's Bar down on Route 7. He hated the bars in town, too goddamn fancy and high-toned, puttin on airs, every last friggin one of them. They were no goddamn good. Eddie's clientele consisted mostly of truck drivers and it smelled and looked like a bar, not all fuckin fancied up like them others. Eddie kept the beer flowin and you could trust the change he gave you as long as you never took your eyes off your money. Work your ass off all week long, ya gotta get out, take your mind off your fuckin troubles, right? Not that he ever talked to anybody. Fuck em, he figured, goddamn truck drivers, pullin down those big bucks, anybody ever offer to buy you a beer? Never. So fuck em, to hell with em. He'd be goddamned if he'd talk to em. They could rot in hell before he'd talk to em. He didn't need nobody to talk to. Man works hard all week, he don't need that shit, right? But he liked Eddie's sometimes on a Saturday night. Man had to get outta the house sometimes, right? He could go to Eddie's and Eddie kept the stuff comin and a man could sit and think, right?

He sat on a barstool by himself at the end of the bar, grumbling half out loud about the fiery pain in his feet, drinking beer after beer because Eddie kept it coming, and thought about his daughter Carla.

Earlier in the evening, on his way down the road from

the Kill to Route 7 and Eddie's, he had thought he saw her ducking back among the bushes as his wavering headlights swept over them on a turn.

He sat there drinking beer at the bar all night, except for when he had to lurch off to the jake to take a piss, until Eddie put him out at closing time.

He stumbled his way across the gravel parking area to the pickup truck. His feet were unreliable on the pedals and his hand unreliable on the stick and the truck was old and he had some trouble getting it in gear. He cursed and slammed the dashboard with the heel of his hand, but then the thing caught at last and he was moving. Leaning forward toward the cloudy windshield, gripping the wheel with both hands, he aimed the truck out at the road and held it in more or less a straight line.

The air was cool and crisp, and by the time he reached the turnoff for the Kill, he was as clear in his mind as ever.

The truck rattled its way up the hill and eventually he was approaching the town, passing Depot Street and the old railroad station and Railroad Street and then coming up the east side of the square. He hauled the wheel over and swung the truck into School Street, past Whitmore's Appliances on the left and, farther along, the church on his right and a little after that over the bridge that spanned the Kill itself that gave the town its name.

Just after the truck jolted across the bridge, as he was passing a dark clump of trees that swept up a short hill on his left, he thought he saw Carla again.

Still later that same Saturday night, a shuffling, grating sound moved down the slope of Deacons Rise, keeping to patches of rock and gravel and shale, where its passing left no mark. The thing hunted at night and ate in the dark. It needed no rest. For the hours of light it had found a place that was safe, a place from which it could watch the hills. But regularly now it ventured out to explore, to learn more about its land, about the slopes of the rise, seeking the patterns that were new, strange, and yet familiar from some distant time before.

It had not yet returned to the open place with the strange smells, where the yellow-eyed monster had roared in the night and the red-eyed monster had threatened and retreated. It had not gone back there yet. It would, later, another time. But not yet. There were still other areas, other directions, to explore. Other places to claim as its own.

It came down the hill, and gradually the ground leveled off. Its heavy, slow steps crushed dead leaves into the forest floor. Ahead of it, the trees ended and there was open space. The thing was wary of open space. It stayed back among the sparse trees, in the darkness of the night's shadows beneath the moon, and it watched.

The big white thing with the straight lines and the sharp angles had many eyes, dark and shiny, two rows of them, one above the other, and yet the thing was not alive. The eyes stared blank and dead at the night and at the woods and at the hill. And the thing's own cold eyes stared back.

Suddenly something happened and the thing that watched in the woods started. Two of the eyes in the upper row had snapped into fiery brilliant life, glaring out at the world, casting beams out and down to the world outside. And within the eyes, first in one and then in the other, something moved. A figure. A figure moved across one of the eyes and then went out of sight, out of existence, perhaps, and then moved across the other eye and then was gone again. And a moment later it reappeared and moved back the other way, one eye, the other eye, and was gone. And a moment after that, the fire disappeared from the eyes and they were as dark, darker, than before.

The thing stood long and silent in the woods, the only sound that of its rasping breath. It stared up at the place where the figure had moved, and it watched and waited. It watched a long time.

The thing stood as still as the night-shrouded trees around it. Its icy, unblinking stare never wavered. After a long while, it turned its body toward the nearest of the trees. Still it stared at the place where the figure had moved. The thing shuddered and a violent stream of urine burst from it, splattered against the rough bark of the tree and seeped, hissing, into the ground. It stopped after a moment, and the thing moved heavily, crushing twigs and fallen branches beneath its stony feet, to another tree. It stood again, eyes still fixed where it was watching, and the urine exploded from it, bestial and angry, soaking the tree and the soil at its base. The urine steamed in the air, acrid and animal-hot. The thing moved again and sprayed another tree. Then it stood silent while its urine dripped from rough bark and pattered on tiny leaves below.

This land, this hill, marked now by its scent, was its own, claimed by itself and open to no other.

Finally, the thing moved away, up the hill, back to its place of safety at the top. Wordless, it wondered what it had seen, and snarled at the night because it did not know. What threat or promise waited down there beyond the end of the trees where the ground grew flat? What dared to invade this territory? It would have to go

back to that place to watch again in the night. And when
it learned what was there, it would kill it.

Jack came back with the tissues, handed the box to
Megan, and snapped off the light.

When she was finished with the tissues, she put the
box on the floor beside the tangle of blankets and
cushions that was serving as a bed. Then she got up and,
naked, walked on her knees to the nearer window of the
bedroom. She folded her arms on the ledge and rested
her chin on them. Jack watched her, admiring the little-
girl line of her body.

"Come here," she said softly. "Look."

She made room for him and Jack joined her at the
window, both of them naked, feeling the cool air on
their bodies.

"Look," Megan said again, softer than before.

They knelt there, nighttime children, looking out at
the moonlit hill.

PART THREE

9

"Not bad for a clunker," Jack said as he maneuvered the old blue Valiant down the turns and slopes of Deacons Road toward Hill Street and the town. He patted the car seat beside him, then for good measure patted Megan's leg.

Megan grinned and said, "Well, it'll do till we can buy the Rolls." Then she patted the car seat too.

The car was the fruit of another favor they owed John Chard. A month before, Chard had gone with them to Honest Bob Booth's, Home of Good Used Cars, down on Railroad Street. Chard had introduced them to the dealer, and they had all greeted each other and chatted pleasantly about the weather for a while. Chard told Honest Bob that they had just moved into the Ferrand place and they were getting settled and needed a good honest car, nothing fancy, to get around with. Maybe Bob could help them out. Bob said heartily that he'd be glad to. Chard took no further part in the proceedings but confined himself to, as Megan called it later, "lending his presence." Apparently his presence was enough because they came away with "a good honest car, nothing fancy," at what certainly seemed a good honest price.

"Ain't good ol' Honest Bob honest any more?" Jack asked afterward.

"He has spells of it still," Chard said drily, but he allowed himself a small smile.

Jack slowed the car at the point where Deacons Road became Hill Street. He and Megan were taking the day off, rewarding themselves for the hard work they'd done in the last month. Megan had invested long hours in her drawing, doing enough pictures to make up a fairly impressive portfolio. She had also put Honest Bob Booth's good honest car to the test by driving it down to the city five times in two weeks for appointments with art directors. It was paying off. On the back seat of the car was a bulky package of drawings on its urgent way to the post office. It was the first job she had completed: a set of cartoon illustrations for a series of young children's activity books. Jack's hustling had paid off too. He now had several clients and a number of inquiries from aspiring and beginning writers seeking an agent. He was working closely with two of the clients on new novels, and one of the books promised to have great commercial appeal. Bob Brockden assured him that he was working like a house afire on his current book. And Jack had actually succeeded in writing two new chapters of his own once-abandoned novel. He and Megan were feeling pretty good these days.

The Ferrand house—they thought of it that way themselves—was serving their needs eminently well. What they weren't accustomed to, however, was the size of the house and the endless list of odds and ends they always seemed to need for it. Hence the shopping list Megan pulled out of her shoulder bag now as Jack drove around the square and headed for the parking lot on School Street.

As they walked back from the lot toward the square and The Feedbag, where they were meeting Nancy Chard for lunch, Jack asked, "What time will you be back from Oneonta?"

"Oh, around five-thirty or six, I guess, after the stores close." She smiled. "Nancy thinks I'm some sort of expert on fashion."

The Chards' daughter had decided, now that she was getting ready to enter her last year of college, that she should stop dressing like a teenager and start looking like a young woman. Her mother had confided to Megan that she thought it was her influence. Megan had laughed but was all the more pleased when Nancy asked her to drive to Oneonta with her and help her pick out some clothes for the fall. Megan had happily agreed.

"You're not having dinner there?"

"I hadn't thought about it, but it sounds like a good idea. I think Nancy would probably enjoy it. Would you mind?"

"Not at all," Jack said. "I'll get the things on that list this afternoon, and I'm going to look for a pair of hiking boots while I'm at it. That place on the other side of the square looks like it should have every hiking boot ever made."

"I'll look for some myself in Oneonta. Promise you'll eat something decent for dinner?"

"I promise. In fact, I was thinking of asking Doc Warren if he wanted to eat out."

"That's a nice idea. Give him my love."

And then they were greeting Nancy in front of The Feedbag.

An hour later, Jack was waving goodbye to them as

they drove off toward Route 7 in Nancy's car. His first
stop was the post office to drop off Megan's package.
The day's mail had brought two more inquiries from
writers and an envelope containing another hundred
pages of a novel by one of his clients. Jack slapped the
envelope against his leg as he jumped down the post
office steps into the bright August sunshine.

He spent the next two hours or so visiting various
stores in town, assembling the items on Megan's shopping list: curtain rods, a window screen, yet another
inexpensive lamp, a supply of file folders for himself and stiff photo mailers for Megan's artwork,
typewriter ribbons, bug spray, a bulletin board for the
kitchen, a fresh supply of charcoal for the grill, and
more. When he had all he could carry, he hauled the
bags and packages back to the parking lot and put them
in the car, then strolled back to the square, feeling even
better than he had before.

At Kite's Kampground, on the same side of the
square as the movie theatre, Norman Kite patiently
helped him try on a variety of hiking boots, carefully
explaining the virtues of each. After some indecision,
Jack finally decided against the expensive Pivattas that
he really liked best, and settled contentedly for the
thirty-dollar pair of Georgia Giants. Then, with the
package under his arm, and feeling lazy in the afternoon, he walked up School Street to Doc Warren's
office.

There were three people in the waiting room, all of
whom Jack knew at least by sight. He greeted them all
and said he only needed to talk with the doctor for a
second. No one objected. When Doc Warren appeared,
they spoke briefly and the doctor readily agreed to meet

him in the Centennial Hotel's Lounge in a couple of
hours.

Jack killed the rest of the afternoon browsing in the
town's one bookstore, where he finally bought half a
dozen new paperbacks. Then he happily sat flipping
through them and nursing a beer in the Lounge until the
doctor arrived.

"How are things?" the older man said.

"Things," Jack said with a sudden and easy grin,
"are fine. Just fine."

The doctor suggested they eat at the Bull's Head Inn
in Cobleskill, and insisted on driving his own car, the
red Mustang. They chatted easily, like old friends, on
the drive, but Jack instantly saw why John Chard was
always warning Doc about speeding.

"You'll put the sheriff in an awkward position if he
catches you," Jack said.

The doctor smiled without taking his eyes from the
road. "I'll just put him in an awkward position next
time he comes by for a checkup." He gunned the car up
the next long incline.

Jack admired the small Bull's Head Inn, standing
where it stood now since 1802, the minute he saw it. He
admired even more the meal he was served.

"You know," he said with satisfaction, "I almost
think this is even better than the Dining Room."

"Where's your town loyalty, son?" Doc Warren said
sternly.

When Jack mentioned the shopping he had done
during the day and the hiking boots he had bought, he
thought the doctor looked a little doubtful about him
and Megan exploring the hills on their own.

"The hills around here can be treacherous," he said. "You keep your eyes open and mind you know where you're going. And mind you know the way back."

"Don't worry about us," Jack told him. "We're out of practice, but we've both been hiking before. We'll be okay."

The waitress asked if they had decided on dessert; they both ordered the peach cobbler.

It was a little after nine o'clock when the doctor dropped him off at the parking lot on School Street. Back in the Valiant, with the heap of packages beside him, Jack turned right into the square in front of the Centennial Hotel, then right again onto Hill Street. As he headed up toward Deacons Road and home, he had forgotten the doctor's mild warning about the hills. He was enjoying the familiar crunch of gravel and shale beneath the tires and thinking instead of how good he had felt when Doc reminded him about "town loyalty." As if he truly belonged.

"I'll show you mine if you'll show me yours," Megan said when he got home.

They spent a happy half hour showing each other what they had bought.

"And these," Megan said, pulling out a pair of hiking boots. They were exactly the same boots Jack had bought at Kite's Kampground.

When they had finished congratulating each other on their good taste, Megan suddenly frowned.

"How much did you pay for yours?" she asked.

"Twenty-nine ninety-five," Jack answered.

"Oh, crap."

"What did you pay?"

"Thirty-one ninety-five."

Jack laughed. "That's what you get for shopping in the big city."

"Well," Megan said, "we better get our money's worth out of them. Especially mine. What do you say we go up Deacons Rise tomorrow?"

"You're on," Jack said. "Let's do it."

They took it easy climbing the hill. Twice they crossed an overgrown road, rutted and almost obscured, that twisted and turned up the slope. It tempted them briefly, but they decided to do it the hard way. They had both worked up a good sweat by the time they emerged from the woods onto the bare rock shelf at the top.

The old firetower at the peak of Deacons Rise seemed to soar against the blue of the sky. Its white paint was long faded and peeled, its wood drying from the action of air and sun. It would not be many years before it suffered the same fate as an old abandoned barn, drying out and turning gray, sagging along stress lines, leaning, and finally collapsing into dust and splintered boards, returning to the earth. The base was wide and solidly planted, the legs embedded in concrete-filled holes drilled into solid rock. The tower's latticed body tapered up to the top, where a small shed was surrounded on four sides by a narrow platform with a railing. The stairs wound their way around the outside.

"Looks pretty rickety," Jack said.

"Sure does. You couldn't get me up there on a bet," Megan said.

They stared up at the tower.

"You know," Megan said, "it doesn't seem to me the world's greatest idea to build a firetower out of wood."

"It was probably the most economical thing to do at the time it was built. Stone or steel would be expensive, and difficult to haul up here, especially years ago. And this thing has been here a long time. Besides, the idea is to spot fires at a distance, not underfoot.''

"Oh," Megan said. "I must have missed that lesson when I was a Brownie." She looked down from the tower. "Jack?"

He was setting the small backpack on the ground and pulling at the zipper.

"I guess the deputies and the State Police checked up here after . . . you know."

"I guess," Jack said. He glanced up again at the tower, then looked back at Megan. "I'm sure they did. Although, really, the thing doesn't look like it would hold a person's weight, at least not all the way to the top. If it looked solid enough, I'd give it a try. I'll bet there's a great view from up there. Besides, I've already climbed to the top of a sort-of mountain today, and I have no desire, believe me, to climb any higher."

"I wonder if that little girl wandered this way. The one we heard about that just disappeared in the hills. I think it was in April."

"Megan," Jack said gently.

"Okay, okay," she said. "I was just wondering, that's all."

"Well, here's something better to wonder about." He pulled some foil-wrapped sandwiches from the pack. "Start wondering how many of these you can eat."

"How many you got?" she said.

They settled on the rough bottom steps of the tower, not saying much, enjoying the air, enjoying the food, enjoying being together. While Jack was finishing the last of the sandwiches, Megan, two steps above him, leaned back on her elbows.

"When I was a kid," she said, "my aunt and uncle

and cousins lived in Toms River, New Jersey, down near Barnegat Bay. They'd been renting a house someplace else, I think, but then they had this little house built in Toms River. There weren't many houses in that section yet and I remember there were a lot of woods around with just roads, streets, cut through them. It's all built up now but then it was all sort of woodsy. Their lot had trees all around on three sides. Cranmoor Manor, that's what the section was called. I always thought it had this really classy sound to it. They lived on Maple Street. All the streets around there had the names of trees.''

Jack rolled the last piece of foil into a ball, gathered up the other papers, and stuffed all the garbage into the pack. He didn't say a word, just waited for Megan to continue.

''My parents and I used to go there for a couple of weeks every summer. I loved it. I really did. Even though I wasn't always comfortable. My cousins always ran around barefoot, for example. I could never get the hang of it. The pavement of the road was always so hot, I couldn't understand how they could do it. I'd be hopping from one foot to the other, feeling like my feet were on fire, and they weren't even noticing it. It used to drive me crazy because I couldn't do it the way they did. And another thing. I remember, sometimes in the woods they'd find a dead animal and they'd get up real close to look at it. I never could. I guess it just reminded me of seeing a dead cat in the gutter or something else disgusting. They were always so matter-of-fact about it, which I guess is a better attitude. But the thing is, they always seemed to *understand* the woods and the country better than I did, better than I ever could. As if there were things about it that only they could know properly because they'd grown up so close to it. And that wasn't even the *real* country, like this.

"Oh, and there was the lagoon. I guess it was just an inlet or something from Barnegat Bay, but it was always called the lagoon. We used to go there to pick blueberries. And we'd go crabbing there, too. That is, my cousins went crabbing and I watched them. They'd dig around in the wet sand and these little crabs would come scooting out. My cousins would pick them up and look at them. They chased after me with them one day and I thought I'd wet myself, I was so scared.

"Then one summer, all of a sudden, there were all these other houses being built all around their house. The woods were still pretty thick because a lot of the trees were left, but you didn't see so many rabbits any more. We used to go and watch the trees being cut and we'd collect the chips, the wood chips. A lot of the trees were cedar, so the chips smelled nice, and we used to make sachets for my grandmother. And one time, when the workmen were digging out a hole for a basement and cutting through a lot of roots, they gave us some and told us we could suck them and they'd taste just like root beer. And they did. They tasted just like root beer.

"There was so much I didn't know about the country that my cousins seemed to be born knowing. They could walk in the woods, for example, and see things I wouldn't notice in a million years. It was just second nature to them, a part of themselves. A secret process, in a way, that I could see but that I couldn't really share. I really loved visiting down there, and I always wished it could be mine as much as it was theirs. I always sort of wished I could live there."

She was silent for a long time. After a while, Jack reached up and put his hand on her leg. She stretched her arm and took hold of his fingers.

"Oh, Jack," she said, "I'm so glad we made this move. I love it here. Everything was just right for it, the time, the circumstances, you, me, everything. I know it sounds corny, but I stand on our porch sometimes and I just feel like a princess in a castle, I really do."

It was patient. It had infinite patience because it knew it was safe.

It stood on the platform of the firetower and watched them move slowly away among the trees. It had attacked at other times, when it was still strange here, uncertain of its territory, uncertain of itself. But now it was secure and it could wait. They were not searching for it, although they had stared at it, unseeing, when they first looked up. It had stood there on the platform, silent, patient, looking down at them, knowing it was safe.

It moved a short distance along the platform and the tower swayed slightly beneath it. The thing took no notice.

There had been a cave and a tree and a hollow in the ground where it had stayed before finding the tower. Instinct demanded a place where escape would be easy. But that was before it knew its domain, before it learned the land. Now it preferred a place where it could watch, a place from which it could survey its world.

From its new position on the platform, the thing could still see the male and the female moving carefully down the hill. They stayed in the open spaces and that made it easier to watch them. Once, in the middle of a large clearing, they stopped and looked back up at the tower. The thing did not move. Then they continued downhill and the thing watched until they were out of sight.

Long after they were gone from view, it went on staring at the spot where they had disappeared. And it felt within it a stirring it had not felt in countless eons of time.

Still staring, eyes fixed, it sniffed the air, seeking again the musky scent of the female.

10

Steve Steiger was sleeping at some girl's apartment, some dive in the village that she thought was really classy. They'd spent the whole day in bed—for a change, he'd gotten lucky, thank God—and sometime in the evening they'd fallen asleep. The next thing he remembered, he was sitting up in the bed, screaming, sweating, trembling, and staring with eyes squeezed shut at the girl named Candy and over her stood . . . nothing.

Nothing.

The girl told him he was a moron and a creep. He left willingly because he hardly knew what he was doing or where he was. Sometime later in the night, he found himself on Hudson Street, his footsteps echoing among the deserted meat packing warehouses. The only thing he remembered clearly was the nightmare.

Candy McBain was squatting on the hillside and suddenly her body was lifted into the air and slammed back down to the ground, and when her body hit the gravel it was suddenly Steve himself, face against the rocks, bleeding, and he was lifted again and this time it was the sheriff, and again, and this time it was nothing, and again he was in the air and then he was awake and screaming.

Three nights later, it happened again.

And the night after that.

And it got even worse when that sheriff started bothering him all over again.

He had called his sister one day to see if he could borrow some money, and all she did was lace into him. The sheriff had called her and wanted to know where he was and for two days she hadn't been able to find him.

So she made him call the sheriff, who asked all sorts of questions, never raised his voice, just asked the same damn things over and over, trying to trip him up. Thinks he's Matt Dillon or something, Steve mumbled when at last, sweating, he was able to get off the phone.

And as if that wasn't enough, the next day two cops come knocking on the door and *they've* got a pile of questions. Detectives. He really needed to have detectives asking him questions. With an ounce of grass in a Pop-Tarts box in the kitchen. And it was Chard who sent them, they said. There were still a few questions. When did you . . .? Where were you . . .? Why did . . .? How did . . .?

Candy died again in his sleep that night.

Now she was haunting him.

Why wouldn't she leave him alone?

He didn't want to think about her.

He didn't want to think about her!

Megan was alone when the telephone rang early on a Tuesday morning. Jack had left at six-thirty for the long drive to the city. He had a lunch date with a publisher who had wondered if he'd be interested in putting together a series for them similar to the ones he had done before. (He would be *very* interested, so long as he could work at home.) Then he had an appointment with one writer for drinks and with another for dinner. The time in between, what little there was of it, would be spent on the phone and in the bookstores to look over all the latest titles. Doing what Jack called the "New York hustle" to this degree was fun and exciting. He had looked forward to the day and the meetings and what might come of them. But he had refused Megan's suggestion that he stay overnight to avoid the drive up after dark. No way, he'd told her, when I hit the big city, I'm like a thief in the night, wham-bam-thank-you-ma'am, in and out and goodbye. Megan expected him home by midnight.

"Tom Vogel, here. Good morning."

"Oh, good morning, Mr. Vogel," Megan said. Tom Vogel was the Cobleskill real estate agent who had sold the Ferrand place to Suzi Steiger. Since Suzi was flying back and forth so often now between New York and Los Angeles, she had arranged for him to collect the monthly rent checks for the house. "What can I do for you?"

"Oh, nothing, really," Vogel said. "Nothing at all, to tell the truth. I just thought . . . . Well, I thought I'd share some news with you, is all."

Megan waited, knowing from the length of the wait that the news was bad. At last she said, "What is it, Mr. Vogel? Something about the house?" And as she said it, she suddenly didn't want to know.

"Well, yes," Vogel said slowly. "Actually, I had a letter from Miss Steiger yesterday and I thought I'd let you folks know what's happening. The fact is, she's instructed me to sell the house.''

"She's *what?*"

"I'm afraid so. Now I really shouldn't be telling you all the details of somebody else's business, but I figure I've seen a lot more of you folks than I have of her. You folks must almost be like natives up there by now, I guess.''

"Almost," Megan said, her voice level. "Tell me the details.''

"Well, I'm instructed to sell the house for whatever I can get for it. She left that part up to me. In fact, the whole thing is left up to me.''

"And?''

"I don't understand you.''

"What else? Did she say anything about us? About our agreement?''

"Nope, not a word. Just told me to sell the house for the best price I can get in the quickest time.''

Megan had to control her voice. What Suzi was doing wasn't Vogel's fault, and it had been nice of him to call right away. "But we can stay until it's sold, can't we?''

"Oh, sure. No problem with that. I just thought I'd let you know so you could be thinking what you'd do. I don't mind the commission, to tell the truth, but it does seem a shame, I'll say that much.''

"Mr. Vogel, how long do you think it might take to sell the house?''

"That's very hard to say, and I'm being honest. She'd like a quick sale—and the truth is, so would I—so we can keep the price reasonable. But even so, with money the way it is nowadays, you just can't tell. But it's a nice piece of property and a nice house, a real nice house, for a good price. I don't suppose you folks would be interested?''

For an instant, Megan almost said yes. Then she closed her eyes. "No," she said. "No, I'm afraid not."

"That's too bad," Vogel said. "That's really too bad. Well, I'll be in touch."

When she was off the phone, Megan didn't know whether to rage around the house swearing at Suzi and the lousy trick she had pulled on them, or whether to just let the tears come now and get the worst of it over with. She thought of Jack and looked at her watch. He was still on the Thruway somewhere. If he called during the day, she thought, she'd tell him everything was fine. No sense in spoiling his day and distracting him from business. When he got home would be soon enough for news like this.

The tears didn't come until she had walked down the hill and was seated at Martha Chard's kitchen table.

Stumbling down the hillside, Jacob Helbig tripped over the tangled roots of a tree. His right hand shot out against the trunk to keep himself from falling, and he only just stopped himself in time from kicking it. He swore, steadied himself, waited for the pain in his toes to subside a little, then continued forward down the hill.

He had taken a dozen lurching steps before the pain in his hand got to his brain. He held the hand out in front of him, as if it were something he carried, and looked at it. Half the nail on his right index finger had been torn away by the rough bark of the tree. As he swore, watching it, a bright red stream of blood ran down the finger onto the back of his hand. He cursed again, then stuck the finger in his mouth.

She was hidin somewhere here, he knew it. Someplace in the woods. She had to be.

Helbig hadn't bothered goin to work at Agway today.

Fuck em. That son-of-a-bitch manager could shove the cartons around himself, let him do some liftin for a change, let him see how he liked it, goddamn lazy bastard. Helbig had more important things to do.

He had to find that goddamn kid, that was clear in his mind now. He had to find the snivelin little brat and haul her ass home and beat the livin shit out of her. He'd teach her to have a smart mouth with her old man. He'd teach her to tell her old man no. Teach her a lot of things.

The afternoon sun angled between the trees where there were open spaces on the hillside. Helbig stumbled often, and the gravel kept getting into his shoes that had the fronts cut off. He swore at the gravel and the shoes and his toes and the woods and the kid, the goddamn kid. He'd fix her ass good, runnin out on her old man. Fix it good. Dark patches of sweat covered his tee-shirt in front and back and under the arms. He wiped a forearm across his face.

Finally, he had to stop. He stood there in the woods, near a road now, panting, running a hand through his hair. His hair was soaked with sweat.

He'd find her. One of these days he'd find her and drag her ass home and teach her a thing or two. He knew she was out here, hidin, but goddamn it, he'd find her. Sooner or later he'd find her.

Jack and Megan both had work to do and plenty to keep their minds occupied. But the edge had gone from their enjoyment of the Ferrand place, now that they knew they'd have to leave it. There seemed little point in doing the minor repairs they'd been planning or in painting the room Megan used for an office, which had been on their schedule for Saturday.

Megan refused to talk to Suzi, but Jack had tried to reach her a dozen times on Wednesday and Thursday, calling her at both her New York and Los Angeles offices. The New York office thought she was in Los Angeles. The Los Angeles office thought she was on vacation. He had left messages at both offices, but Suzi did not return his calls. At first he had been furious, raging that failure to return a phone call was the height of rudeness.

"Sure," he said, stalking back and forth in the living room, "she knows exactly what she's doing and she doesn't want to admit she's being so shitty, not even telling us what she was planning, so she has all her little secretaries and assistants do the dirty work for her. Nice. Really nice. Well, I may learn slow, but I learn. You never know what people are like till you do business with them."

When he finally calmed down on Thursday afternoon, he called Tom Vogel. Vogel expressed his regrets to Jack as he had to Megan on Tuesday. Jack thanked him for letting them know what was going on, and asked if the realtor knew where they could reach Suzi Steiger. He didn't.

Jack asked Vogel to keep an eye out for another place that might be suitable for them. Vogel said he'd be very glad to do that and promised to keep them posted about the house.

As soon as he got off the phone with Vogel, Jack drove down to the Kill and visited the real estate agent there, asking him to watch for a place too. There was no question in his or Megan's mind that Deacons Kill was the place they preferred.

Late Thursday afternoon, they both had to get out of

the house. They strolled hand in hand along the edge of
the woods, neither saying much, looking at the dark
shadows on the hill and occasionally pointing out some
pretty wildflowers to each other. The ground here was
rocky, with patches of gravel and shale, and the vegetation was coarse and tough. Once, they stopped and
poked in the gravel for the blue-gray stones that split
apart to reveal the fossil imprints of ancient seashells.
Megan found an especially pretty one, perfectly preserved, and started to slip it into the pocket of her jeans.
At least it would make a nice souvenir of the Ferrand
place. But then the thought of *needing* a souvenir of the
Ferrand place bothered her and she dropped the stone
on the ground. It blended in with all the others. She
tapped Jack on the shoulder and they strolled on,
farther away from the house, following the line of the
woods.

"Over there," Jack said suddenly. "Look at that."

Ahead of them, on their left, near the first trees that
started up the slope of the hill, was an unusual patch of
dirt and rocks. It was large: eight or ten feet wide and
maybe fifteen or twenty in length. The surface looked
raw, scattered with stones. One end of the area rose in a
slight mound, but the other end had sunk a little lower
than the surrounding earth. Despite a light covering of
grass and straggling weeds, the rectangular outline was
clearly visible.

"Jack, it looks like a grave," Megan said.

"I hate to say this, but you're right. It does. God,
look at the size of it."

"What do you think it is? Do you think it could just
be something to do with farming or . . .?"

Jack shook his head, still looking at the odd patch of
dirt at their feet. "Beats me." He crouched beside it and

laid a hand on the dirt. "It looks like it might be a couple of months old. But then I'm a city boy. I really can't judge." He shook his head again and stood up and put his hands on his hips. "It still looks like a grave," he said.

"Jack, I'm frightened. Let's get out of here. C'mon, let's go back."

"Okay," he said, but he stood a moment longer, looking at the patch of raw earth.

As they walked back to the house, with the shadows of the trees sliding rapidly toward them across the ground, Jack said, "I think we ought to tell John about that. Just to be on the safe side."

Megan held his hand tightly and walked a little closer as they headed for the house.

The thing stood still as a boulder and watched them move away. As they walked up the slope, it took one gritty step forward to keep them in sight a little longer. Only when they were completely gone from view did it turn away.

It looked at the place where they had stood. It looked at the mound of dirt. It thought it remembered this place. Then it moved slowly forward to the outermost tree and looked again up the slope. The figures were not in sight.

As it had before, it stared a long time at the place where they had disappeared. Its breath rasped harshly as it thought about them. And about the female in particular.

And it felt again the stirring it had felt before.

John Chard came up the hill as soon as he arrived home for dinner and Martha told him Jack and Megan had asked for him. They were waiting on the porch. He accepted a cup of coffee and listened while they told him what they'd found. There wasn't much to tell.

"That's it," Jack said. "We just didn't know what it was and it looked so strange that we thought we'd tell you about it. It's probably nothing."

Chard placed his coffee mug on the floor beside his chair. "Where is it exactly?" he asked.

Megan pointed out past the small vegetable garden they had started too late in the summer. "A little way past that far dip in the hillside. Near the line of trees."

Chard stood up and walked to the steps. He glanced up at the sky. "Let's go while there's still some light," he said.

Megan bent to pick up the coffee mugs and take them inside, but Chard was already walking away from the house. She left the mugs where they were.

She and Jack had already caught Chard's mood. None of them spoke until they reached the odd patch of dirt.

"That's it," Jack said.

Chard stood silently looking at the ground. He studied it a long time, then raised his eyes to the nearby woods that were growing dark now as evening approached. Unconsciously, he kneaded his stiff fingers. Then he walked slowly around the area, keeping back a couple of feet from the perimeter.

"All right," he said at last, almost to himself. "All right."

They looked at him but his face was expressionless.

"We'll need some things," he said. "Let's go back."

"What is it?" Megan said as they hurried after him. "What do you think it is?"

"We'll have to see," he said without stopping.

In front of the house, he said, "Call Doc Warren. Ask him to come up right away. I'll be back." He got into his car, swung it around quickly, and was gone.

Jack, Megan, and the doctor sat on the porch, waiting for Chard. Jack had turned on the yellow lights, but instead of making the place look warm and friendly, they seemed to isolate the house in the middle of a pool of darkness beyond. To ease their nervousness a little, Doc Warren was talking steadily, telling them the history of Deacons Kill.

"Have you seen the Centennial's ballroom?" he asked Megan.

She shook her head.

"It's a beaut," the doctor said. "Kept just the way it was the day it opened. That was in 1876, as you might guess. Of course, there was a hotel or inn on that spot for pretty near a hundred years before that. Three of them, all burned down. Indian raids got the first two. Chief Joseph, whom you may have read about, led raids through this whole area several times. Must have had bad service at the inn." The doctor studied his audience critically in the dim light. "When the third one burned, around 1872, a local man named Gayle decided to put up a new one for the centennial celebration. It opened on time, too, in 1876."

"It's a beautiful building," Jack said. He was watching the road, waiting for Chard.

"It is that," the doctor said. "But I guess if you haven't seen the ballroom upstairs, then you haven't seen the quilt."

He waited. Finally Megan said, "What sort of a quilt?"

"Well, as a kind of centennial project, all the women

in the Kill made an enormous quilt for the wall in the
ballroom, the long wall, the one that faces the windows.
It's something to see, I can tell you that. The design
shows the whole history of the town, right from its
founding by the deacon himself in the eighteenth century. Took about a year to get the whole thing done, so
they say, and every family in town was responsible for a
little part of it. It was unveiled as part of the centennial
celebration when the hotel opened. My grandmother
was a girl of nineteen then, and she was there to see it. I
remember her telling me the strangest story about that
day. She was one of three girls who were in the room
where the—"

"Here he is," Jack said and went to the steps of the
porch.

Megan and the doctor came and stood beside him.

Chard had hitched a trailer behind his car. It rattled
loudly as it bounced across the uneven ground and
stopped before the porch. On the trailer was a small
yellow Caterpillar bulldozer.

"Is there anything you want me to bring?" Jack
asked.

Chard looked up at him from the car, and Jack was
immediately reminded of the first time they had met. A
chill went through him at the thought of that morning.
"I have everything we'll need," Chard said.

Without a word, Jack opened the rear door and he
and Megan climbed in. Doc Warren was already hurrying around to the other side and got in beside Chard.

"Is that Vredenburgh's dozer?" the doctor asked
quietly.

"Yes," Chard said, and concentrated on his driving.
The car bounced roughly over rocks and once it

bottomed out so hard, when the front wheels dropped into a hole, that they all caught their breath sharply. But the car kept moving forward, Chard holding it at a steady pace. He did his best to avoid the worst of the holes and rocks but couldn't miss some of them. The headlights seemed to skitter ahead, bouncing around with the irregular movement of the car, barely illuminating the ground. Behind them, the trailer with the bulldozer clanked along. Jack turned in the seat to look back at it. It loomed at him like a monster relentlessly following their trail. Beside him, Megan squeezed hard at his knee.

Chard had the brights on now as they came close to the odd patch of earth. Off to the left, the line of trees was a solid wall of pitch black darkness, lacking even shadows to give it life. The car bounced to a halt.

"You'll have to get out here, Jack, and find it," Chard said. He held something up at the top of the front seat. Jack took it. It was a flashlight.

"Jack, be careful," Megan said quickly. "Stay in front of the headlights."

"I'll be careful," he said, and opened the door and got out.

Behind him, Megan pulled the door over without latching it closed. Quickly, she rolled down the window, then leaned forward, hands squeezing the back of the seat in front of her. The three of them watched Jack as he moved out in front of the car.

Jack thought it was the blackest night he had ever seen in his life. The moon was almost full, but tonight it was obscured by a solid cloud cover. He thought that, except for the headlights, he wouldn't be able to see his hand in front of his face. He stole one quick glance at the woods on his left, then tried not to think about all the primitive, unnamed fears that suddenly assailed him as he realized that he was surrounded by dark. A chill crept up his back and involuntarily he shivered.

Moving carefully on the rocky ground, he stepped in front of the car, into the welcome glare from the headlights, and switched on the flashlight with his thumb. It was one of the heavy square utility lights; he was glad to have the solid weight of it in his hand. He began walking slowly forward.

The night engulfed him, crept in around his ankles and caught at him. He shivered, felt stupid about it, then shivered again. Admit you're afraid, he tried to tell himself angrily, admit it, then get the hell over it. What is there to be afriad of? The dark? An odd patch of ground? For God's sake, this isn't some John Carpenter movie. Against his will, he shuddered, and the chill prickled the hair on the back of his neck.

He was at the edge of the light from the headlights now. He swung the flashlight slowly in a wide arc in front of him. He couldn't see the place. He looked up again at the darkness of the trees to try to orient himself. Where the hell was it? He took two more steps forward, and the car suddenly seemed very far behind him. The darkness washed like a tide around his feet.

He jumped when the car rolled forward and its lights bounced around him on the ground. Goose bumps covered his arms; he suddenly realized the evening had grown chilly. Of all nights for the moon to be hidden, he thought. He made another wide arc with the flashlight beam.

His ears suddenly seemed to pop open, the way they do sometimes on a plane, and the night was filled with strange sounds: the chittering of insects, crickets, something that squeaked with a high-pitched sound in the darkness beyond the lights. Behind him, comforting him, was the deep familiar hum of the car's powerful engine. Stones crunched beneath its tires as it rolled slowly in his wake, keeping his feet in a pool of dim light that shuddered as the car jounced over rocks. He kept the flashlight aimed ahead of the light from the car.

There! He saw it at last and breathed a sigh of relief. There was no mistaking the outlines of the area now. His flashlight cast harsh shadows on the low mound at one end of the area. He aimed the light at it and pointed with the other arm.

Chard brought the car a little closer so the headlights shone full on the spot. Jack stepped aside and when Megan came up beside him, he put his arm around her. She was shivering and hugging herself against the night. Something hard touched his side. He looked down and saw that she had a flashlight too.

"God, it's creepy here," she said. Her trembling voice was barely a whisper. Jack said nothing, only squeezed her shoulder tighter.

Chard and Doc Warren moved to the other side of the patch of dirt, out of the beam of the headlights.

"Megan, turn on your flashlight," Chard said.

She turned it on and the four of them aimed their lights at the place on the ground. Even more than it had in daylight, it looked like an enormous grave.

"I think I want my mother," Megan said softly, so only Jack would hear her. But, determined to take her part in whatever they had to do, she inched away from him a little to stand on her own.

Chard moved back to the trailer and the three others followed him, as much for company against the dark as to give him light to work in. It took several minutes to release the bulldozer from the trailer. When it was free,

Chard climbed up onto the hard metal seat and got it started. It roared like a beast in the night.

He brought it around in front of the car and stopped it. He pointed with his left hand. "Bring the car over here and aim the lights," he said.

Doc Warren was already moving the sheriff's car. He had to swing it in a wide circle until he could bring it to the left side of the area, its headlights shining on the spot. Chard backed up the dozer, studied the area for a moment, then went to work.

The bulldozer snorted angrily when he changed gears and when he experimented with the controls for the heavy-duty blade. After a couple of attempts, he was certain of the pattern of movement he needed for the blade.

"Keep your lights where I'm working," he said above the noise. "Don't block the lights from the car."

Then he backed up the dozer, aimed it carefully, and brought it forward to the edge of the area. The blade bit into the dirt. The engine whined at the sudden strain, but the blade sank in and lifted a crumbling chunk of dirt and rock. Chard backed off but lost the load by not lifting the blade in time. It took a couple of experiments before he got the rhythm right and then slowly, very slowly, the mound of dirt at the right side of the area began to grow.

It took ages for the hole at their feet to deepen. Each of them, Jack, Megan, Doc Warren, glanced up at the night that pressed in at their backs and at the woods that seemed filled with creatures, creatures who watched them and who were resentful of their presence and their violation of the soil.

Chard rode the dozer, hauling on the handles that moved the blade, making it bite into the earth, pull back, turn, dump its load, come back and bite again. He sat in darkness, all the light in front of him, and seemed to be one with the machine, forcing it to do his will, forcing it to dig and find for him what he needed to know. A few times the blade scraped against a large rock and the dozer bucked. Once he almost fell from the seat when that happened. Then he backed off, changed the aim of the dozer slightly, and attacked again.

Slowly the hole deepened as the dozer cut a ragged ramp that led down into the earth.

The three of them stared down where they aimed the beams of the flashlights. As the hole grew, the light from the car did little good. They moved closer to the edge, and the flashlights revealed broken soil and rocks. Slowly, the blade of the bulldozer nosed its way deeper.

As the bulldozer tilted more and more steeply, growling down into the hole, it seemed more and more to be following work that had been done before. When Chard angled the blade too sharply, it caught hard on tighter-packed dirt below the track made by the dozer. At the sides, softer dirt crumbled easily from what seemed a solid, undisturbed wall. Gradually, the dozer removed the remaining dirt that crumbled at the deeper end of the hole, at the far end of what had been the rectangular shape on the ground.

The others watched, shifting from foot to foot, and waited. Around them, behind them, on all sides of them, the night pressed in and the darkness of the woods seemed to move a little closer. When they looked up from the hole, as all of them did from time to time, they were blinded from following their own lightbeams. And there was nothing to see but the darkness itself.

Then Chard backed the dozer up the ramp and this time there was no load of dirt. He moved it back just to

level ground and shifted gears. At last the thing stood
still, poised at the top of the ramp.

They shone the flashlights in his direction to give him
light, and as they did so, they realized as one that there
was no light shining into the hole for a moment and
there was something there! Chard reached the top of the
ramp and they quickly swung the lights back to the hole.

Standing close beside each other, they peered down.
There was still a mound of crumbly dirt there that the
dozer hadn't lifted out.

"What is it?" Jack asked. His voice was hoarse and
he cleared his throat.

"I don't know," Chard said, and there was something in his voice that Jack and Megan had not heard
before. "There are shovels in the trunk," he said.
"Would you get them?" He did not take his eyes off the
dirt at the bottom of the hole.

Jack handed his light to Megan, got the keys from
inside the car and opened the trunk. There were two
shovels there. He brought them back and stood beside
Chard.

"No," Chard said. "I'll do it." Then he added, as explanation, "It's mine to do." He sounded very tired.

Carefully, planting his feet sideways to get purchase
on the soil, Chard moved down the ramp.

The others stood side by side at the edge of the hole.
Jack had the second shovel and realized suddenly that
he was gripping it like a club, ready to swing. He could
hear Doc Warren breathing at his side. The doctor and
Megan each held two lights. They kept them aimed on
the dirt at Chard's feet as he neared the bottom of the
hole. The darkness seemed to follow him down.

Chard stopped close to the mound of loose dirt and
carefully set his feet, bracing them wide apart for

balance. He leaned forward and studied it.

Jack, watching his every move, felt his flesh crawl with fear and suddenly wondered how old Chard was. Too old for this, he thought. We're all too old for this.

Chard held out the shovel with one hand and dropped its edge into the mound of dirt. It penetrated a few inches into the soft soil. Nothing happened. He withdrew the shovel, moved a little closer, and planted his feet firmly once again. This time he took a solid grip, right hand on the handle, left hand holding the shaft. He bent forward a little and shoved it solidly into the dirt. The third time he did it, the blade hit something solid.

Megan saw it first and her scream rang out in the darkness among the hills.

Jacob Helbig heard the scream as he staggered along the road that circled the base of Deacons Rise. He stopped and looked up, but the hills disguised the direction of the sound. He thought it was Carla's voice, and for a second he almost started back the way he had come. Then he decided against it. The hell with tonight, he thought. Let her scream in the woods all fuckin night if she wants. Right now he was more interested in getting back to where he had left his truck somewhere along this road.

He'd get the little brat tomorrow. Or tomorrow night. Or the night after that.

He knew how to do it now.

Martha and Nancy Chard heard the scream as they sat talking quietly together on the front steps of their house.

Nancy leaped to her feet. Martha Chard moved more

slowly, but in an instant she too stood at the edge of the
tiny porch, peering anxiously into the night. The older
woman held her right hand to the side of her face.

"Dear God, what was that?"

"It came from the hill," Nancy said. She swung
around toward the open front door.

Martha grabbed her daughter's arm. "Where are you
going?"

"I'm going up there."

"No!"

"I need a flashlight."

"You're not going!"

"Daddy's up there! I have to go. Mom, that sounded
like Megan."

"Oh, God," Martha said, but she released her
daughter's arm.

Helbig slammed the door of the truck, then fumbled
the key into the ignition and turned it. Reluctantly the
motor coughed into life. He swung the wheel hard to the
left and the truck bounced over the rough edge onto the
black tarmac of the road.

The aim of the truck's headlights hadn't been
adjusted in years, and the dim light they cast was dissi-
pated by the darkness. Helbig leaned forward over the
wheel, straining to see ahead. The solid painted line in
the middle of the road was badly worn by traffic. He
could barely see it. There were no lines painted at the
edge of the tarmac surface, and twice the truck's right
wheels dropped off the edge into the shale and weeds
that lined the road.

That was her, he knew it, and she was screamin just
to drive him crazy. Little bitch. He'd get her. He'd get
her! He'd get her now for sure because now he knew

how to get her. He'd find her and get her and beat the livin shit out of her for makin a fool of her old man. Tryin to.

He took his right hand off the wheel and felt on the ragged seat beside him for the—

Shit! The fuckin thing wasn't there! He'd had it a minute ago, it was right in his—

Shit! He'd dropped it! He must have dropped it when the little bitch screamed back there. Goddamn it to hell, now he'd have to go back and walk along the fuckin road in the dark and look for it. No. Wait. He could get it tomorrow. Sure. He could look for it in the daylight, find it easy. Yeah.

And once he had it again, he'd get her. Because he was smarter than that little bitch. He could come back in the daylight and find it along the road where he'd dropped it, and once the goddamn brat saw it, she'd do anythin he said. Goddamn her, that kid cared more about that fuckin Raggedy Ann doll than she cared about her old man. Yeah. He'd come back and find it, then he'd carry it in the woods again and when she saw it she'd come runnin and then he'd fix her ass.

The truck veered off the edge of the tarmac again, tires spitting gravel. Helbig yanked the wheel over, got the truck back on the road, and pressed down on the gas.

He'd get her with the doll, all right, he was sure of it, and he grinned at the rushing night.

The eyes were long-since rotted away, leaving only black dirt-filled sockets. The lips had dried out and pulled back grotesquely from the large irregular teeth. The stench itself was gruesome, rising like a solid wave out of the hole to fill their nostrils.

Megan clapped a hand over her mouth and took an involuntary step backward, away from the edge of the hole. Her movement made the beams of her flashlights dance nervously over the awful shape lying in the dirt at Chard's feet. She quickly steadied herself and aimed them again.

They stared in silence at the thing in the hole. After a long while, Chard was the first to move. He lifted the shovel and carefully scraped away the remaining dirt that covered it.

The cow must have been dead for months. It had been buried in the raw earth and much of the body was gone, rotted back into the soil. The mottled hide lay slack and fleshless, partially decomposed, displaying the bones beneath. One of the animal's legs had been broken and lay now at an impossible angle to the body. But the worst was the head. The flesh was gone from the cow's face, and the skin lay slack and moldy over the skull. The skull itself had been crushed. Where once the broad forehead had been, now there was a long depression. The hide had split and a jagged point of broken yellowed bone protruded. The bare teeth made the long face seem to leer up from the bottom of the hole. The eyeless sockets stared at nothing and seemed to see everything.

No one moved, but each of them could hear the others breathing.

"John," the doctor said at last.

Chard stood motionless in the hole, the shovel still poised in his hand.

"John," the doctor said again.

"God, the smell," Megan murmured.

Jack put his arm around her and took one of the flashlights. After a moment, he took his eyes away from the bottom of the hole—the huge grave—in the earth and looked at the doctor. There had been something in his voice when he spoke to Chard . . . .

"John," the doctor said again, and at last Chard turned and looked up. His face was gaunt, exhausted, deeply lined in the dim light that spilled from the flashlights. He looked at them a moment, scanning their faces, then focused on Doc Warren. Jack saw their eyes meet.

"Take this," Chard said wearily, and handed up the shovel. Jack took it from him and threw it on the ground. He moved quickly to his right and stretched out a hand to help Chard up the slope and out of the hole. Chard's fingers felt stiff in his grasp.

The four of them stood together, breathing heavily, surrounded by the night, the blackness of the hole deepening at their feet.

Doc Warren straightened up. "We'll leave all this," he said. His voice was stronger now. "Tomorrow's time enough."

They moved in silence toward the car and climbed into the same seats they had come in. The doors thudded solidly closed against the night. In front of the car, the headlights shone across the hole onto the mound of dirt the dozer had lifted out of it.

Without a word, Chard started the car and swung it slowly in a tight circle away from the hole. Behind them, the trailer, relieved of the weight of the dozer, rattled and clashed loudly over the rocky ground like an angry monster snapping at their heels.

Finally they drew close to the house. The only lights on were the yellow ones on the porch. Chard brought the car around to the front, facing toward the gate, and drove a little past the steps before stopping, almost as if his mind were miles away and the house not even visible.

Megan's heart nearly stopped as a figure loomed at her window. She clutched at Jack's arm.

"Daddy?" Nancy said. "Are you guys okay? Is everybody okay? We heard—"

"Everybody's fine," Doc Warren told her. "Everything's all right." He turned to look at Chard.

The sheriff clutched the steering wheel and stared forward through the windshield. "There was something else," he said quietly, his voice low and level, "something you couldn't see from above. Before it was pushed in the hole and buried, that cow's stomach was torn open the length of her belly."

They lay in bed, in the dark, not sleeping.

"I'm sorry I screamed," Megan said.

"It's all right."

"I couldn't help it."

"It's all right."

"When I saw what it was . . . . I don't know what I was expecting. I guess it could have been worse. I just feel so stupid."

"Don't. If you hadn't screamed, I would have done it for you."

"What kind of person could do a thing like that? Do you think it was Martin Ferrand?"

"I don't know. But I do know there's something about Ferrand that John Chard and Doc Warren don't really want to talk about. But I think they're going to have to, now. I'm going to go see the doctor in the morning, when John's not around."

"Do you really think you should?"

"Yes, I do. We may not own this place but for the time being, at least, we live here. And we may live here for a while yet, until it's sold." He remembered the doctor referring to "town loyalty" that night at dinner. "I may have to press him, but the doctor will tell me."

"Tomorrow, then?"

"First thing in the morning."

"I keep thinking about . . . what's out there in that hole."

"If I can figure out how to run that bulldozer, I'll cover it up tomorrow myself."

"Okay. You know . . . ."

"What?"

"There's a lot we don't know about living in the country, isn't there?"

"Yes," Jack said. "An awful lot."

They lay silent, thoughtful, in the dark, with the house standing solid around them.

"Are you still happy here?" he asked.

"I don't ever want to leave," she answered.

11

On Friday morning, Steve Steiger woke up shivering. The nightmare had filled his dreams again all through the night.

His pillow was soaked with sweat. He pushed it aside and it fell to the floor. He didn't bother to pick it up.

Still shivering, he lifted himself on his elbows, swung his feet to the floor, and sat unsteadily on the edge of the rumpled bed. He ran a hand through his hair, pushing it back from his face. Coffee. He needed a cup of coffee.

He stood up from the bed, balancing with one hand against the wall. He made it to the doorway without stumbling, then had to hold on again. His foot touched a stack of record albums propped against the wall and they slid down to the floor. Steve didn't bend to straighten them.

There was no milk and he hated black coffee but he gagged it down anyway. At first he thought he was going to be sick, but he doggedly kept sipping at the coffee until his head began to clear.

That nightmare. That goddamn nightmare.

It was the same every time, the same scene that he had viewed through the camera up on that damn hill by that damn house in that damn town in the sticks. Then there was his dumb sister who'd gotten him into this mess in the first place. People were always getting him into messes! Now she told him she was selling the house. He wished she'd never bought the house in the first place. Then none of this would be happening. That girl Candy wouldn't have gotten killed and he wouldn't be having *this goddamn nightmare!*

He dumped another spoonful of instant coffee into the wet cup, debated for a second, then poured in hot water from the kettle without boiling it.

This nightmare was driving him crazy. And why did that damn sheriff have to keep coming after him? People were always coming after him! And the tape. He wished he had the tape. It was the tape that was playing over and over in his head, the tape the sheriff had taken from him.

He set the cup down so hard on the table that some of the coffee slopped out.

It was in his head again, the whole scenario, the scene on the hillside, Candy squatting, then sprawling in the dirt, and himself running down the hill and the sheriff talking to him in the barn, and himself telling the sheriff there was nothing there, nothing on the hill besides the girl, nothing, *nothing!*

But that couldn't be. There *had* to be something, somebody, there. There had to be.

Using both hands to hold the cup, he sipped the vile stuff again.

It wasn't the sheriff or even the girl that haunted him most. It was the remembrance of seeing nothing where

there should have been something. Or someone, he corrected himself. If he had the tape, he could look at it
again. He could . . . .

Look at it again.

He stood up quickly from the table and went back to
the bedroom and sat beside the phone on the night-
stand. He punched in a number and waited impatiently,
listening to it ring at the other end.

"Yeah, Frankie, it's Steve," he said when the phone
was answered. "Yeah, I know what time it is . . . . Listen to me! I need a favor. I have to borrow your car for
the weekend. I have to . . . . Will you listen to me? I
need your car for the weekend . . . . Never mind, just
someplace I have to be."

He talked fast, hardly thinking, and at last Frankie
agreed. When Steve hung up the phone, he was sweating. Silently he swore at his sister, who had controlled
the family purse strings since their parents died. And she
held those purse strings so tight, he was always having
to ask for money. He'd asked her three times for a car
but he still didn't have one. Why wouldn't anybody ever
trust him with anything?

Well, at least he'd been able to talk Frankie into loan-
ing him a car. Steve was pleased with himself about
that. Usually, he wasn't able to talk anybody into anything. He brightened a little. He was beginning to feel
determined, capable, resourceful, purposeful, now that
he was actually taking charge of things. Yes, that's what
he was doing; he was taking charge of things!

The nightmares were driving him crazy and if he
couldn't see the tape again, at least he could go back to
where the thing had happened. Maybe that would help.
Maybe he could figure out what had happened that day.
Maybe if he could see it all better, know more about it,

the nightmare would leave him alone.

He hurried back to the bedroom and put on some clothes from the pile on a chair, then pulled an orange backpack out of the closet and began throwing a few things into it. Then he stopped and straightened up. The hell with it, he wasn't going to stay up there or camp out, he was just going to look around, see what he could see. Why weigh himself down? Hey, he was on the right track now, thinking clearly. Okay, everything was going to be okay now, he was taking charge of things. Right. He shoved the backpack into the closet, then turned to the bureau and scooped his remaining cash out of a drawer. He hesitated, then walked out to the kitchen. He pulled open a drawer and lifted out a heavy carving knife. He held it in his hand a moment, weighing it, suddenly frightened, looking at its polished edge and sharp point. He squeezed the wooden handle and it felt heavy and solid in his hand. He thought about it, trying to be as thorough and resourceful as he had been about the car. Better take it, he thought. Just in case.

And then he was on his way.

"Are you sure you don't want to call first?" Megan said. They were standing on the porch. Above them, the morning sky was gray, threatening rain.

"No," Jack said. "If I call, he can say he's loaded with patients or make some other excuse, put me off some way. I don't think he will, but he could. If I just show up, he'll have to deal with me."

"Oh, you're right," Megan said. "And I want to know everything he has to tell. I guess there's just a part of me that doesn't want to know, too." She looked out across the yard and the hill sloping gently away beyond the barn. "I love this place, Jack, even if we have to leave here soon. I don't want to know anything bad about it." Her eyes came back to Jack and met his. "But if there is something, I want to know it. And if there's something we have to do about it, I want to do it."

"We'll see," Jack said. "I won't be long." He kissed her, then stepped off the porch and headed for the car at the side of the house.

Megan stood on the steps and waited until the car had disappeared down the road. Then she went inside to the kitchen and poured herself another cup of coffee. She was going to take it up to her studio—she had been calling the room that for some while now—but instead she sat down and stared out the kitchen window. She could see the barn and the fields and a broad expanse of gray sky.

Life was so different here. Cleaner, somehow. More civilized. Well, it's more civilized in some ways, she thought, remembering the evening before, and trying to put it from her mind. Less civilized in other ways, more primitive. No, more *basic*, that was a better way of putting it. Closer to the earth, with a greater faith in the old, traditional values.

She thought of John Chard and Doc Warren. There was Deacons Kill in a nutshell. John Chard, who wanted nothing more in life than a decent place to live for his neighbors and himself, and who would devote all of his energies to a single-minded pursuit of that ideal. And Doc Warren, who was perfectly satisfied being a country doctor, doing his best to serve his own community. Were these men without ambition? Chard gave no thought to a political career, despite his popularity in the Kill and the popularity he could no doubt win elsewhere, on a broader field. In fact, Martha had told Megan that he'd passed up more than one offer from powerful people in county politics. Doc Warren sought no comfortable position in a group practice or in a hospital, where he could keep regular hours and leave the work behind him in the office. Certainly he was an educated man—they had talked with him enough to know that and Jack had been to his house and seen the size and range of his library—and certainly he knew the possibilities the world could offer. Yet, like Chard, he stayed where he was. It was another kind of ambition that motivated these men, the ambition to do the work that needed to be done, and to see it done well.

And something else too. Jack had told her about Doc Warren referring to "town loyalty." That was part of it. A sense of pride and tradition. A sense of permanence, stability, continuity. A sense of place.

God, I'm getting sappy, she thought. Then she thought: But, oh, I love it here.

Her gaze focused on the scene outside the window. The rough grass and weeds were starting to lean as a stiff breeze swept across the hill. It rattled a window in the living room. She leaned forward to see more of the sky. It looked a little darker than before. Rain coming soon, she thought.

Then she remembered the hole in the ground and the horrible thing in it and what it would be like if it rained before the hole was filled in. She shivered and hoped Jack would get back soon.

She finished the coffee, rinsed out the cup, then went upstairs to work on some sketches. Ten minutes later, she heard Nancy calling from the porch.

"Megan? Are you home?"

Megan made more coffee and they sat talking in the kitchen. Nancy wanted a first-hand account of what had happened the night before. Her eyes grew wide as Megan told her.

"Boy, that Mr. Ferrand must have gone really weird," she said when Megan finished.

"Why do you say that?"

"Well, I don't know much about it because I was at school most of the time then, but my folks wouldn't say very much, which was really strange. The Ferrands just packed up and moved, practically overnight, I think, and didn't even tell anybody what they were doing." She glanced toward the window. "And then for Mr. Ferrand to bury a cow like that." She shook her head. "It's really weird."

"To make no mention of the skull being crushed."

Nancy grimaced. "That too," she said.

Megan was silent a minute, looking out the window at the gray sky. She sipped slowly at the coffee she no longer wanted. Then she put the cup down and said, "I don't suppose you know how to run a bulldozer."

Nancy stared at her a second, then grinned. "Is it still out there?"

Megan nodded.

"I used to go with a guy in high school who thought he was doing me a big favor by giving me a ride on a tractor. He let me run it a couple of times."

"If the rain starts before this evening," Megan said, "that hole will be one godawful mess. Will you help me fill it in?"

"I may regret this in the morning," Nancy said, "but I'm game if you are."

They stood up from the table.

There were no patients waiting in the outer office
when Jack arrived. Doc Warren showed no surprise
when he greeted him and showed him into the
consulting room. An old leather couch, covered with
stacks of manila folders, stood against one wall. The
doctor lifted three piles of them to the floor to make
room for Jack, then settled comfortably in his own
chair, one elbow resting on the rolltop desk.

"It's amazing what a good night's sleep will do," the
doctor said.

"Too bad I didn't have one."

Doc Warren nodded. "I imagine there's a lot of that
going around," he said. "After last night."

Jack leaned forward. "I was hoping you'd tell me
what that was all about. You and John were acting very
mysterious, to put it mildly. And all this business about
Martin Ferrand. I never met the man, and yet I keep
hearing his name. And I keep seeing the two of you
looking at each other every time it comes up. And I keep
hearing you *not* talking about him. And then that business last night is the capper. I assume it was Ferrand
who buried the cow. Is it normal for a dairy farmer to
dig a grave for a cow?"

Doc Warren's face remained impassive. He looked at
Jack a moment longer before replying.

"No, Jack, it's not. It's not normal for a cow's skull
to be crushed, either. Nor its belly torn open. But if
you're asking me for explanations, I don't have them.
I'll tell you what there is to tell about Martin Ferrand,
but I don't think it will answer your questions."

Jack sat back on the couch and straightened a pile of
folders that was threatening to topple over. Then he
looked up at the doctor.

"Tell me about Martin Ferrand," he said.

"Oh, it's so gross!" Nancy said. She had one hand over her nose and mouth as she edged toward the lip of the hole, stretching forward for a better look at the carcass of the cow. A thick swarm of flies swirled above it, creating a buzzing, shifting cloud.

"Gross isn't the word for it," Megan said. She stayed farther back from the hole. "C'mon. If we can get the bulldozer going, we can just shove that mound of dirt right in on top of it and have it covered in a couple of minutes."

Nancy backed away from the hole and turned to face her. "Its head really is bashed in."

"Don't say you weren't warned."

"Do you know how hard a cow's head is?"

"Not exactly," Megan answered. She looked up at the sky. "We should get started if we're going to do it."

They turned away from the hole and walked toward the bulldozer.

Doc Warren was telling Jack about Martin Ferrand.

"He never exactly reveled in the life of a farmer, of course. No man would. It's a hard life, even with all the advances of science a farmer has available today. But it was Martin's life and it mattered to him. You know, there are some people who it's easy to picture doing something other than what they do, some other kind of work. You couldn't do that with Martin."

"Like you and John," Jack said quietly.

Doc Warren dropped his eyes from Jack's face. "I suppose you might say that. Something like that."

"So what happened? He just walked away?"

"Very close to it. It couldn't have been more than a

month or so from the time John or I or anybody else
saw something was wrong until he and Edith were
packed and gone. They moved to Cambridge, Massachusetts. They have a son there who teaches at Harvard.
Martin was always very proud of him.''

"So he's a man of . . . about your age?"

A tiny smile flickered across the doctor's face.
"About," he said.

"So you probably grew up together, and John too."

"Everybody in the Kill more or less grows up together. What you mean is, were we close friends? We
were, the three of us.''

"Haven't you been in touch with him?"

"He never gave us an address. Martha had one letter
from Edith but it didn't really tell anything, except to let
us know where to reach them." He hesitated briefly. "I
wrote once after that, but had no reply."

"It doesn't make sense."

"No, it doesn't. Jack, think about yourself for a
second, or Megan, for that matter. You work for yourself, push yourself hard, live by your wits. You enjoy it
too, or I'm very mistaken. Tell me when you plan to
retire."

Jack saw where he was going and shook his head.
"Never," he said. "I'll just slump over my typewriter
some day."

The doctor nodded. "Yes," he said. "And they'll no
doubt find me with my face on this old desk." He
patted the desk fondly, as if it were an old friend,
always ready to welcome him. Then he looked up at
Jack. "Martin was like that," he said. "Just like that."

They got the bulldozer started and figured out how to
work the controls that moved the blade but, no matter

how hard they tried, they couldn't manage to lock the blade in the elevated position. And unless they did that, they couldn't move the machine.

"Want me to kick the tires?" Nancy finally said in frustration.

"Only if I get the first shot," Megan said. She brushed an arm across her forehead, then turned off the motor and climbed down.

A brilliant flicker of lightning flashed across the sky. A few seconds later, thunder crashed above them, the sound echoing back and forth among the hills.

Megan glanced up at the dark cloud cover that seemed very close above them.

"Just for good measure," she said. "Oh, well, let's go. There's no point in drowning too."

As they started back toward the house, another bolt of lightning flashed across the sky. This time the thunder came with it. Seconds later, they were pelted with huge drops of rain. They started running.

It knew this place. It had been here before.

It stood at the edge of the trees and watched them turn away from the monster that had roared. For a moment, it looked back at the monster. It was still silent, unmoving, and the thing in the trees saw that the monsters were tame. It was not yet ready to go near them, but it knew them now. It turned its gaze back to the two females.

Thunder crashed in the skies above. The thing recoiled and moved back among the trees but its eyes stayed with the two figures. They were moving away more rapidly.

The rain hissed down all around it, pattering loudly on leaves and branches.

The females were running.

Thunder split the air.

They were almost up the slope.

It turned and slashed through the undergrowth to follow them. It could just see them through the outer trees of the woods. It could still smell them. It wanted them now and even the thunder would not keep it off. The gritty sound of its passing was lost in the noise of the storm.

Helbig found the doll a minute before the storm crashed over him.

Grunting, he bent to pick it up, swore, shook it in anger, then held it above his head and shook it violently again.

"Here!" he shouted at the darkening sky. "Here's the fuckin doll! Come get it!"

Then the heavens opened and in a second he was drenched. His hair was plastered to his face and his feet were soaked. He was wearing only green workpants and a yellowed tee-shirt. The cold rain sent an icy shiver through him.

He stood in the middle of the road, hunched over against the pounding rain, breathing hard, shivering, muttering to himself. He held the doll with one thick hand around a ragged foot. The doll hung upside down, the free leg dangling from only a few threads.

"Here!" he shouted again, still bent over. The rain hammered at his head and back and ran down his face in icy rivulets.

He bent over more, and suddenly he was holding the doll by the one leg and beating it against the wet black pavement, smashing its head against the road, bellowing "Here!" every time it struck.

At last, he stopped and straightened. His mouth was open as he gasped for air, his barrel chest heaving. Rain ran across his face in sheets. He shook the doll again. "Here!" he tried to shout once more, but choked on the word.

He swung glazed eyes around to orient himself, then, unsteady, his left arm out for balance, his right holding the battered doll, he lurched slowly toward the trees.

Behind him, in the middle of the road, muddy and soaked by the rain, torn from its body in the beating, lay the doll's other leg.

Some of the eyes in the bottom row came alive with light, and it knew they were in there. They had gone in at the other side, away from the woods. This must be the back of the thing they lived in.

It watched the house.

Rain sheeted across the open space, a curtain of gleaming arrows. It hissed into the dirt, turning it to mud. All around, it beat against the leaves.

The thing watched the house. It had watched here before and it knew that sometimes there were monsters here that roared. It would have to be careful, although it was no longer afraid of the monsters.

Slowly it stepped out from the trees, into the rain, and moved across the open ground. The mud plucked at its legs as it cautiously moved toward the house. Finally it had gone far enough from the trees to see the front of the house. It could see where they had gone in. It stood still and, finally, in the bright space inside, it saw one of them move. It took a step closer, the grating sound of its movement lost in the noise of the rain. Nothing happened. It took another step closer.

And then the monster roared.

The mud in the yard looked axle-deep, and Jack reminded himself that they would have to put in a concrete driveway from the road to the end of the porch. Then he remembered that they wouldn't be living here very much longer, and the thought filled him with a sudden piercing sadness. He had come to think of this as their home. The habit would be hard to break.

He was afraid the car would lose momentum in the mud, so he gunned the engine, aiming to come in alongside the steps of the porch. The car slid to a halt a foot away from the bottom step. There was just enough room to open the door, jump onto the steps and up to the shelter of the porch. He made it to the screen door safe and sound, with hardly a drop of rain on him.

The sudden roar had surprised it and the thing stood now among the trees, glaring coldly at the house. Its breathing was harsh, raw, guttural, louder than the rain driving into the ground in front of it.

Dark was a better time to hunt.

It would come back again.

The females. It could still smell them.

It would come back.

It turned away and moved off heavily between the trees, and as it turned, a sudden anger exploded within it. It struck out at a thick branch that blocked its way. The branch split, and the thing ripped it from the tree, hurled it down and crushed it, ground it, into the earth. Fury welling within, it tore viciously at another branch and flung it crashing through the undergrowth. The thing roared in rage, then attacked the treetrunk itself, clubbing it ferociously until the bark was raw and shredded and the naked wood beneath bled sap. The sounds of harsh feral breath, of breaking branches and tearing wood, of stone grating harshly on stone, were lost in the pounding of the rain.

Martin Ferrand knew it was his fault. He should have been home, instead of out walking the streets of this strange city. He should have been home with Edith. If he'd been home, this might not have happened.

That thought brought him up short and he stopped where he was, on the steps of the hospital. Two nurses bumped into him. They apologized without interrupting their conversation, and hurried on.

He and Edith should have been *home*. And home was the farm in the Kill, among their friends and their own people. Not here. Definitely not here. With Edith in a strange hospital in a strange city.

He went to the bottom of the steps and sat on a low wall at the side. The sky was clouding over; it was getting dark early. Rain tomorrow, he thought. A sudden vision of the farm snapped into his mind, and another of Edith upstairs in the bed, and he had to stifle a sob.

He had been out at midday for another of his walks, filling the hours with the only kind of exercise he could get now and managing, as he did each day with less success, to keep himself from thinking. And when he got home at last, he found Edith on the floor at the bottom of the stairs, her face streaked with tears from the pain of her ankle. How long had she been there? She didn't know.

The hours after that had passed as in a fog: the call to the police, the wait for the ambulance, the ride to Mt. Auburn Hospital's Emergency Room, the television on wall brackets in the waiting area which he had stared at sightlessly until someone came to say that he could see her now. And the lump in his throat that choked him when he tried to tell her how sorry he was, for this, for the pain, for everything.

From where he sat, he could see the Charles River and it looked flat and gray beneath the cloudy sky. He looked from there to the concrete and glass of the hospital behind him, and then again at the traffic passing by on Memorial Drive that skirted the river. And wished they could be home.

He stood at last and began walking.

When finally he reached home, he realized he should have called Ramsey. He badly needed to lie down and rest, but he went to the phone, looked up the number and dialed.

Susan answered and told him that Ramsey was working in the library and she had no way of reaching him. He told her about Edith. Susan said it was just terrible, but thank God it was only a bad sprain and not a break. She'd be glad to come right over, except that she was due to leave the house ten minutes ago, she had some people to pick up and she'd promised to drive, and wasn't it something how things always worked out this way?

Martin hung up the phone while his daughter-in-law was still talking. He slowly climbed the stairs to the bedroom, set the alarm for six o'clock, so he'd have plenty of time to get back to the hospital to see Edith again this evening, and lay down on the bed. He was reminding himself that he'd have to find out about a taxi to bring Edith home tomorrow when his eyes were suddenly very heavy and he fell asleep.

It was raining and getting dark when Steve Steiger finally reached Deacons Rise. The damn car, wouldn't you know it, had blown two hoses, and he'd spent four hours—four hours!—in a gas station in East Durham, waiting while a couple of country bumpkins scratched their heads and tried different hoses to see if they'd fit and finally had to send to some other town for the right ones.

Nothing ever worked out right!

And now it was raining and getting dark. This whole thing was turning into a whole new nightmare of its own.

Some thought. That was what had him here in the first place. Oh God, what a mess!

He'd been halfway up Deacons Road, the car splashing through puddles in the gravel, before he'd remembered that the sheriff lived just below the farmhouse. If he went this way, he'd have to drive right by the sheriff's place. Just his luck, the guy would be standing out in the rain watching the traffic. And the way his luck usually went, he was sure of it. When he reached a fork in the road, just before the last stretch uphill, he turned right to avoid being seen. After that, if he kept going left whenever he could, he'd come to that damn hill from the other side.

As he drove, he debated calling the whole thing off or finding a place to stay for the night—he thought he remembered the town had a hotel—and going up to the hill in the morning, in the daylight, when at least he'd be able to see what he was looking at. It was getting dark fast now. Besides, he didn't even know what he was looking for.

No. No, he'd started it and he was going to see it through. He was taking charge of things at last, wasn't he? He decided to keep going, get as close to the hill as he could, and get out and walk. So he'd get wet, big deal. All he wanted to do was to get this over with.

If he could just get into those woods, see them again, find that same place, and look at it with a sane man's eyes, calmly and rationally. Maybe that would drive the crazy image out of his mind and drive away the nightmare once and for all. He clutched the steering wheel tighter.

But then his luck changed, and by the time he figured he was back at the base of the hill, the rain had stopped and the sky was getting a little brighter. There were still a couple of hours of daylight left, so it should be enough time. He could get in and out before dark. His spirits began to pick up.

He pulled the car to the side of the road, tires crunching on wet gravel, and turned off the motor. He got out and looked around. It was hard to tell, but if he was figuring right, the place he wanted was off in . . . that direction. He turned back quickly to the car and lifted the carving knife, wrapped in a towel, from the front seat. When he had it wedged securely in his belt, he felt a little more secure.

He locked the car and dropped the keys in his pocket. Then he looked up at the hill that rose on the other side of the road. He tried to find some sort of marker to aim for and that he could use later to help him locate the car. There was nothing, only a dark and solid mass of foliage.

Well, he thought, there's always Rule One. When in doubt, go downhill. He touched the knife in his belt again, took a deep breath, crossed the road, and started up the slope.

Helbig knew she was here somewhere in the woods.

He was very confused now—about the time and how many days he had been searching and his location on Deacons Rise—but he knew for certain that she was here, she was hiding in order to make a fool of him, but he would find her and then she would learn her lesson once and for all. That much he knew.

It had finally stopped raining and the sky had grown a little brighter, but Helbig was barely conscious of the change. He splashed doggedly through the narrow streams that now ran down the hillside, cutting channels through the dirt and broken rock. His feet had stopped hurting at some point, but he hardly noticed the absence of pain. The numbness only caused him to clutch at the trunks and branches of trees to support his progress, and that was all right because it meant he was closer to his prey. His face and arms and hands were scratched now by branches and the trees he clung to, and the blood would not dry. A branch he had carelessly shoved aside had whipped back viciously at his face and cut the hard ridge over his right eye. The blood trickled into the eye and left his vision a red-stained blur.

But he was closer every second and he knew it.

The bright sky that followed the rain had fooled Steve Steiger. He was no outdoorsman, but he knew from camping trips at Lake George and canoeing trips at the Delaware Water Gap—he hated those trips because he always fell in the water and everyone always laughed at him, but he had to go because all of his friends went—that, above all, you don't get lost in the woods with night coming on fast. And now he was lost.

He'd thought for sure he knew where he was, both in relation to the car and in relation to the curve of the hill

itself. But the light had betrayed him and the hill had
tricked him. When he'd realized the light was fading
rapidly, he had given up at once—what a stupid idea to
come up here in the first place!—and had started downhill. Rule One. His route didn't look familiar, but then
nothing looked familiar. Then downhill suddenly
turned into uphill and he knew he'd gone wrong. He
caught his breath, felt for the carving knife again, and
moved to his left until he found another downhill slope.
When he came to a wide ledge of rock jutting out from
the rough hillside, he shivered and knew for sure he was
lost.

It could see at night as well as it did in the day, and it
shoved roughly through the undergrowth, heedless of
the noise, secure in its solitary strength. Darkness
hugged the Rise, but the thing cared not at all.

Then suddenly it stopped, its sandy wheezing the only
sound in the darkness.

The sky had cleared enough for the moon to shine between scudding clouds. It shone brightly now, and a
breeze stirred across the slope. The mottled ground
shimmered darkly with the shadows of swaying
branches, but no shadow marked the place where the
thing stood.

It looked up toward the sky and the moon, but a
cloud like a blanket of dark gray smoke drifted quickly
before the light, and darkness again took the hill.

More slowly now, the thing moved on.

When the moon shone for a minute between the
clouds, Helbig saw Carla on the hill below him.

Now he had her.

He crouched behind a tree and watched. He had to be

certain. But it was her, of course it was her. Slowly he stood and rubbed his meaty hands across his face to clear the blood from his eyes. He had stuffed the ragged doll into the top of his pants earlier to free his hands, but now he pulled it loose and held it out to look at it. It was waterlogged now, wet and muddy, and it was missing one leg. But it was all he needed. He wiped the other hand across his mouth and started down the hill.

Steve Steiger sat with his knees pulled up against his chest for warmth and cursed his own stupidity. The air was damp, chilly, and the rock beneath him wet, and all he had was a shirt, no jacket, no nothing. Oh Christ, he thought, I'm lost in the woods at night.

And the woods! God, they were creepy. And all the sounds he couldn't identify. Animals pushing through the tangled undergrowth, things moving out there in the dark, things watching him, their eyes making him shiver and his skin prickle all over. And he thought of what he had seen, or not seen, on this same hill that other time, and he shuddered violently, skin crawling, in the dark. Thank God for the moon, he thought, at least there's some light. And just then the moon disappeared behind a cloud and the light went with it.

He shivered and the skin at the back of his neck prickled. A hard, choking lump formed in his throat.

And in the darkness something grabbed his shoulder tight and spun him around, lifting him from the rock. Steve was too shocked, too terrified, to make a sound. His arms flailed and he tried to get his feet under him but couldn't, and he tried to shout but his throat was choked with fear. Whatever it was growled as it held on to him and shook him hard again and wrapped its arms around him and squeezed. His fingers groped at his belt

and then miraculously the knife was in his hand and he
was stabbing, stabbing, and then the knife hit something soft and sank in, but the impact threw him off
balance and the thing that held him let go and he was
clawing at the edge of the rock shelf and then he was
over and falling and sobbing as he wondered for an
instant at the hardness of the branch that stabbed
upward at his chest as he plunged down and then there
was nothing at all.

Then the moonlight returned, and on the rocky ledge
on the hillside, Jacob Helbig stared dumbly at the knife
embedded in the doll.

They gathered that evening at John Chard's house,
and this time he kept nothing from his wife and
daughter. He had called Jack and Megan and Doc
Warren that afternoon to ask them to come, and from
the sound of his voice, they knew that the evening would
be solemn.

There were straight chairs on either side of the
fireplace and Chard took one of those himself. Martha
sat on the edge of the other one, watching him. Jack
thought it looked like a war conference, with Doc
Warren impassive in an easy chair on one side of the
room, Nancy sitting cross-legged on the floor in front of
another, and Megan and himself on the couch facing
Chard. Chard's fingers were stiff and he clutched the
right hand with his left as he talked. It made him look
very prim, Jack thought, for a man his size.

A videocassette deck sat on the floor in front of the
television set and Jack couldn't remember seeing it before. When Doc Warren had come into the room, he
had glanced briefly at it, then at Chard, but had not
looked that way again.

"All of you," Chard said suddenly, as if bringing troops to attention for a briefing, "know at least a part of this. I want you all to know everything."

And he told them. Told them again of the disappearance of Carla Helbig months before and of the failure to find a trace of her. Told them again of the investigation into the death of Candy McBain, including the medical findings, at which the doctor nodded. Told them next of Martin Ferrand's odd behavior, his sudden silence, his unannounced departure from the Kill and his failure to respond to letters. Told them about the cow buried on the hillside not very far away. Told them everything, whether they knew it already or not, told them everything he had been thinking for the last—how many?—months. And then he told them about the videotape and warned them it wasn't easy to look at, and then he showed it to them.

"There was nothing there," Megan breathed at the end.

Chard lowered his head and looked at the floor.

"And you're an experienced observer," Doc Warren said quietly.

"I think it's all one," Chard said, still looking at the floor. Then he raised his head and looked around the room. "Whatever it is that did one thing, it did the others. I don't know what it is but I want to stop it."

"Martin," his wife said. She was almost sobbing.

"Yes. It's Martin we have to talk to."

"Why haven't you called him, talked to him?" Jack asked, looking only at Chard.

The big man let his eyes come to rest on Doc Warren for a second before he looked at Jack.

"I don't believe in handing burdens to others unless the burden is rightfully theirs. A man has a right to his own life. I wish Martin had spoken to us, but he didn't, and that was his right. As far as we knew. And there was nothing in the disappearance of the child, except that it happened around the same time Martin sold the farm, and nothing in the death of that girl, to make me feel we needed Martin. But now there is. The cow was buried on Martin's property, and it was buried the way a man would do it if he was in a hurry. And we saw what had been done to it first."

They were silent, all six of them, searching each other's faces.

"Well, John?" Doc Warren said softly at last.

The rain began in Cambridge as Martin Ferrand walked home from the hospital at the end of the evening visiting hours. He was crossing Brattle Street toward the Harvard Coop when it started, and he stood with other people in the Coop's entranceway to see if it would let up. After a few minutes, the rain settled into a steady downpour. Martin lowered his head and hurried across the street, then through the gate into Harvard Yard and the shortcut back to Trowbridge.

Harvard Yard sat quiet around him in the rain. A few hunched figures hurried along the paths beneath the great oaks and disappeared amid the shadows. The red brick buildings that formed the Yard stood stolid in the rain. Two girls in red slickers, unmindful of the weather, stood near the statue of John Harvard, their laughter floating on the breeze.

Martin halted just past the statue and looked across the Yard, ignoring the rain that wet his face. This place had impressed him the first time he had seen it, not least because it was part of his son's life. It impressed him too because it had a sense of age to it, a solidity, a peaceful strength against the changes of the moment. It reminded him—not in its details but in its mass—of home.

He stood a moment watching a dark figure pass from one dim pool of light beneath a lamppost to another, as if fading in and out of existence before disappearing entirely. Behind him, the girls laughed again.

But the handsome brick buildings were not his, nor were the libraries, nor the trees, nor the young people who came here, nor the laughter of the girls in the rain. And, as he had discovered, neither was his son, nor his son's wife, nor his son's children.

It was a long slow walk home in the chilly rain.

When he reached the house, he went upstairs to the bedroom and changed all his clothes. But he still felt wet even with the dry clothing, and he took a blanket from the closet and carried it downstairs and wrapped himself in it on the couch.

He thought about Edith and how patient she had been with him, never complaining, trusting him, trusting his judgment—his judgment!—and trying only gently to change his mind, months ago, about the farm, and, when his mind would not change, standing by him still.

He thought about Ramsey and Susan and about the work and meetings and "hassles" and promises to drive that filled their lives. Edith was in the hospital but a stranger must not be inconvenienced because Susan had promised she'd drive. Ah. He looked at his watch. Could Susan still be driving? Could Ramsey still be working in the library? At this hour? There had been no return call when he was home before. He'd been home for three quarters of an hour now and there had been no calls.

Yes, it was true, he had loved his son more at a distance.

And then the dry clothes and the blanket finally did their job, and he dozed off on the couch.

And when the telephone rang, he woke up but did not move to answer it. It rang eleven times before finally it stopped.

"There was no answer," Chard said when he returned to the living room.

"Maybe they're out," Megan said, but she didn't sound as if she believed it.

"They're not," Chard said in the same flat voice. "Not at this hour."

"I'll go."

They turned to look at Jack.

"I'll go and see him," he said, looking steadily at Chard. "If I can, I'll bring him back. If not, I'll talk to him."

"What if he won't talk to you?" Megan said.

"He will. We live in his house and on his land, even if it's only for a while. And while we live there, it may not *be* ours but it *feels* like ours, which in a lot of ways means the same thing." His eyes met Chard's for a moment. "We'll be able to talk."

Chard and the doctor nodded at the same time.

Megan went out to the kitchen to talk with Nancy and Martha for a minute before leaving. Doc Warren pleaded a very long day and left right away. For once, the rear wheels of his Mustang didn't squeal as he backed out of the driveway.

A few minutes later, as Megan stood waiting for him on the steps and Jack said goodnight to Chard at the door, he suddenly remembered something he had meant to mention earlier.

"The bulldozer," he said. "It's still out there. Megan and Nancy tried to move it today but had some problem. I'd do it myself, but I wouldn't be any better than they were with it."

Chard closed his eyes for a second.

"I'll get it in the morning," he said wearily. "I'm just too tired tonight. I really am just too tired."

12

On Saturday morning, the sky over Deacons Kill was still gray with clouds, promising more rain. It had rained again during the night, and pools of water in the fields and yards reflected the false brightness of the day. In weather like this, the gravel roads of the Kill were safer than those that were paved. The paved ones were slick with silt and mud washed across them from the fields, and a wise driver would treat them as if they were ice.

At a little before seven o'clock that Saturday, morning, a truck driver named Ernie Flagg, who had started out from San Luis Obispo, California, eleven days earlier, was traveling east on Route 7. He was driving the truck cab that he owned himself and hauling a huge trailer that contained the entire household belongings of two families who had moved east from the golden west. One of the loads was going to Colonie, just outside Albany, and the other to Pawtucket, Rhode Island. When Ernie wasn't on the road, he lived in Santa Barbara, on the hill up near the Spanish mission, where you could see the mountains in the background, and he was already looking forward to the trip west as soon as he picked up another job in Hartford, Connecticut. He had a container of hot coffee nestling snugly between his legs and he was thinking pleasant thoughts about Santa Barbara and the beach and wondering why anybody would want to move from California to the east, when the rear end of the trailer suddenly fishtailed on the slick surface of the road. He felt the shift in weight, felt the truck go out from under him, and in one instant had checked the road ahead and the space on either side of the road, looking for an escape route, but it was already too late. The trailer swung around to the left and smashed into his side of the cab and wedged itself in tight. The door beside him buckled. Ernie's hands were clamped on the wheel but it was all happening too fast and the truck was sliding off the road and there was nothing he could do anyway. The last thing he ever thought was that the hot coffee was soaking into his crotch and then a woman's body flew up from in front of him and smashed through the windshield, driving shards of glass into his face. The truck, with Ernie dead inside and the woman's dead body in his lap, came to rest, after scattering tables and chairs and bodies and food in its wake, inside a roadside place called Danny's Diner, where fourteen people had been eating breakfast.

The diner was located just over the line into Deacons Kill. Three of Chard's deputies, Phil Aymar, Bob Carroll, and Richie Mead, were on the scene within minutes, and the troopers arrived immediately after them. Truckers and other drivers in the area with CB radios picked up the news and headed for the scene to help.

When Chard got there fifteen minutes later, the place was in chaos. It was still chaos when Doc Warren arrived, and a few minutes after that, Route 7 was impassable and Chard had to send Richie Mead out to clear the traffic so the ambulances could get through. Then, just as the first ambulance slid to a halt near the ruins of the diner, the rain began again. The driver of the ambulance hurried through the shattered front of the diner to where the deputies were bent over a woman whose face was gray with pain. More intent on the wreckage around him than the mess at his feet, he slipped in a puddle of broken eggs and blood and landed hard on his right arm. The deputies heard the bone crack. Later, one of the other ambulances, speeding back with two victims to Fox Memorial in Oneonta, slid off the road into a ditch and couldn't be moved until a tow truck came and hauled it out.

By the time Chard finally got home, it was nearly two in the afternoon. He told Martha he was going to shower and put on clean clothes and then go back to the office to keep tabs on things, but she wouldn't hear of it.

When Jack came down at two-thirty to say he hadn't been able to get his car started all day because the rain had soaked the wiring, Martha told him what had happened and that John was in bed.

Jack approached the bedroom feeling suddenly very awkward about seeing Chard in what the sheriff himself would regard as a position of weakness. He pushed the door back and found Chard sitting up in bed.

"I thought you'd be there by now," Chard said. His voice was the same as ever, but he looked more tired than Jack had ever seen him.

Jack told him about the car, then added, "But it

should be okay shortly, if the rain stays off till I get going. I was just wondering if there was something in particular I should say or do that would get Martin to cooperate."

Chard pushed himself a little higher in the bed and studied Jack for a few seconds. "No," he said at last. "Just tell him where you live. And that he's needed. Tell him the truth."

Twenty minutes later, Chard heard Jack blow the horn twice as he passed the house on his way to Cambridge.

Chard waited ten minutes more, watching the clock on the dresser, then got dressed, told Martha he'd had all the rest he needed, and went back to the office.

Several hours later, by the time Jack finally hit the last dull stretch of the "Mass Pike" heading into Boston, he was having a hard time keeping his foot light on the gas. The meeting, as he couldn't help thinking of it, last night at Chard's house had brought together all the vague hints and worries that had been just below the surface all summer: Chard's theory, if that was the word, made sense of all the odd comments he'd heard from him and Doc Warren. And there was the tape of Candy's death. He was going over it yet another time in his mind when he finally saw the exit sign for Storrow Drive and Cambridge. He swung left into the exit with a sense of relief.

He had friends in Cambridge, writers, and although he hadn't been there for a while, he thought he remembered where Trowbridge Street was. He crossed the bridge, turned left into Putnam Street, crossed "Mass Ave" and then was driving slowly on Trowbridge, trying to read the house numbers. It was a little after seven o'clock; the sky had cleared in Cambridge, and there was still an hour or so of light. When he located the house, he had parked the car and was heading up the path toward the door before he had figured out what he was going to say first.

John Chard came home at seven o'clock that Saturday evening. Martha had made roast chicken. "It's easy to digest," she told him. "It's good for you, and you need your strength." He didn't feel like eating, but he washed his hands and sat down at the table anyway to do the best he could.

Two hours earlier, he had been standing in a light drizzle beside the wreckage of Danny's Diner, grateful that the rain had washed away at least the more gruesome evidence of the morning's carnage.

The scene had turned into a major local attraction that lasted all afternoon, and he'd had to station a deputy there to hold back the sightseers and keep traffic moving on Route 7. He stood in the rain, massaging the fingers of each hand alternately, and shook his head at the sight. Danny Lester had been a friend for years, and Chard had sat at that now-wrecked counter thousands of times. He knew the man's family, had watched his daughter grow up; she and his own Nancy were the same age. The last he'd seen of Danny, he was being loaded into the back of an ambulance. Doc Warren had had to give him a shot before he could be moved; when the truck hit, Danny had landed face-down on his own grill.

Chard was just turning away to go to his car when the deputy on duty, Richie Mead, walked over. They talked quietly for a few minutes about the accident. Richie had been here all day. He looked exhausted, and Chard promised to send someone to relieve him.

"Oh, hey," Richie said, "I've got a small thing that might take your mind off . . . ." He nodded toward the wreckage. "Just before I got the call this morning, I was up on Castle Road. Found that old pickup of Jacob Helbig's up there, pulled off to the side. I was just going back to the car to call it in when I saw another one, a car, a little further down the road. I looked it over but I didn't recognize it. Not from around here. Then I got the call and I forgot all about them. Never knew that Helbig to be a nature freak, especially in weather like we've been having."

Chard thanked him and said he'd investigate the car and Helbig's truck and promised again to send a replacement for Richie as soon as he could. Then he got back in his car and drove slowly and alone to Fox Memorial Hospital. Of the victims who were still alive when they reached the Emergency Room, two had been released, two had died, and the others had been admitted for treatment of their injuries. Danny Lester was in the Intensive Care Unit and Chard was not permitted to see him. He spent some time in the waiting room, talking with the families of the injured, then drove slowly back to the Kill and home.

At the dinner table, as he tried to make a show of enjoying Martha's roast chicken, he did his best to clear his mind of the day's events. He thought about Jack and wondered if he had reached Cambridge and seen Martin yet, and he wondered what, if anything, Martin could tell him. Then he remembered the bulldozer still sitting out on the hillside. And that hideous hole still exposed to the air and the rain. It would have to be filled in and the dozer returned to Al Vredenburgh.

He put down his fork and, needing something else but afraid coffee would upset his stomach, asked Martha for a cup of tea. By then, he was thinking only of the bulldozer and the buried cow with the smashed skull and the rain that was again rattling at the windows, and had forgotten all about Richie Mead's report of a strange car and Jacob Helbig's truck parked up on Castle Road on the other side of Deacons Rise.

Jack heard the bell ring inside the house. Nothing happened. He waited for what seemed a decent interval, then rang it again. This time, he thought he heard a voice call out inside. He waited again, wondering why no one came to the door, then tentatively touched the handle. The door swung open a few inches.

"Who's there?" a woman's voice called through a doorway on the right.

Feeling suddenly like an intruder—and feeling too that this was the *second* Ferrand home he had intruded on—Jack pushed the door back and stepped inside.

Edith Ferrand sat alone on the couch in the living room. Her right leg was stretched out in front of her, the ankle tightly bandaged. She was a small, fine-boned woman, and the strain of her injury and incapacity showed in the narrow features of her face.

"Mrs. Ferrand?"

"Yes," she said, her eyes fixed on his face. There was caution but no fear in her voice and expression, and Jack thought how a typical woman in New York City would react to a strange man walking into her living room.

"My name is Jack Casey. I live in Deacons Kill. In fact, I live in your . . . former home."

She stared at him for several seconds and then said simply, "Oh. I see." Suddenly there was a mixture of fear and relief in her eyes.

"Please sit down," she said. "I'm afraid I've had an accident, or I'd get up."

Jack sat awkwardly across the room from her, not knowing how to begin, startled by her acceptance of him and of his presence here, understanding the moment of fear in her eyes but puzzled by the unmistakable look of relief. And the story he had come here to tell, and the questions he had come to ask, suddenly sounded like the sheerest madness.

"Mrs. Ferrand . . . ," he began, then caught a movement out of the corner of his eye.

"Martin," Mrs. Ferrand said, "this is Jack Casey from the Kill. He lives in our house."

Jack stood up again, and he and Martin Ferrand looked at each other. Jack was instantly aware that Martin was looking at him with the same combination of fear and relief that he had seen in the man's wife. Maybe Chard was right, Jack thought. Maybe there is something he can tell us. Ferrand shifted a brown paper bag he held in his arms.

"I'll just be a minute," he said, avoiding Jack's eyes, and disappeared toward the rear of the house.

Jack sat down again. When he looked at Edith Ferrand, her eyes were closed and deep frown lines creased her forehead. She's in pain from that ankle, he thought.

It seemed a long time before Martin Ferrand returned from putting the bag away. When he did reappear, his face looked grim, set, his mouth a hard tight line. Jack couldn't tell if the look was defiance or resignation. Ferrand stood a moment in the doorway, looking at him, then crossed the room slowly and sat on the couch beside his wife. Then his eyes met Jack's. This time they didn't waver, and Jack began to think the look was resignation.

"Mr. Ferrand," he said quickly, "I understand you may be upset by my visit, but I hope you'll listen to what I have to say. I'm also speaking for John Chard and Doc Warren."

Edith had been studying her hands, which were clasped in her lap, but now she raised her head and looked sideways at her husband.

Martin didn't move, just kept looking at Jack, until Jack finally thought he would have to look away. When Martin spoke at last, his voice was low but steady.

"I've been expecting you," he said. "You or somebody else from the Kill. I knew . . . ." He had to pause to clear his throat. "I knew sooner or later it would happen."

"Mr. Ferrand, I—"

"You live in our house now?"

"Yes."

Martin nodded and cleared his throat quietly again. "Please call me Martin," he said. "I'd like you to tell me first if everyone is all right."

"If you mean the Chards and Doc Warren, yes."

Martin Ferrand had dropped his gaze, as if prepared to avoid the answer he might receive. Now he visibly relaxed a little at the news and looked up again at Jack. His expression seemed resigned, although a suggestion of his initial relief still lingered. Above all, Jack thought, he looked weary.

"I'd better start at the beginning," he said, and Edith touched his arm and said, "Oh, Martin," very gently.

The rain beat loudly on John Chard's yellow hat and slicker, and when the breeze whipped around to another direction, it caught him hard in the face. The temperature had dropped into the sixties at nightfall and the rain touched him with icy needles.

The heavy downpour had been more than the sodden earth could absorb, and a pool of slimy water had formed at the bottom of the cow's makeshift grave. Chard stood back from the edge for a moment, fighting a wave of nausea caused by the smell that even the pounding rain couldn't wash away. Then he forced himself to step closer, drawn to the sight as if it could magically reveal the answers to all the questions that he barely knew how to form. He took a step and the mud sucked at his boots. He had aimed the headlights of his car at the hole, but their beams cut a gleaming white swath across it, glistening on the sheets of rain, and leaving the hole itself in even deeper darkness.

The pit of hell, he thought, then reproved himself for being melodramatic. It was foolish to think that way. And it was useless. The only sensible way to be about all of this . . . strangeness . . . was: realistic and practical. And one other thing.

He lifted his face into the rain, ignoring—and accepting—the drops that pelted his face. All around him, beyond the light from the car, the slope was in darkness. The hill above him, Deacons Rise, was nothing more than a dark and indistinct bulk against the greater darkness of the night. He looked to his right, where the hill fell gradually away. Out there were other hills, slopes, valleys, other fields like this one, other places that perhaps held their own dark secrets. Chard had, at one time or another over the years, looked upon, if not actually walked upon, pretty near every square foot of land in Deacons Kill, every foot of land for which he was responsible. And he had learned that there were things one could not learn, things that one could not prepare for. The hills, he had long since come to know, would permit themselves to be tamed, but they would forever hold back—impenetrable—some secrets in reserve. Fields could be cleared and sown, towns built, human lives conducted well or ill, but the hills would remain ever and always silent, private, primitive.

He lowered his head and turned back to the mud-filled hole at his feet. When he switched on the flashlight he carried, its light revealed only the slimy surface of the water at the bottom, and nothing of what lay beneath. He shivered, and blamed it on the evening's chill and the rain.

Then he turned away, lumpy wet mud clinging to his boots. He walked slowly back to the bulldozer, picking his way with the narrow, fragile beam of the flashlight.

"My God," Megan said when Nancy suddenly appeared at the door, "you must be half drowned! Come on in here."

She helped Nancy off with her dripping slicker and hung that and her hat on wall pegs while Nancy yanked off her floppy yellow boots.

"This is the very latest thing for the 'farmer's daughter' look," Nancy said as she set the boots on the porch outside the door. "It's all the rage this season."

"Well, you won't end up in any 'farmer's daughter' jokes wearing an outfit like that," Megan said.

Nancy pouted, said, "Oh, no, I was counting on it!" and they both laughed.

"*Annie Hall* is on television tonight," Megan said. "Can you stay to watch it with me?"

"I sure can. Where's the popcorn?"

As they headed for the kitchen, Megan said, "Your father stopped by a little while ago. He's getting that bulldozer out of the field. I offered to help and hold a

light or something, but he refused. I hope he's not
having any trouble with it."

"If he is, we won't hear about it. Daddy has to be
desperate before he'll ask for help. You know how he
is."

Megan found the jar of Orville Redenbacher popcorn
and opened the refrigerator to get butter.

The telephone rang.

Nancy sighed. "Dollars to donuts, that's my mother
calling to see if I made it up the hill safely. And to see if
Daddy's here."

"So answer it. My hands are full."

Nancy lifted the phone, said hello, then nodded to
Megan. She assured her mother that they were both
okay and told her that Daddy was still out with the bulldozer and, yes, she was absolutely certain he didn't
want her to go and hold an umbrella over his head.

When she had replaced the phone, she said, "On
second thought, let's not talk about all that stuff tonight. We'll have to think about it soon enough, anyway."

Megan was putting oil in the pot on the stove. "What
do you mean?"

"I mean that my father is very upset and very
worried," Nancy said seriously. "And I think he's
very . . . well, I guess *frightened* is the right word,
although it doesn't suit him at all. And for another
thing, he's getting in touch with the Ferrands. Jack
went, I know, but my father has confidence in Jack, so
it's really almost the same as Daddy going himself. So
Jack will either come back with some information or
he'll come back with the Ferrands."

"You think your father is right, then. I mean, about
these things all being connected."

"Oh, he's right. Believe me, he's right. It's not the sort of thing he'd be wrong about."

"That's what I was afraid you were going to say."

"So when Jack gets back from Cambridge, the problem will have to be solved somehow. And since whatever is happening, is happening very close to home, that's where it'll have to be settled." She paused, then looked critically at the pot that Megan was still holding over the stove. "We need more popcorn than that."

Megan looked into the pot and slowly nodded her head. "You're right," she said. "You are absolutely right. Pass over the jar."

As Nancy handed it to her, she said, "Have you seen the new Brooke Shields movie? God, she's so beautiful. I really hate her a lot!"

"You only *think* you hate her now," Megan said. "Wait till you're a few years older!"

Then they were laughing again, and in a few minutes the popcorn was starting to pop and the kitchen smelled warm and sweet.

Martin Ferrand's voice was low and husky, as if he were too weary even to bother speaking louder. He leaned forward, elbows on knees, hands clasped before him, and Jack could see the farmer's scarred fingers and swollen knuckles. Martin kept his gaze on the floor at Jack's feet and looked up only rarely. When he did, his eyes seemed to search Jack's face, seeking a clue that the younger man understood both the things he was saying and the things he was ashamed to say. All the while he spoke, Edith kept her thin hand on her husband's arm.

"I have two grandchildren," he began, the words coming slowly, "a boy and a girl. They're good children, I suppose, in their way. Well, that doesn't really matter, but they are. Anyhow, last March they were here to . . . . I mean, they were at the farm for a visit. Spring break, I think they call it. They're very self-sufficient children, both of them. The parents just put them on the bus and they ride all the way here . . . to the Kill, I mean . . . by themselves. But I'll tell you the truth, I just can't see parents doing that, putting young children on a bus all by themselves for almost five hours. I can't see it and I don't like it. Anyhow, we had them on the farm with us for a week.

"Now I have to tell you something else. Those hills there, all those Catskill Mountains, were formed a long time ago. And at some point in . . . prehistoric times, it's called . . . that whole part of the country, all those mountains, was underneath an ocean. There's still signs of it you can see. Have you ever noticed?"

He looked up, and Jack thought he could see in Martin's face a kind of pride in the sheer size and age of the mountains, the land.

"Yes," Jack said quietly, "I knew that. It was the bottom of a sea. And I've seen the seashell fossils in the shale along the road. There's a lot of it, especially on the Rise."

Martin watched his face for a moment without speaking and Jack wondered if it was because he had referred to the hill as "the Rise," the way any resident of the Kill would, rather than calling it formally "Deacons Rise." And with that thought came the sudden realization, stronger than any Jack had felt before this, that he *was* a resident of the Kill, that it belonged to him and he to it, and he saw in the same instant what it must truly mean to Martin Ferrand and his wife that the farm and the Kill and the land were no longer theirs.

Finally, Martin nodded. "Yes," he said, "that's

right. There's a lot of it on the Rise, more than some other places, anyway. It's light stuff, too. You can break it up with your fingers. Just dried mud, really, is all it is. Prehistoric mud.

"Well, my grandson found some seashell fossils in the stuff by the gate, so he started looking for more. Spent hours out there, looking for the good ones, you know, nice clear ones. Found a few, too. He got real good at breaking them open the right way, nice and easy, just separating the layers so you wouldn't damage what was inside. Funny how those things are formed, just mud burying them and they lay there for millions of years. At least, I suppose it's millions, I don't know too much about those things. And then you pick it up one day and there's the perfect clear impression of the thing. Of course, the shell itself or the plant or whatever it is, that's all gone, but the impression of it is right there, all this while later.

"So then the week was up and the children had to leave to go back to school. They both wanted to come back in the summer for another visit, and of course we said that'd be fine. Robert—that's my grandson— thought it was just great to find seashells on top of a mountain. Or at least the place where a seashell had been. He told me he was going to read up all about fossils before he came back, said he was going to start a collection. He's a very bright boy."

Martin paused and squeezed his hands together so tightly that Jack could see the whites of the knuckles.

"It was a week or so after that, after the children went home. That was the week of that terrible storm. Rain and thunder like you never see, and I was glad it didn't do that while the children were with us or they would have had to stay indoors the whole week. Terrible storm." He shook his head, remembering. "Terrible. Lasted for days. Brought down a lot of trees. We were worried for the soil. Even had the livestock upset. Fellow who has a farm, about thirty head of cows, on the other side of the Rise, said he had mudslides on his place, trees and rocks coming right down the hill into his pastureland.

"Well, the following week, when the weather cleared, I took some time out from chores one afternoon and took a walk up on the Rise. I thought I'd see if I could find something really nice up there for Robert. Well, eventually, I found a place that was good for what I was looking for. Looked like a big boulder had come down the hill and smashed to pieces. They'll do that, especially after the snow and rain have been working on the ground for a while. And, depending on what kind they are, sometimes they'll split up, just smash all up, when they hit another boulder below. That's what it looked like had happened in that spot. There were chunks of rock all over, jagged ones with raw edges, the way they are before the weather wears them down and smoothes the surface. It must have been a big one that came loose and rolled down, then broke apart, because there were fresh-looking pieces all over. There was one chunk a little distant from the rest and that one caught my eye. It had . . . a hole in it, just a sort of round hole. I thought it might be something for Robert. So I was careful about breaking it open. I wanted a clean break, you know, just split it in half so you get the top and bottom impressions clear . . . ."

His voice trailed off as he stood again on the Rise with the broken stone in his hands.

Jack waited, willing to let the man go at his own pace.

Finally, Martin looked up from the floor and his gaze

met Jack's. Then, slowly, he unclasped his hands and stretched out the left one toward Jack, palm turned up, fingers curled.

"It was a hand," he said. "The impression of a hand, just like that, top and bottom, only bigger. A lot bigger. The end of the stone with the round hole in it was flat, like it had snapped off from a bigger rock. That hole was where the wrist or forearm had been." He paused, but this time his gaze didn't waver from Jack's face. "It was a human hand," he said.

John Chard didn't stop the car until it was safely through the gateway and onto the solid surface of the road. He'd had a hard enough time getting it and the trailer, even without the bulldozer, across the field through the mud, and he didn't want it getting mired again in front of the house. Bad enough he had to do this in the dark, but he couldn't leave that grave open another night.

Once he'd gotten the dozer's blade into position, he had quickly pushed enough wet earth into the gaping hole to fill it in, trying not to think of what he was covering up as he did it, and then he'd driven the dozer to the barn and parked it there for the night. But he'd still had to go back for the car and trailer, and as he'd wrestled them through the muddy field, he was wondering whatever had possessed him to bring them out there in the first place. This whole strange business was getting to him, distracting him, making him careless. He wondered too if the same sort of thing had happened to Martin Ferrand back in the spring.

Despite the chill, his shirt was soaked with sweat beneath the slicker as he slogged back to the house.

When Megan came to the door, Chard was surprised

to see Nancy inside. They urged him to come in and sit while Megan made fresh coffee, but he refused, saying he just wanted to let them know he was finished and that he wanted to get home to put on dry clothing.

"You haven't heard from Jack, I suppose," he said, using his hand to wipe sweat and rain from his face.

"Not yet," Megan answered, and the three of them were silent, all thinking how they wished the unanswered questions weren't hovering in the air around them.

"Well, I'll be getting back, then," he said. "If he calls tonight—"

"I'll call you right away," Megan said quickly.

Chard hesitated a moment, his gaze lingering on Megan and his daughter, then said goodnight and turned to go.

The rain had eased off a little from its furious pounding and, although the sky was still dark with clouds, the moon shone for a moment through a break in the cover.

He halted at the bottom step and glanced back at Megan, who stood just inside the screen door.

"Watch your step in all that mud," she said. "And remind me to do something about it before the next storm." She smiled at him.

Chard thought how much like his daughter she was. "Goodnight, then," he said.

He made his way back to the car and got in, then started the engine and pulled away from the gate. But he only drove a hundred feet before stopping the car at the side of the road. The high banks that formed the edge of the field, and the line of tall weeds and thistles beside the road, hid the car from the house. Chard climbed out, suddenly conscious of what a wearying long day this had been, and stood a moment in the rain, which was mercifully light just now. Then he decided he had to do it and started back up the hill. As he walked, the moon disappeared again behind a cloud and the hillside was swallowed by night.

It sounded like madness, but Martin Ferrand looked more frightened than mad. And he looked ashamed.

Jack could hardly even form questions. A fossilized hand? Or, rather, the impression of a hand? Was that possible? How old were the mountains? When was there first human life in the area? He didn't have the answers, and every question that sprang to mind had a dozen more trailing after it. Better wait with the questions, he thought. Let the man tell it his own way, now that he was started. For an instant, he wondered how John Chard and Doc Warren would react if they were sitting here now.

"There must be more," he said.

Martin nodded.

"Tell me," Jack said gently.

Martin took a deep breath and visibly forced himself to sit back on the couch. At least the worst of it is over, his expression seemed to say, at least it's being told now.

"I didn't know what to think," he said heavily. "I don't know a lot about such things. I put down the rock with the hand—the fossil of the hand—and went to look at the other broken pieces of rock. Most of the rest were smaller than the one I'd been looking at. Almost like the rock had really burst apart when it hit. The way it might if . . . if there was something inside it. I found a piece that looked like it might have had part of a foot in it.

And I found another piece that had the impression of an ear, the top part of an ear. I . . . stopped looking after that.

"I stood there a long time, just looking at all that broken rock scattered all over the hill. It didn't make sense, but I knew what I was looking at. I could see it. Then I wanted to get out of there. That was all I wanted to do: I just wanted to get out of there. Then, the next thing I know, I spot another piece of rock that has a sort of curve in it, like it might match the one with the hole. It's split open, so there's only half. I looked at it and, I swear, it looked like it had an arm in it at one time. I . . . ."

He had to pause to steady his breathing. Edith squeezed his hand.

"I picked it up and took it over to the other one, the one I said looked like it had a wrist. I put the two broken pieces together and the two of them fit perfect. You could see the impression, like a fossil of a hand and an arm, like right up to the elbow.

"I just dropped them. Dropped them right there at my feet. It . . . frightened me. I swear, it frightened me . . . ."

Jack waited a moment, then said, "What did you do then?"

Martin shook his head, as if in wonder at his own answer. "I didn't do anything," he said. "I didn't do anything at all. I just left them and ran. That's all I did."

Martin lowered his head and pressed his chin down to his chest. Jack had to wait this time until Martin had control of himself.

"There's more," the older man said. "I found something else there, too. A couple of things."

Despite himself, Jack felt goosebumps on his arms and a shiver prickled the skin at the back of his neck.

At first Chard thought his vision was blurred by the night and the rain and his own weariness. He blinked and turned his eyes away, then instantly looked back to the spot where he thought something had moved toward the house. There was nothing there now, only the rain and the uncertain dark.

He pulled the collar of the slicker tighter around his throat and hoped he wouldn't come down with pneumonia after all this. The rain had steadied into a constant drizzle, but it no longer mattered to him. His feet were wet and cold, his slacks soaked through completely. But he thought that some of the chill might have gone out of the air, and he was grateful that the cloud cover was breaking up a little, letting moonlight shine through every now and again. Thin wisps of mist were drifting lightly over the ground. The dampness made his fingers ache. He rubbed them together hard, trying to drive out the pain.

He stood at the edge of the road, just a foot from the side of the gateway, behind the tall bank of weeds. He could just see the front of the house. One step forward would give him a view of the whole place.

He finished his sweep over the yard, where there was nothing at all to see, and looked back at the house. He knew better than to keep staring in one direction; if you did that, very shortly you couldn't see anything. And in the dark, he knew, peripheral vision is best. Now he looked at the house and was glad that Megan had left the porch lights on, although he wished she had closed the inner door and not left only the flimsy screen door to guard the house against the night.

He made another slow sweep of the yard and, as before and as expected, saw nothing. But still . . . .

He thought of the two girls in the house—the two *women*, he corrected himself; Nancy was growing up so quickly—and rejected the idea of going home. He longed for dry clothes and a warm bed and Martha's comforting body, but his day had done something to him, made him nervous, made him see shadows where there were none. He couldn't stay here all night, but he could stay a little while longer.

He looked out again across the yard to the barn and then back to the house. Nothing moved but the rain that occasionally gleamed in the watery moonlight. The mist was getting thicker. There'll be heavy fog in the morning, he thought.

He looked at the porch, bathed in yellow light from the doorway. The steady downpour caught yellow reflections across the steps to the porch, making the rain a golden sheet. He told himself he was being foolish even thinking such things and standing out here in the rain and the night. Well, foolish or not, he thought, nothing can move across that curtain of rain without being seen.

And then for a moment the curtain disappeared, winked out of existence, and then came back.

Martin Ferrand's voice wavered from resolute to shaken, but he continued his story, determined to get it all out.

"It was about a week later, about a week after I found the rocks. One of the cows was missing at evening milking time. I went to look for her. Sometimes one of them will do that, just stay way out in the field. If you have a broken fence, sometimes one of them will just wander off and not even think about coming home. So anyway, I went looking for her. And I found her. She was out near the edge of that upper pasture, up near where the trees start. Being a farmer, I've seen plenty of dead animals, you get used to it. But you don't get anything like this. This was no natural death. The animal was killed. Her head was smashed in, like she was clubbed. And her belly was torn open, like an animal done it, and she was . . . . Her belly was partly eaten out. Like you might think by a wolf or something. Her bag was gone too, ripped right off her.''

"We found her," Jack said.

Martin nodded. "Somebody had to, sooner or later, I suppose." He shook his head sadly. "All this while too, and nobody out in the field."

"You said nothing to anyone?"

"Nothing."

"What . . .? What happened to the cow? What do you think it was?"

"It was the thing I found in the rock," Martin answered, his voice suddenly clear and firm, convinced. "It was the thing I found, I was sure of it. I'm sure of it now!"

"But . . . ." Jack shook his head, trying to clear his thoughts. "I just don't understand," he said.

"All right, then," Martin said, coming alive now as the weight of his secret left him. "Listen. There was something in those rocks. What I found was like one of them fossils, but it wasn't. It wasn't a fossil. I mean, it wasn't gone, all dried up or rotted away or whatever happens to them. It was . . . encased . . . in the rock. It was there, inside the rock, and when the rock broke apart, it came out. It was a man . . . . It was some kind of a man, with its left arm and hand gone where that piece of rock had broken off. It killed the cow for food and ate her belly and her milkbag. *It was some kind of a man!* I know it was.''

"Fossils aren't like that," Jack said. It sounded like the stupidest thing he had ever said in his life. His mind was racing, but with every logical step it tried to take, it tripped over some piece of illogic.

"But how did it kill the cow?" he asked. "A man couldn't do that."

"It hit the cow with the stump of its arm, the one with the hand missing," Martin said steadily. "That arm must be like a club. It hit her over the head and crushed her skull."

"It can't be," Jack said almost before he realized he was speaking.

"Yes," Martin said. His manner had changed now. He looked and sounded stronger, bolder, determined to convince Jack of what he was saying. "I examined the animal's head before . . . I did anything. Before I buried it. There was stone, like little flakes of stone, in the hair where the head was crushed. I saw it. I know."

"Why did you just bury it?"

Martin's hesitation was barely noticeable. "I was afraid," he said.

"Why didn't you tell anyone?"

"I was afraid. And three days later, I was more afraid than before."

They were sitting at opposite ends of the couch, legs tucked up beneath them, and sharing a second heaping bowl of popcorn that sat between them. As a concession to their figures, they hadn't put melted butter on this one. On the TV screen, Woody Allen was yearning for Diane Keaton. Nancy and Megan were both laughing when the telephone rang.

Megan uncurled her legs and stood up to get it.

"Megan, this is Martha."

"Oh, hi," Megan started to say, but Martha cut her off.

"Megan, is John there?"

"No. Isn't he home? No, of course he's not or you wouldn't be asking. I don't—"

"I thought maybe he stayed with you for a while, but now I'm worried, and if he's not there, where is he?"

"I'm sure he's all right, Martha. Just stay calm. Maybe he got a call on the car radio. Or maybe he had some trouble with the car or with the bulldozer." No, she thought instantly, he said he had put the dozer in the barn. "Listen, I'll call you back in a couple of minutes. Let me just look around here."

She hung up the phone. Nancy was looking at her anxiously, the movie forgotten.

"Your father's not home yet," Megan said, trying to make her tone sound casual. She walked across the living room to the screen door with Nancy close behind her.

Megan opened the door and stepped out onto the yellow-lit porch. She could see wispy fingers of mist creeping slowly up the wet steps, but the darkness left the rest of the yard invisible.

She was turning around to speak to Nancy when, out of the darkness and the rain, a savage hand clawed at her breast and something hard, erect, rocklike, prodded at her crotch.

"Why?" Jack asked.

"I found something else. And I don't think you know about this. It may even be a crime, what I did; I don't know."

Edith Ferrand had remained silent through her husband's story, never letting go of his hand, never taking
her eyes from his face. Now she looked across the room
at Jack, her eyes pleading for her husband.

"Go on," Jack said.

"Does the name Helbig mean anything to you?"

Jack nodded.

"That poor little girl who disappeared. We searched
all over for her. I found her. I found her on the Rise. I
was alone, the rest of the search party was scattered over
the hill, so I was alone when I found her. I had a shovel
with me, we all did, and I knew as soon as I looked at
her what had happened, what had killed her. I buried
her."

His words were all the more chilling for the monotone
in which he spoke them. Jack's mind was filled with
images he didn't want to be looking at: the dead and
mangled cow in the grave on the hillside, the little girl he
had never seen who must have looked the same, and
Candy McBain in the last moments of her life, recorded
on tape, as something attacked her, something that
must be . . . must be invisible.

"Martin, why did you do it?" he managed to say.
"Why didn't you tell someone?" But suddenly it didn't
matter now as Jack thought of Megan alone in the
house and realized in the same instant that he believed
everything Martin had said.

"It frightened me," Martin whispered, and suddenly
he was sobbing, a man who looked as if he hadn't cried
in more than half a century. "The very thought of it
frightened me to death."

"You have to go back," Jack said.

"Yes," Martin said. "I know."

John Chard was starting to shiver with the cold and the dampness of the air. His fingers felt numb. He knew that they must be white and bloodless, but at least they had stopped aching.

He squinted again through the rain and the dark, straining to see without even knowing what he was looking for. Everything—the months of wondering, that terrible image moving on the television screen, the accident this morning at Danny's Diner—everything was conspiring to make him jump at shadows.

For the briefest of instants he thought something had moved on the porch.

Then, from inside the house, he heard the ringing of the telephone. It rang twice, then stopped, and there was only the silence of the night, broken by the pattering of the rain all around him. He shivered again.

Then Megan was at the screen door, looking out, and Nancy was just behind her. Chard froze, watching, not knowing what to expect, what to think. Megan opened the door and stepped outside, the yellow porch lights illuminating her face. She looked around, then turned back toward Nancy and suddenly she screamed and fell . . . .

Chard was running, slipping in the mud. His hat fell off and the rain stung his eyes and he was fumbling under the slicker for the gun he wore at his belt. His stiff, numb fingers clutched at it, lost it, clutched again, and closed around it. Then the mud betrayed him and he slid and flailed his arms for balance and he was on his knees. But now he had the gun out and somehow his thumb released the safety and his finger squeezed the trigger and the gunshot crashed against the night and echoed back from the hill and on the porch the girls were screaming.

Then, wet mud chilling his legs, rain in his hair and his eyes, he was on the porch. Megan lay at his feet, her eyes wide with terror. Nancy was pressed flat against the wall by the open door. He held the gun out in front of him.

"What . . .?"

To his right, at the end of the porch, the wooden railing exploded outward, split apart, splintered wood flying into the night with a loud crack. Something heavy splashed in the mud and a harsh, stony grinding sound faded into the dark.

Chard dashed to the end of the porch, gun held out before him, stood in the space where the railing had been, but there was nothing there.

"Oh, Daddy," Nancy wailed behind him and Megan started to cry.

Jack was on his feet now. "Tonight," he said. "We're going back tonight. Right now."

"Yes, all right," Martin said.

Jack looked at Edith and the bandage on her ankle. "Will you be all right?" he said quickly.

"I'll—"

"Yes," Martin said suddenly. "I'll call my son. He'll take care of her." He looked at his wife. "He'll take care of you, Edith. I'll see to it."

Edith was crying now. Jack ignored her.

"I have to call home," he said. "Where's your phone?"

"In the kitchen. I'll get ready while you're calling."

As Jack raced for the phone, he saw Martin and his wife come together on the couch, grasping at each other as if the world would end that night.

Then he was at the phone and was punching his own

number at Martin Ferrand's former home and praying that Megan would be there to answer.

Chard picked it up on the third ring.

Megan and Nancy were on the couch in the living room, still shaken. Megan had been trying to tell him coherently what had happened, what had touched her, grabbed her, what she had felt.

"Yes," he said into the phone and realized he was short of breath. Then: "Jack, you—"

But Megan was suddenly beside him and grabbing the phone from his hand and crying, "Oh, Jack, please come home, *please!*"

"Are you all right?" he said. "What happened? *Are you all right?*"

He listened, then said again, "But you're all right?"

Then he looked quickly at his watch. "We're leaving now. We'll be there between two and two-thirty . . . . A few hours, babe. Just a few hours."

Then he was standing in the hallway, looking into the living room, and telling Martin Ferrand: "We're leaving *now!* This minute!"

He ran for the car and a breathless Martin Ferrand hurried after him.

Chard got Megan and Nancy out of the house to the car, then down the hill and into his own home, where he closed the doors and windows against the unknown thing outside in the night.

He told the story quickly to Martha, who first hugged the two young women and then held him. Then quickly she made them all go out to the kitchen, where she took a bottle of brandy from a cabinet, something to warm them all up and calm their nerves.

Chard was at the phone, dialing quickly with fingers that were stiff and cold. The phone was answered on the first ring.

"Doc," he said. "Please come. I'll tell you when you're here."

By the time he hung up the phone, Martha was ready with a towel to dry his hair.

It climbed slowly upward, homeward, breath rasping harshly in its throat, the sound of its movement the same as the crushing of gravel underfoot.

The rain had stopped now and only a few drops fell from branches stirred by the breeze. The overcast sky had cleared, and the moon shone full and bright on the mountain.

The thing continued its slow climb uphill. Then, in a clearing on the slope, it noticed, as it had before, the shimmering shadows of trees in the light of the moon. It stopped, studied the ground at its feet, but found no image of itself, and slowly resumed its climb.

It reached the bare shelf of rock at the top, where its place of safety rose higher still. Slowly it climbed, the structure swaying and crackling beneath its feet, until it reached the highest point. Then it raised its head and looked up, lifted its eyes to gaze in stony silence upon the radiant face of the moon.

13

They gathered in John Chard's living room, the same ones who had gathered before, Martin Ferrand joining them now, and this time it was a council of war.

Ferrand's meeting with the Chards and Doc Warren had been awkward, and the younger people had quickly left them alone.

Jack and Megan sat knee to knee in the kitchen, filling each other in quickly on what had happened. Jack held both of Megan's hands while they talked. When she described the attack at the house, he got up at once and stood beside her, arms around her shoulders, her head pressed against his stomach.

When she was done, she put her arms around his waist and held him tight and said, "Oh, Jack, I'm so glad you're here. This whole thing is . . . ." She shook her head. "Jack, it was right on the porch of the house. And we don't even know what it is!"

Jack said, "We might," then eased away from her and sat down again. Talking rapidly, he told her of his

meeting with Ferrand and what the man had said. While
he was talking, both Nancy and her mother came into
the kitchen, listening in silence until he finished.

"God save us," Martha whispered.

Megan looked at him in silence, then glanced past his
shoulder at Nancy. The younger woman came and
crouched beside her chair.

"It makes sense, Jack," Megan said softly. "I don't
know how such a thing can be, but it makes sense."

In the silence that followed, they could hear the low
murmur of John Chard, Doc Warren, and Martin
Ferrand talking in the living room.

Abruptly, Jack stood up. The muscles in his face were
hard, knotted, and his voice was strained.

"Come on," he said. "Let's get on with it."

They followed him into the living room.

Martin Ferrand, as if doing penance for his sins, was
seated on a straight chair, by himself, at one end of the
room. Doc Warren sat in the easy chair closest to Ferrand. Chard stood near the fireplace, his hands joined
behind his back.

Without a word, Martha, Nancy, and Megan sat together on the couch. Jack, too keyed up from the events
of the night and the long drive from Cambridge, remained standing in the doorway.

They all avoided meeting Martin Ferrand's eyes.

John Chard drew a long breath and straightened up,
wincing at the pull of weary muscles in his back. He
looked pale, worn, the strain of this long day and night
adding lines to his face. When he spoke, the words came
slowly.

"I believe what Martin says." He looked around the
room, as if to impress his conviction on the others, then

turned toward Ferrand. "Tell it again, Martin," he said. "All of it."

"John, please sit down," Martha said. "You're so tired."

Chard reached for the other straight chair and pulled it to him. He sat down without saying anything else. They looked at Martin Ferrand now, who finally raised his head and met their eyes.

He told them the story again, the whole thing, what he had told Jack in Cambridge and told quickly to Chard and the doctor just now, told it all slowly and carefully, straining to recite the details of each event, wanting them to see it as he had seen it. No one interrupted.

When he was finished, Doc Warren turned his head slightly toward Jack and said, "That storm was the worst we ever had here."

They were all silent and Martin Ferrand dropped his gaze to the floor.

Finally, Jack said, "What became of the rocks? Are they still there?"

Ferrand shook his head. "No."

"What happened to them?" Jack said, the impatience sharp in his voice.

"I went back once more," Ferrand said. "I went back and found them and shattered them all, smashed them up as small as I could."

"Why?" Jack said, but the impatience was suddenly gone from his voice and he sounded as if he already knew the answer.

"I thought it would save us," Ferrand said. He spoke the words so quietly that they hung in the air for a moment like the whisper of a ghost.

Chard cleared his throat and the others looked at him.

"I believe it," he said simply. "I can't account for what Martin did or didn't do. That's a matter for him to think about some other time. But I do believe what he says, and I think his idea is right." He paused, a new expression of pain coming into his face, and looked toward Doc Warren.

The doctor pushed himself up with his hands flat on the arms of the chair. He looked quickly around the room, and Jack instantly noted the contrast between him and Chard. The doctor, who was often content to let the sheriff take the lead in conversations, now assumed that position himself. It was going on three o'clock in the morning, and everyone looked tired and strained, but none of them more so than Chard.

"Let's just be certain we're all talking about the same thing," the doctor said, his tone very matter-of-fact. "Martin tells us he found what appeared to be the fossil of a man, presumably a prehistoric man, in the rocks on the Rise. If we're to believe this at all, I think we'd have to agree that it's a unique event, never to be duplicated. An ancient boulder was released from its place in the soil, which was eroded by the rain and wind of the storm, and rolled down the hillside and smashed apart when it hit other boulders. As for what was . . . or might have been . . . inside it . . . . Well, I just don't know. If there *was* something there, I can't tell you how it got there." He paused and thought for a moment, frowning. "In any event, the impression in the stone was clear enough to convince Martin that it really was the fossil impression of . . . of a man. Then Martin found one of his cows slaughtered in a way that suggested it was done by this . . . this man. When Carla

Helbig disappeared and the Rise was searched, Martin found her body and again believed she was killed in the same way."

He glanced at Martin without interrupting his recital. "We told you, Martin, about the girl who was killed. Candy. We've watched the videotape that we told you about, too, and John, at least, is satisfied that he understands it now. John feels that he was correct all along in thinking that nothing or no one could be seen— no murderer, that is—because there was nothing there that *could* be seen. That is, she was killed by something invisible. And there's something else, too. At the time of her death, John questioned the young man who followed her up the Rise and took the pictures. The young man told John then that he had seen nothing near the girl."

The others sat still, almost frozen, listening to the doctor's dry, uninflected voice. He was obviously being deliberate about showing no emotion, his courtroom-trial tone intentional.

"So far," he said, "if we accept all of this, we have an invisible prehistoric man living wild on Deacons Rise. The dead cow—assuming we accept the basic idea —can be explained as food, I suppose. There was evidence of its being eaten by whatever killed it. The two murders, if we can call them that, are harder to explain. On the other hand, the fact that the two human bodies were *not* eaten"—Martha Chard gasped at this but the doctor ignored her—"tends to verify the reason for the cow's death."

Suddenly the doctor looked weary himself, as tired as Chard and as frightened as Martin Ferrand. His body sagged and he wiped a hand across his eyes.

"Without considering what happened tonight," he

went on more slowly, "I think that's as much as we know and one way, however strange, of explaining it."

"No," Ferrand said. "There's the hand. The missing hand."

"Yes, all right," the doctor said. "The left hand is missing, broken at the wrist. There's one bit of medical evidence too. When Candy McBain was killed, I examined the body, and there were unusual scraped areas of the skin, marks that could have been made by very rough sandpaper, say, or stone, something like that. For the sake of argument, we could say that it fits in with the other bits of . . . well, let's call it information, also for the sake of argument."

He looked at Megan on the couch.

"Megan, what exactly happened tonight?"

Jack stepped in from the doorway and rested his hand on her shoulder as she spoke.

"It was . . . . Something grabbed me by the neck. Or someone . . . . No, wait a minute, let me start again." She took a deep breath. "I stepped out on the porch and stood there for a second. I was looking for John, so I looked out from the porch, all over the yard, all around. This all happened very quickly. Then . . . something grabbed me. It . . . it was a hand. I know it was a hand. And it felt like stone."

"Where did it touch you?" Jack asked.

"Here," Megan said and raised a hand to touch her left breast. "Like this," she said, and shivered.

Beside her on the couch, Nancy's eyes were wide. Her voice trembled but she asked, "Megan, was it one hand or two?"

Megan hesitated, looked around at all the faces watching her, and said, very slowly, "It was just one. The right one. I know how it felt."

They could all hear each other's breathing in the room.

"There was nothing there," Megan said. "There was *absolutely nothing there* that I could see. But it was a man, I know it was. He . . . ."

When she hesitated, it was Doc Warren who finally said gently, as he might have urged a patient in the office, "Go on, Megan."

"I could feel it against me. It pressed against me . . . lower down. Then . . . I don't know if he . . . it . . . knocked me down or I just lost my balance, or what, but I went down and . . . and my arm brushed against him as I fell." She was on the verge of tears. "I . . . I could feel him. When I fell. I know. I know what was there." And the tears came, softly, her shoulders shook as she tried to hold them back.

"Well, then," the doctor said with a long sigh.

"Could something like that actually happen?" Nancy asked, looking at the doctor. "I mean, it sounds like . . . the spirit of a fossil or something."

"It does, a little," the doctor said. "This is not really my field, and I only know a little about it. I think you—"

"Doc," Jack said, "maybe you should clear something up for us before we go too far. What *is* a fossil, anyway? Isn't it just the impression of a plant or animal, preserved in mud or something? Like a negative image?"

The doctor shook his head. "No," he said. "There are two kinds, and a fossil can also be solid. If a body were buried very quickly, even immersed by accident— drowning, for example—in the right kind of moist sediment, which then hardened, the tissue would be protected from both oxygen and bacteria and—again, under the right conditions—it might be protected against decay. Sometimes mineral matter, over a long period of times, mixes with the tissue matter. A process like that produces what we know as petrified wood.''

They were watching him closely, trying to understand what had happened on Deacons Rise last spring.

''I remember reading about a paleontologist in New Mexico,'' the doctor went on slowly. ''It was sometime last year. He found the fossilized jawbone of some tiny mammal no one had known existed before. Whole animals, big ones, like mammoths, have been found preserved.'' He shook his head. ''We just don't know all there is to know. And it's very late at night for an old doctor to be lecturing,'' he added quietly.

''Doc,'' Chard said, his voice startling the others in the room. ''Do you think that's what it is?''

It was a long time before the doctor answered. But when he did, he said, ''I do.'' And said again, ''Yes, I do.''

''There are so many secrets here that we'll never know,'' Chard said sadly. ''A man.''

''Let's say the ghost or . . . the shadow . . . of a man, something like that. At least for the sake of argument. I don't know what else to say.''

''I guess I believe it,'' Nancy said quietly, ''but it just doesn't seem possible.''

''No,'' Doc said. ''It doesn't. But it does explain what we know, or at least what we think we know. I don't have an explanation for how such a thing can be. But at the same time, I can't tell you that it's out of the question.''

If any of the listeners were still doubtful, the simple

flatness of his voice convinced them.

"You're satisfied with the explanation," Chard said, his eyes searching his friend's face.

Doc Warren closed his eyes and nodded. "I am, John," he said.

"All right, then," Chard said. His face was still pale and lined, but his voice was strong. "We'll have to get it."

"Kill it," Martin Ferrand said.

"Yes," Chard agreed, his voice barely audible. "I guess we'll have to kill it."

"We'll have to find it first," Doc said. "And from what we know, or think we know, it can't be seen."

Chard was silent a moment, then rose and walked out of the room. They heard him open the front door for a second, then close it. When he returned to the room, he said, "There's ground fog. We could see it in that, I think."

"Possibly," Doc said.

"Where will you look?" Martha asked, watching her husband. She had one hand pressed to the side of her face.

"On the Rise."

"I know where," Jack said. They looked at him. "There's an old firetower on the peak." He looked quickly at the sheriff and saw him nodding. "I know this sounds crazy, but the whole thing sounds crazy." He took a deep breath. "If I were suddenly in a new world, a world totally new to me, I'd want to be where I could see as much of it as possible."

"Yes," Martin Ferrand said.

"Maybe," the doctor said. "Dawn would be the best time, wouldn't it?" he asked Chard.

"Yes."

Doc Warren stood up slowly from his chair. "Let's continue this in three hours," he said. "I prescribe three hours' rest for all of us."

As they stood up, Megan said, "We'll try the tower first."

"Oh, Megan," Martha said, taking her arm, "you're not going. Let the—"

"I *am* going! I—"

"So am I!" Nancy said at the same time. Martha looked at her daughter in panic.

"I am!" Megan said, her voice tight. "I was attacked at my own front door. I've been driven from my home. I may not own it but I love it, and I won't be driven from it. I won't!" She was trembling but refused to acknowledge it.

Jack put his arm around her shoulder. "We'll do it," he said. "We'll all do it."

Then Martin Ferrand took a step forward. "I don't have much to say in this," he said quietly. "I guess I've lost the right. But I . . . I'm glad you're living in that house. On that land. That's all I . . . ." But he couldn't say anything more.

They stood in silence a moment. Then Nancy broke it, her question a whisper in the silent room.

"How do we kill it?"

Her father looked at her. "I don't know," he said. He looked at Doc Warren.

Doc Warren lifted his eyebrows a fraction and smiled a sad half smile. "I don't know, either," he said. "I just don't know."

14

"It's cold," Megan said, and had to concentrate to keep her teeth from chattering.

It was six o'clock and they'd be leaving in a few minutes. They were sitting at the big table in the kitchen, drinking coffee, holding the heavy mugs with both hands to keep them warm. Martin Ferrand held his without drinking. Jack sipped carefully from his. Nancy was retying her boots. It had stopped raining, but the dampness and chill seemed determined to get into the house and touch each of them. Across the room, at the counter, Martha was getting ready to make another pot of coffee, filling the time by keeping her hands moving. But then there was nothing left to do and she turned around from the counter.

"What could be taking him so long?" she asked the silent room.

"He'll be all right, Martha," Doc Warren said. "Don't you worry about him. He drove down and he'll be driving back."

Chard had gone down to Al Vredenburgh's place. When Chard had borrowed the bulldozer from him, he had asked nothing more than a casual question and didn't object to Chard's equally casual answer. He wouldn't object now, either, when Chard asked to borrow his four-wheel drive pickup.

As if to confirm the doctor's comforting reply, they heard the motor of the truck as it turned in at the driveway. Martha went to the front door to meet her husband, then walked back with him to the kitchen.

Chard stood in the doorway, unconsciously rubbing his hands together. With a glance, he took in all the faces. Martha stayed close at his side.

"Nancy," he said, "you know I don't want you to come with us. There's no need for you to come."

"Daddy, I'm going with you," she said. "I live here too."

Martha pressed her lips together and blinked but said nothing.

"All right, then," Chard said and, after a second, looked away from his daughter. "I have the truck. We'll go in that."

"To the tower?" Jack asked.

"We'll take the truck up that road, what there is of it. We'll go as far as we can and we'll stay in the truck. We may end up at the tower. We'll have to see what happens." His gaze wavered for a second and came to rest on Doc Warren. "We'll just have to see what we find once we're on the Rise."

Jack stood up. "Well, let's go," he said, and then the others moved.

Chard had parked the red Ford pickup near the front door. When they got to it, he said, "I'd rather ride in the back, but I think I should handle this thing going up the hill. That road is overgrown and pretty rough. Doc, you ride up front with me.'' He hesitated for the briefest of seconds, then leaned forward, and his lips touched his wife's cheek. "We'll be back," he said. "You stay inside." Then he was getting into the truck and Doc Warren was opening the door on the other side. Martin Ferrand moved quickly, as if coming alive now after a long sleep. He climbed into the bed of the pickup and extended a hand to help Megan, Nancy, and Jack.

They settled themselves quickly in the back, Ferrand sitting on the spare gasoline can, all of them facing backward, their eyes scanning the familiar house and road in the dim grayness of morning. At the living room window, Martha held the curtain aside and watched them. Then Chard started the engine, backed the truck into the road, and they were starting up the hill.

No one spoke as the truck reached the crest and they drove, without slowing, past the Ferrand place. Megan put her hand on Jack's shoulder and squeezed it in a silent message. Martin Ferrand let his eyes sweep over the house, the barn, the yard, that had been his home all his life, then dropped his gaze to the bed of the truck. The others just caught a glimpse of the broken railing on the porch, then the house fell away behind them and the woods closed in.

Deacons Road ran level past the house for a little distance, with the woods growing thicker on the right and a cleared pasture, stony and weedy, on the left. But then the road quickly narrowed, grew rutted and rocky, with the branches of trees crossing above it. It was dark beneath the trees, and the dampness rose from the ground in misty swirls.

Then the truck swung sharply to the right, onto a still
narrower road, little more than a track between thickly
growing trees. The rocky path wound a twisting route
up the Rise, ending eventually at the firetower on top,
but it had been unused for years now and the woods
were reclaiming it for their own. Trees and undergrowth
had edged onto the sides of the track, young branches
stretched eagerly to fill the open space, and years of
rainwater and melting snow had run down the hill and
deepened the furrows, shifted stones and gravel and re-
designed the road to suit other needs. In a few more
years the road would be gone, swallowed by the life of
the hill.

The truck bounced violently, engine roaring, as it
struggled to keep all four wheels on the ground.
Branches scraped sometimes at its sides, more often as it
made its way higher up the slope, following the twisting
track.

They were silent, watching the woods. There was
nothing to see, only darkness beneath the trees and
gray-white mist drifting slowly between them.

Twice, Chard stopped the truck. They sat in silence,
watching, listening, but still there was nothing to see.
The morning mist drifted back to the narrow open track
of the road, touched the truck, and closed in slowly
around it. The only sound was the steady growling of
the engine.

Each time the truck stopped, they shivered without
speaking, eyes searching the dark and the moving mist,
then Chard shifted gears and the truck lurched upward
again.

And then finally it reached a level stretch and halted
at the edge of the broad rock shelf at the top, where the

tower rose higher still. Birds, startled into silence by the roaring of the truck, slowly resumed their morning calls. The dampness here was thick and chill, misty, as if a cloud enveloped the top of the Rise. It moved against the truck, touched the sides with questing fingers, and closed in around it. The truck vibrated beneath them, its rumbling the only source of comfort on the hill. Then Chard turned off the engine and even that was gone.

"What do we do now?" Nancy whispered.

After a moment, Megan reached over and touched her arm, but no one answered.

They watched the growing light in the sky and listened to the whisper of the woods.

Instinct decreed that it eat and it had hunted, after all. Now, sated for the day, it moved slowly up the hill.

A wild thing, it still was a creature of habit and pattern, and its months of hunting had worn a path through the undergrowth where it neared the top of the hill and the shelf of rock. Its immediate need now satisfied, it followed that path, unthinking, slapping branches out of its way, and as one gritty foot touched solid rock, it suddenly saw the monster.

"There's nothing here," Chard said, and turned to face the doctor.

Doc Warren shook his head sadly. "I don't know what to do, John," he said, his voice hoarse. "We can't just sit here, waiting for something we can't even see. I thought maybe the mist, the fog . . . ."

"So did I," Chard said.

"We might as well go," the doctor said quietly. He turned in his seat and looked back through the narrow window of the cab at the others who crouched in the back. Jack turned to look at him and Doc Warren silently shook his head.

Beside him in the front, Chard turned the key in the ignition, pressed the gas pedal, and the truck roared into life.

The thing held its ground.

The gray light of morning shone off the monster's single broad eye, fixed steadily on the thing from the other side of the rock. But the place of safety was between the thing and the monster, and it had to get there to be safe, even if the monster attacked. It had to go forward. Slowly, watching the silent monster, it took a step, stone sliding on stone. Nothing happened. It stepped forward again, and again, across the long distance to the place of safety, with the monster glaring silent and deadly beyond it, but at last it reached the bottom and stood between the legs of the tower, and now it could be safe if the beast attacked.

Then the beast roared and the thing fled up the tower.

The truck lurched across the rough surface of rock, coughed once and threatened to stall, then caught and bounced again. Chard was looking for a flat spot to turn around to head back down the hill. The flattest place was at the base of the tower, where concrete had once been poured over the naked rock. It was cracked and broken now, clawed at by the weather for years and years, but it was the flattest area at the top and Chard aimed for it.

He let the truck move slowly, letting the tires find purchase on the rock, and they had crossed half the distance to the tower when they heard the scream from above.

The thing fled up the steps of the tower, hauling itself faster with its one hand as if, all its life, stairs had been familiar. Its breath came harsh and ragged now. Could the beast climb up and get it?

Panting, breath rasping in its throat, it reached the platform on top of the tower, hurled itself flat, and, with freezing shock, felt something soft that should not have been there touch its face.

Chard's foot smashed down on the brake and he flung his door open. Doc Warren leaped out on the other side.

The others crouched in the back of the truck, and all stared up at the tower. The scream had come from there, from the top.

"Oh, my God!" Megan cried.

"What . . . ?" somebody said, but the words died as another scream came from the tower.

It had been days since Jacob Helbig was human. His mind had faltered somewhere on the Rise, somewhere on the rocks and in the mud and between the trees. He had stumbled and fallen, tripped, splashed through mud, shivered in the icy rain, and barely heard even the wheezing of his own tortured breath. One eye was swollen shut, crusted with blood, where a whipping branch had sliced through it. Three of his nails were torn off, his fingers raw and bleeding, from crawling on the rocks. His shoes were gone but his feet were long-since numb to pain.

Some time in the night, he had crawled to the base of the tower and a need, wordless and automatic, had driven him, on hands and knees, up the shaky steps to the top. He had lain there, half asleep, half dead, and mumbling at the dark, and only came awake when the tower swayed beneath him and a heavy step made the platform shiver. He flung out an arm, stretched out bloody fingers to ward off death, touched a cold and stony face and screamed with the last of his voice, and screamed again.

It moved with instinct, struck out with the blunt stump of its handless arm, crushed the skull of the man before it, then struck it again, the stump sinking into wet brain matter. The scream turned into a rattle, a choking bubbling sound that lasted only a moment, and then was gone. The corpse flopped twice and was still.

The thing stood, lifted the dead body by the throat with its one hand, and tossed it across the railing of the platform. It leaned over to see the monster below.

There were figures around the monster now and they were looking up. The monster itself was growling. It was hard to see, looking down, because the morning mist was a swirling cloud around the top of the hill and the tower. But it could see the figures dimly, and the monster. It straightened quickly, snatched at the neck of the body on the railing, lifted it high, then hurled it at the beast below.

"Helbig!" Chard breathed.

They watched the body as it was lifted invisibly, floating, back and up from the railing, then as it hovered in the air, limp, like a puppy held by the neck or a soft and boneless doll, and then the corpse was hurled at them. All this in silence. The body, dark against the growing brightness of the sky, spread out its arms and legs at awkward angles, as if trying to catch the currents and fly. It began turning over in the air as it plummeted toward the rock below, and then it struck. It made a brief, wet thud and then the silence returned.

None of them saw it.

Even the flailing body tumbling through the air could not move their gaze from the top of the tower. Something had lifted the body to the railing, then lifted it off, raised it high and thrown it to the ground. While the body was up there, they could see nothing but it, a human body floating weightless above them. But in that icy instant of shock when the body fell toward them, they saw, outlined in the swirling, pearly mists at the top of the tower, one arm still outstretched, the hideous phantasm of a man.

"Dear God," Chard said out loud.

"John!" Jack said beside him. *"John!"*

But still they stood frozen another second before anyone moved.

Then Doc Warren was hurrying around the front of the truck, away from the place where the body had fallen, where a pool of dark blood was spreading out to mark the spot.

Jack looked quickly up again, his eyes seeking the figure on the tower. It was . . . . Yes, it was still there.

"How can we . . .?" he started.

"Watch it!" Doc Warren snapped. "Don't take your eyes off it!" He grabbed Chard's arm. "John!" Then: *"John!"*

At last Chard stirred, tore his eyes from the sight, looked at them, at each of them, and said only, "Doc," very sadly, and then his eyes sought Martin Ferrand, and then suddenly everyone was moving.

"We can burn it!" Jack said. "Can we burn it? Burn the tower? Blow it up?"

Nancy and Megan scrambled over the side of the truck. One of Megan's feet kicked the side panel as she went over. The sound rang hollow in the air. Behind them, Martin Ferrand lowered himself to the ground.

"It's wet," Chard said. "It's wet from the rain. It won't burn." He turned his head, swept his gaze around the shelf of rock. "We could . . . ."

They were staring up again. The thing on the tower was still visible, its misty outline shifting as the currents of air stirred the drifting fog. Still there.

"We could burn the truck," Doc Warren said. "Explode it. Blow it up."

"The trees," Megan said. "The woods."

"They're wet. They won't burn," Jack said.

"The tower?"

"Gas. Gasoline!" the doctor snapped.

Chard grunted and threw himself toward the back of the truck, but Martin Ferrand, breathing heavily, was already hauling the spare can of gasoline over the side and setting it clumsily on the ground.

"Here!" he said, voice husky, work-hardened fingers twisting at the cap.

Chard knelt beside him, reaching for the can. "The truck!" he yelled to Doc. "Move the truck!"

Doc Warren instantly jumped for the truck, into the cab, and slammed it into gear. The truck lurched forward, springs complaining loudly as it bounced on the furrowed rock of the mountain.

They were all shouting, hardly knowing their own voices.

The damp mist of morning drifted around them, chilling them, moisture and fear making their hands clammy.

"Will it burn?"

"How do . . . ?"

"Watch the thing!" Chard shouted, his voice hoarse. *"Watch the thing!"*

Then he and Martin were on their feet. "Get away!" the sheriff shouted. "Get back in the trees. *Go on!* All of you!"

"Here!" Megan said. She was pulling a sweater over her head, one arm still tangled in it.

The time lasted seconds and years, ages, time both frozen and racing, time stopped dead and time blurred with its own speed, their voices, words, tangled together.

"Here!" Megan said again.

"I need—" Chard said, his head swinging around, looking everywhere, hand already extended.

"Here!" Megan said. "Use this!" She thrust the sweater at him.

"Oh, God!"

"A fuse! Douse it, John." Martin Ferrand was pale, his gnarled hands trembling with the weight of the gasoline can as he held its slippery sides and tried to tip it toward the sweater.

"Watch the thing!" Chard shouted again as he crushed the pink sweater into a ball and Martin poured gasoline onto it.

"More! Soak it!"

Doc Warren was stumbling back from the truck, realized what they were doing, and went back, grabbing at the truck's gas cap. He pulled it free as Chard jumped toward him, holding the dripping sweater. Together they stuffed in the cloth, shoved it down the pipe, all moving as one. Chard was in the middle of it, and Ferrand, and their hands and minds worked together as one, reading each other and moving, moving.

Doc had driven the truck under the tower, between the straddling legs of the tower, motor running, doors open. The sweater hung from the open gas pipe. Martin Ferrand, chest wheezing as he gasped for air, hauled the partly empty can by himself and twisted away as Chard reached out to help. Mouth open with the effort, Martin sloshed the bed of the truck with gasoline from the can and dumped the can after it.

It was still only seconds, yet time stretched around them like fog, stretched and lengthened and took on dark shapes and they moved at the same speed but everything was both slow and blurred with speed.

"I'll do it!" Ferrand gasped. "Me! I'll do it myself! *Go on!*"

It was ready, the truck was ready, the truck that was now a bomb, the fuse ready, ready themselves, and *"I'll do it!"* Ferrand shouted again at Chard.

They stood, breathing, suddenly still with the readiness, ready to do it, just one thing to do, and they stood, staring, wild-eyed, breathing, hearts pounding.

"I'll do it!" Ferrand shouted into Chard's face. And then more calmly, "Let me do it, John," he said, eyes pleading. "Let me."

"Martin," Chard breathed, and nodded once, and touched Martin on the shoulder.

Then he twisted away and shouted, "Run!" and they were running, bounding over the rocks, diving for the trees, hiding among the trees, panting, lungs aching with the strain, gasping for air: Chard, Doc Warren, Jack, Megan, Nancy. And stopping, crouching, arms up to faces, waiting, watching to see it happen.

Above them, alone on the rock, Martin Ferrand stood and looked up once at the thing, turned his face alone to the thing and, for an instant, defied it. Then he stepped close to the truck, to the rear of the truck and the fuse, the gas-soaked sweater. He fumbled a book of matches from his pocket and, trembling, struck one and, trembling, it sputtered out. He flung it away, tore loose another, struck it, held it out to the wet cloth and saw the burst of flame, and ran, hurled himself away down the rock toward the faces in the trees.

A dull *whump* thudded out from the truck and, an instant later, another. The truck burst apart, roared upward in jagged shreds, a fireball slamming at the tower, a cloud of black smoke enveloping it. The air stirred violently, trees whipping back from the blast, greasy smoke rolling and billowing, killing the pearly mist and then drifting away.

The truck, the flying steel, roared up between the legs of the tower. The force of the explosion, flung savagely down at the rock, rebounded, drove up for release. The rain-soaked wood of the tower steamed, white steam mixing with black smoke, hissed in the heat of the blast, and tiny tongues of flame licked hungrily at it, flickering, working at the wood as it dried in the sudden, shocking heat. The tower sagged, seemed to gather itself, shuddered, and settled to one side, trembling. Beams cracked, split, flew away but, for an instant, clung together.

Torn and ragged steel, like shrapnel, ripped at the

tower, tore upward at the platform on top, burst and burned through the floor at the top, the beams of the floor that were drier than the rest, and then the top was wrapped in flame, the platform was smoking and burning, wood hissing and spitting. It sagged, then wavered, and hung for an instant, before its death. And outlined in the swirling curtain of black smoke and the dust of cracking wood and the hiss of steam and the gray mist of the mountain at dawn, there, for its final moment, was the thing on the platform, gripping the railing, and then, as the platform sagged and fell inward and plunged back to the earth amid shooting flames, letting go and falling with it, crashing with it to the ground and shattering when it hit the rocks below.

Much later, when the fire had died out and even the smell of burning rubber had been carried away by the morning breeze, they came and stood close and surveyed the little that remained of the charred wreckage on the rock.

"It's over," one of them said for the others. "It's over now."

"Yes," another said.

And, "Yes," said another.

And another merely nodded.

"Let's go home now," Megan said. "Please let's go home."

"Yes," Jack said. "All right."

"All right, then," Chard said, and at last they turned away.

Epilogue

It was the last evening in October, Halloween, the air brittle and clear, with a million pinpoint stars in the sky.

Megan held the door open and called back to Jack, "I'll be outside," then stepped out on the porch. She stood on the top step for a minute in the yellow light, breathing the air deep into her lungs, tasting its crystal sweetness. Then she stepped quickly back to the door, opened it, switched off the lights, and went back to the darkened porch. She turned up the collar of her jacket—not because the air was so cold but because it felt snug that way—and folded her arms beneath her breasts and hugged herself for warmth.

After a while, she strolled to the left, to the end of the porch that angled closer to the woods and the slope of Deacons Rise, and for a moment her legs pressed against the now solid railing that enclosed the porch. Except for the rustling of dry, brittle leaves, blowing across the porch and in the yard before the house, the evening was still. Cool weather had come late this year and the woods, by day, were still a flame of color. Even now, in the dark of evening, she could still see the red and gold of the leaves that littered the porch. She shuffled her feet through them, liking the sound, and strolled back to the steps.

Jack switched off the inside lights as he came out, then realized that the porch lights were already off.

"Are you hiding out here?"

Megan could hear the smile in his voice. "On the contrary," she said. "I stayed right here where you'd be sure to find me." She stayed where she was, leaning against the pillar at the side of the steps.

Jack stood behind her and wrapped her in his arms, slipped a hand beneath her jacket and held lightly the warmth of her breast, and she leaned back against him. He bent forward and kissed her temple and she squeezed his hand tighter against her.

"This should be fun tonight," he said, and she nodded, her head moving against his shoulder.

Every year on Halloween in Deacons Kill—every year since there was a Deacons Kill, some people said—a bonfire was built in the middle of town, in the park in the square. And in the light of the roaring fire, the children of the Kill could play and laugh and stay up until long past midnight, then go home safe with the goblins put to rest for another long year.

"We did the right thing, you know, Jack," she said.

"I know," he said.

And then John Chard's car came up the hill and turned in at the gate. Near the porch, it swung in a wide circle to face the road again.

"Happy Halloween!" Nancy called as they stepped off the porch and walked to the car. She was in the back and Martha sat beside her husband in the front.

They climbed into the back beside Nancy and they all greeted each other, and Martha said something about the clear weather, but Chard still had not started the car again.

"We'll have to do something about this driveway," he said after a moment.

"What do you mean?" Jack said.

Chard continued looking out through the windshield, the palms of his hands against the wheel. "Well . . . ." he said, his voice strange. "Well, I own the house now, you see, and a man should improve his property as best he can."

"You—" Jack said.

"I bought it in August," Chard said quickly, hurrying the words, "when Tom Vogel said it was for sale. Got a good price, too." He turned his head a little at that and a small smile moved his lips. "I'd be willing to sell to decent people, of course, once they're ready to buy. Meanwhile, I have to remind you that the rent's due tomorrow."

"Count on it," Jack said.

"John, we—" Megan began.

"Where's the pumpkin?" Chard asked. "That jack-o-lantern?"

"Oh!" Megan said. "It's all carved out, has a candle all ready and everything. I put it on the windowsill in the living room, but we forgot to light it."

"Better light it," Chard said.

Without a word, Jack got out of the car and walked back to the house and went inside. A moment later, a match flared in the darkness behind the window and the candle inside the pumpkin jumped to life. Its orange light cast flickering shadows from the window onto the porch and the rustling leaves.

Then Jack returned to the car and they drove slowly out of the yard to the road to Deacons Kill, and knew that, behind them in the night, the house was safe.

Best-Selling Horror and Occult from TOR

☐ 48-042-3   **The Wells of Hell** $2.95
            Graham Masterton

☐ 48-043-1   **Night Vision** $2.95
            Frank King

☐ 48-036-9   **Last Come the Children** $2.95
            David Hagberg

☐ 48-041-5   **The Possession of Jessica Young** $2.95
            Russ Martin

☐ 48-046-6   **The Playground** $2.95
            T.M. Wright

☐ 48-055-5   **The Kill** $2.95
            Alan Ryan

☐ 48-054-7   **The Obsession of Sally Wing** $2.95
            Russ Martin
            March 83

☐ 48-061-X   **Tengu** $3.50
            Graham Masterton
            April 83

Buy them at your local bookstore or use this handy coupon:
Clip and mail this page with your order

PINNACLE BOOKS, INC. – Reader Service Dept.
1430 Broadway, New York, NY 10018

Please send me the book(s) I have checked above. I am enclosing $_____ (please add 75¢ to cover postage and handling). Send check or money order only—no cash or C.O.D.'s.

Mr./Mrs./Miss_____

Address_____

City_____ State/Zip_____

Please allow six weeks for delivery. Prices subject to change without notice.
Canadian orders must be paid with U.S. Bank check or U.S. Postal money order only.

Best-Selling Science Fiction from TOR

Best-Selling Science Fiction from TOR

☐	48-547-6	**Test of Fire** Ben Bova	$2.95
☐	48-542-5	**The Descent of Anansi** Larry Niven and Steven Barnes	$2.95
☐	48-531-X	**The Taking of Satcon Station** Barney Cohen and Jim Baen	$2.95
☐	48-555-7	**There Will Be War** J.E. Pournelle	$2.95
☐	48-512-2	**Not This August** C.M. Kornbluth revised by Frederik Pohl	$2.75
☐	48-543-3	**The Syndic** C.M. Kornbluth revised by Frederik Pohl	$2.75
☐	48-570-0	**Gunner Cade/Takeoff** C.M. Kornbluth and C.L. Moore *April 83*	$2.95

Harry Harrison

☐	48-505-0	A Transatlantic Tunnel, Hurrah!	$2.50
☐	48-505-9	The Technicolor Time Machine	$2.50
☐	48-540-9	The Jupiter Plague	$2.95
☐	48-521-2	Planet of the Damned	$2.50
☐	48-519-0	Planet of No Return	$2.50
☐	48-031-8	The QE2 Is Missing	$2.95
☐	48-554-9	A Rebel in Time *February 83*	$3.50

Fred Saberhagen

☐	48-501-8	The Water of Thought	$2.50
☐	48-564-6	Earth Descended	$2.95
☐	48-520-4	The Berserker Wars	$2.95
☐	48-536-0	Dominion	$2.95
☐	48-539-5	Coils with Roger Zelazny	$2.95
☐	48-560-3	The Sword Game The First Book of Swords March 83	$5.95
☐	48-568-9	A Century of Progress May 83	$2.95
☐	48-573-5	Berserker's Throne July 83	$2.95

Philip José Farmer

☐	48-511-5	The Cache	$2.50
☐	48-508-5	The Other Log of Phileas Fogg	$2.50
☐	48-504-2	Father to the Stars	$2.75
☐	48-535-2	Greatheart Silver	$2.75
☐	48-522-0	Stations of the Nightmare	$2.75
☐	48-529-8	The Purple Book	$2.95